ECLIPSE

ON THE

NILE

T. A. MANLY

**Castlewhite Press,
16 Eden Avenue,
Dublin 16 P2C5**

Independently Published by Castlewhite Press 2023.
All rights reserved

© T. A. Manly 2023

A CIP record for this book is available from the British Library

eISBN 978-1-7392538-0-6

ISBN   978-1-7392538-1-3 (paperback)

Book Cover Design by Masa Radanic, BooksGoSocial.com
Book Setting out by Jacqui Corn-Uys, BooksGoSocial.com

'Man cannot do without Beauty,' Albert Camus

AUTHOR'S NOTE

Introduction

Eclipse on the Nile can be read as a romance, a psychological thriller, a Bildungsroman, or a discussion on contemporary roles and relationships, but it is ultimately a story of the difficulties of moving on in a marriage for all involved. To this end, the novel switches perspectives between Sara, husband Andy, and son Rick in a close and immediate writing style that captures each character's motivation and provides deep insights – as well as proffering a triangulated view of the elusive James.

If your intent is to approach the novel as a good narrative then read on, and please enjoy. For the more inquisitive reader, I have included some notes below that may assist with ideas explored and the layering and sequencing of the book.

The Idea

The premise of the novel is an essential truth behind a relationship, how in that first instant each recognises in the other that 'beauty' that will keep them together. This is a quality that is free of all constraints and that each person knows intuitively, and it is the recognition of this in another that becomes the cornerstone of the bond in the relationship. But there is a dichotomy that a relationship needs to develop, open up and become something deeper, more caring, complicated, and whole – while at the same time retaining and revisiting that initial recognition.

What is behind this transition, and how can it be mapped?

Joyce points us towards a possible explanation when in 'A Portrait of the Artist as a Young Man' he argues for 'static' emotions in the case of (aesthetic) beauty rather than transient emotions – and that beauty look two ways towards terror and toward pity. This can be interpreted as terror at the power that human beauty can have over the beholder leading to pity (empathy) that such human beauty is mortal and must struggle, diminish, and die. There is a completeness in this.

There can be problems on this usually rocky road to a more expansive relationship. For instance, this initial connection can be perverted or halted from opening if it is undermined through fear, uncertainty, or force rather than accepting beauty's power to lead to a broader relationship. Arguably, these initial situations are also more prone to indulging the more extreme practices of power and indulgence, which can inadvertently or otherwise be a result of a failure to open out into something more. The interplay between these two stages can also be read as the balance between passion and compassion as applies in a relationship, with the possibility of never opening from the particularly exciting interplay of passions that exists early on.

What the novel explores is when those initial passions begin to run out of momentum without the relationship having opened out, and the limiting effect such a relationship has eventually on those involved. Is all that can be done to remove the issues preventing opening out to return, renew and realign?

Why Egypt

Setting the Novel in Egypt arose from a chance discussion late into the night and then into the early morning after a long day attending literary sessions at a book festival in Ireland. The late-night discussion was on how one experiences something for which one does not have a recognised vocabulary. It was a wide-ranging discussion involving half a dozen of us. In the early hours, the discussion moved to mythology as the starting point, and especially their narratives. This coincided with the return of the hordes who had been attending a disco that closed about this time, so that there was suddenly a forest of farming legs around our low-level table and a cacophony of voices overhead – perhaps reverting to those opening memes.

We struggled on in our artistic endeavours, excusing ourselves when necessary to talk around whatever obstacles presented themselves, and to reach a tentative conclusion somewhere around 5 a.m., if I remember rightly. The limited answer is to return to the common first order human stories of mythology that sustained mankind through numerous millennia, and then to link to their archetypes and paradigms.

This reminded me immediately of Egypt, where ancient mythologies are still palpably alive among those that I had previously encountered there, and where the Ancient Egyptians believed that the deeds of man were reflected in the action of Gods represented in the sky. In the novel, Egyptian mythology is introduced to parallel the unconscious issues beneath the surface for both male and female – to ask if the ancient myths that are common throughout human cultures still apply in a modern context. Can or should mankind adopt new role-models, and can these somehow be aligned with archetypes that have existed from the dawn of humanity and are layered into mankind's psyche? Must we somehow connect and build upon the male and female norms of our common ancestral past?

Consider Goddess Aset (the Egyptian name), whose cult, as the Goddess Isis, was adopted by Romans and whose influence spanned from Britain to the near East. She is the Goddess of Womanhood – not a Goddess of

Love, but of what it is to be a woman. Could Aset have significance today for modern women moving away from traditional roles into Aset's iconic image spreading wings to soar? The Gods and Goddesses of Ancient Egypt encountered during the Nile cruise (particularly) provide comparison and contrast.

Writing Style and Perspective

'Lily, the caretaker's daughter, was literally run off her feet.' – the opening sentence of Joyce's famous short story, *The Dead*, is a wonderful example of third-person free-indirect. There is stylistic infection to the personality of the character under focus using the word 'literally' and the phrase 'run off her feet' as Lily would have said it, while retaining a third-person perspective. I wish to expand upon this, so that there is even more of the vibrancy of what it is to live and experience being 'run off her feet'.

To get one step closer, I determined to adopt a style and perspective more immediate that would hopefully bring the reader closer to the character's experience. I wanted to pick up the spin off the sub-conscious as it translated directly into thoughts, words, and actions to expose the character's true intent, personality, and experience, as it occurred. Where does a person operate except at the intersection of the external, with internal memories, emotions, experience, and reason, and that is what this book is trying to capture: words and actions breaking through into consciousness to interact with the exterior world. Yet, I wanted to be able to pull back for reflection, as needed, and then to be able to mix them, while continuing with a third person perspective.

My solution is that expressions, actions, guffaws, thoughts, and actions all get incorporated into the moment without prefix, comment, or explanation, while continuing to use third-person free-indirect. The moment of interaction is a much bigger deal. It is not a first-person narrative nor an internal monologue – but rather an 'in-the-moment' free-indirect. It allows for each character's outpouring with honesty while retaining authorial editing input, and is that interfacing of reality, thought, emotion and, subconscious. Note: Authorial editing continues to provide overview, and cognisance of modern conventions and sensibilities.

I am pleased with what has emerged, and I believe that when used, there is a sense of honesty that comes from the immediacy and links to the present experience. It is intended to create a closer connection between the reader and the character, and perhaps it is one step closer to experiencing who we are.

Some Further Notes:

Cross-cultural exchanges from my experience can produce altered expression with nuances from the parent language imposing themselves, and yet the recipient ear generally does not have a problem either understanding or interpreting. I have therefore remained true to tripping into original language phraseology and sometimes, the original language; where characters perform the latter, I have included a translation.

There are numerous references to publicly known artistic masterpieces and works from history that affect the characters, and that capture for the characters, particularly Sara, understanding and connection with civilisations and cultures and that extend common consciousness. Where these works are referenced, the originating artist is noted in the text, in all cases I believe, and the reader can easily search online or visit museums, bookstores, and other institutions to better appreciate the significance of the work for the character.

The novel switches between three perspectives, and these generally follow the same timeline, one handing off the next. However, as in the last three chapters, where characters separate to pursue their individual private paths, we follow each's individual journey in parallel or in overlapping timelines.

Texting acronyms are used, primarily by Rick, as would be normal for a modern adolescent: I have not provided the original phrases as these can be sourced online with ease, imho.

Please enjoy reading Eclipse on the Nile.

T.A. Manly MFACW

ECLIPSE

ON THE

NILE

Book 1: Cairo

Chapter 1,

Sky High Flight

Sara

Nobody died! Sara startled in her seat. That thought train catching her again. She would try letting her mind take her away into the possibilities ahead. Strange how the past continued to resurrect after seventeen years. Poetic justice in a way for her trying to massage two months onto Rick's pregnancy – all will out now.

She must have dozed off while they were taxiing over the tarmac in Istanbul, because only vaguely did she recall the plane's subsequent manoeuvres. She remembered the flash of silver wings flexing the sunlight when the pilot roared the turbines into a frenzy and the giant fuselage surging until its bullet acceleration had melded her into her seat. That release at lift-off and sitting into the smoothness of flight with a sigh, and, oh again, that rolling about when the pilot was finding the flight path and she g-forcing to plunge to earth except for the safety belt. An impressive proficiency over the skies had her pilot, easing them in gentle full-body movements.

Nobody died? Not easily banished. She would try wry amusement instead. Very melodramatic. Nobody was even hospitalised, not if she didn't include an emergency Medevac from Hurghada on the coral Red Sea, and by then Andy was fully on board with Rick. Who was complaining? Nobody, except James that is, right from the off appearing at every student gig and party, telling everyone that he was Rick's real father – whatever that was. Even after he had settled with the ultimate trophy wife and him a mover-and-shaker of the Celtic Tiger – before it crashed and him along with it! She in her more desperate moments before his bankruptcy had thought she could ask for one of his apartments on account, but if truth be known she always felt indebted to him for funding her student high-life. Still, decent to a fault, and he was the one who sent the wives of his racing and business circles her way for ensembles after – and what successful business entrepreneur of the boom didn't own a *thoroughbred* racehorse. Couldn't tell Andy that he had checked in with her by phone whenever he had a potential client to refer – and wouldn't have gotten started in her fashion business otherwise.

Here she was returning to the scene of the crime – not 'zactly a crime, except there would be a resolution once the paternity test results came through.

Her best friend since school, Ucind, it was, who had advised when James's paternity subpoena had come out of nowhere: 'Go to Egypt and sort matters out with him in a civilised manner.' She had been reluctant: Egypt was not the safest country, having had both a revolution and a coup in the previous few years, and a militant opposition faction conducting terrorist acts that made it into Western media. However, her attempts to contact him had seen no response, neither through his company nor via his relations. They did not want to hear his name despite their running his remaining business interests in Ireland and him being hugely successful in his adopted land; decorated him with an honorary title if you don't mind, James Sullivan Al Bahr Al Ahmar Bey. There was mention of him in the Irish news recently – probably because of his notoriety from the financial crash – taking over massive contracts in the New Cairo when that disaffected Egyptian developer had fled to Europe, leaving construction works uncompleted. That same individual too was pursuing a media campaign from abroad against the current regime, she saw, a threat Egypt was taking very seriously given how quickly the previous revolution had hyperbolized. Although she told herself that James was nothing to her now, her heart had raced with worry that he might be in danger when she saw he had taken over those New Cairo contracts.

Unable to make contact, and with no clear plan except to connect with him from Egypt, she decided she would go after all. Some things you do. Tourist areas were safe on all the government websites. She decided on an organised tour, and then she had the idea of killing two birds with one stone by turning the trip into a family holiday of a lifetime – to bring about a *rapprochement* with Andy as well as ironing out that little paternity misunderstanding with James. Another *éloignement* with Andy arising from the sudden arrival of the subpoena, and always one these days – off more than on. A woman had to be careful because who wanted to end up husbandless?

She wasn't going to think about it anymore. Good to be away from the dreary drizzle and the incessant cloud, brave sleek plane nose-poking into a new hazy heat on this connecting flight – and those diaphanous cushions in the pure air – thrusting forward into the cerulean, and here came the sun for sure. No water trails from the windows to run batik patterns over her as previously from Dublin, but, instead, inner glow as the sun came through, infusing her legs sensitive-tender; and how did they do that – legs spreading into each other mermaid style together and then reforming singly, sleekly; oh, nothing compares to a woman and what a wonder she was. Never lost it, did she? Even when she was pregnant with Rick never lost a hint of shape and fully back in six weeks and couldn't keep their eyes off her, the young doctors on rounds in the hospital – still had it. Good muscle tone that she had no idea why and her mother had said that she had a swanky, toned figure like she had grown up in luxury, with good definition from perfect diet, exercise, and treatments.

In the calm of the luminous cabin, she had time to observe a scene from which she felt strangely distanced, an observer. The couple her own age beside her who had ignored her greeting earlier were now both engrossed in reading material, she in a book and he closest to her in the airline magazine. His magazine might contain articles on their destination, its exotic ancient lands and mythological gods, animal-headed and only half-human. She would throw an eye over his muscular shoulder as there was no sense in them both perusing it. It would provide an excuse to get talking by the by – and he could tell her about those gods, who had held sway for nearly four thousand years and of whom she had an inkling from her fated first trip. Much better to have him relating it to her than to have to go to the trouble of reading it herself.

Wisps of cloud whizzed past the windows at crazy speeds as the wings went tripping off the endless soft white that stepped towards the horizon. That Georgia O'Keefe's, *Sky above Clouds*, in Chicago's Art Institute that she had to visit now that her career was thriving. Unlike that gigantic painting, where pink tinted clouds stepped towards a distant pale blue sunset, their plane was racing south towards the hot desert sun.

Oh, for a drink – of water even – and how was there always those *boings* of the attention bells and amplified the conversations all around. Rick was opposite on the aisle two forward, where she could keep an eye on him without having to sit with him; she wouldn't do that for anything with his pranks, and aviators on him – Maverick or Iceman in Top Gun – give her patience. Not to be hard on him, he had had a tough year when he didn't integrate into his new school, and Andy had to drive him around the country to paraglide that had become his new fad – and that had been a success. Rick had brought along the gear for later in the trip. That and the gym had saved him and ripped in muscles now – could pass for twenty. No trouble on the unscheduled layover; but imagine using layover for an airplane – no longer a stopover – as if it had folded its wings and gone to sleep. Always able to keep himself busy these days and replaying the same video on his tablet all the while – that she needed to ask him about. Besides, a more open discussion was possible without him if she ever got to talk to her neighbours – haven't said a betty-boo to each other even.

Might as well be travelling all alone with Andy gone ahead, to walk down the Egyptian Revolution if you don't mind, and him losing the plot since the subpoena. Suddenly, he is interested in his student days and the marches against the Iraqi War from long ago, as if he had personally organised the largest anti-war protest that the world has ever seen. Give her a break there too. At least that would be over when they arrived, and WhatsApp from him this morning so he was alive, and she didn't want to know more. Never mind, they would be fresher for the layover and not arriving in the early hours that Andy had complained about. Fortunate in an unfortunate way, as her father had always said of her.

Like that change in routing. Instead of Istanbul, she had wanted to go via Schiphol that would have been a dawdle where connecting passengers walked between arrival and departure gates without leaving the international side, and where the clever finger-in-the-wall-Zuiderzee's had installed limitless shopping and restaurants to amuse the curious wayfarer. She had been planning a stopover there to rekindle memories of that school tour in Amsterdam that had become the defining moment in catapulting her into her now-successful career. The cultural side and not that the red-light area and cannabis bars from which their teachers had steered their class of thirty back then.

Thirty girls full of protest innocence and mock daring away! 'Teacher, Teacher? Why are those women modelling glowing swimwear in those little glass-fronted booths?' *New line of swimwear.* 'Why is that woman waving her foot from that upstairs window?' *Cooling it, I expect.* 'Why is that man going into the booth and the curtain drawn?' *Discretion.* On and on with the Teacher, Teacher, questions to Ms Brophy and Ms Malone, as they had dragged their class away through the toy-town streets and past the lighting-strung over house-boats on the waterways – in their school uniforms that Ucind had said, *What were they like?* – and to the Rijksmuseum and the Van Gogh the next day.

'These are the images that will remain in your memories, girls, in twenty years, in forty years, not the street nightlife. This is the real night-watch,' Ms Brophy announced in front of the Rembrandt's *Nachtwacht*, her cleverness causing a smile to creep onto the ruddy cheeks of her unmade face and crinkling around her blue eyes. *'Militia Company of District II under the Command of Captain Frans Banninck Cocq.'* Hilarity reigned. Ms Brophy persisted: 'These are the real attractions of Amsterdam, uniformed and armed with plumed hats, and musketry, leather, and gunpowder, menace lurking in the corners of their eyes. Painted in the golden age of exploration!' Ms Brophy got as close as she could to the painting, studying the soldiers, clearly enthralled. More of it later in the Van Gogh while introducing the *Wheatfield with Crows*. 'It was one of Van Gogh's last paintings – a harbinger of death!'

Of course, they had paid not a smidgin of attention, Ucind and her, except to interrupt, and she given the nudge to let her know it was her turn to invent and contrive.

'Ms Brophy, Ms Brophy? Isn't it true that Van Gogh died from a wound that, although self-inflicted, should not have killed him? So, he could not have been anticipating his death? Isn't it also true that he was attended by a certain

Dr Gachet, whose daughter was reputed to be having a relationship with Van Gogh – of which the good doctor may not have entirely approved? Could the good doctor not therefore have committed a great sin of omission against art by not speedily attending the artist? Isn't it therefore ironic-peculiar that Van Gogh's paintings of him should be one of the most revered, and—?'

'Sara Loughlin, enough! Ironic-peculiar, indeed! We know who put you up to this, don't we, Ucind Gorman?' She even had the teachers dropping the *l* and the *a*, calling her Ucind instead of Lucinda and them not knowing that it was a *sounds-like*. 'I was counting on you, Sara, to provide elucidation for the less artistically endowed girls in the class.'

Felt sorry for her then and did try to compensate. 'The *Almond Blossoms*, Ms Brophy, against that beautiful azure blue sky with the turquoise hue draining out, spring sunrise or an early afternoon sunset. The gilded tint is there whenever the painting catches the light from outside. The blossoms were a symbol of hope for Van Gogh, against the last of the turquoise until the autumn when the sun would be low and golden again, an autumn that he never saw. It is the colour that is truly magical.' Ucind had given her a delighted kick, except the real irony was that she had been serious.

'What a lovely memory! Thank you, Sara. Girls, you will never forget that colour now. Wasted – such talent wasted on ironic-peculiars,' she had gone on to deplore. Poor Ms Brophy had been given early retirement the following year on the grounds of anxiety – those lurking menaces?

Ms Brophy had been wrong about what Sara would remember from the trip: it was the expression on the faces of one of the ethereal booth-women, not much older than herself with a dazed, smiling face. As her memory of the school trip when they got back, she had painted her in a luminous yellow swimsuit, dancing back and forth in a trance. She was not brilliant at faces and had used the light in the booth to blur her features, making it into a modern Munch's *Madonna* complete with a glowing red crown. The painting had caused a minor scandal when she had submitted it, but in fairness to Ms Brophy and the nuns, they had awarded it first prize! It was hung up for parent-teacher day where it raised eyebrows, to say the least, saved only by its title: *Cast the First Stone*.

It was from there that art poured into her life: art leading to fashion that had become her thing. Colour, texture, design, material, and the effects on both the wearer and the beholder, combined with that quality that Ms Brophy had so deplored: ironic-peculiar. But serious intent – there were always features of any woman's presence that she could capture to create a statement and hint at a possibility. She would like to retrace those beginnings.

To her surprise that morning when they returned to Istanbul Airport, it turned out to have a huge shopping foyer with all those designer labels that she was hoping to see in Schiphol. Even the control tower rising into a giant cobra sent her as it reflected rose into the morning light, and she had thought of Cleopatra's asp. Rick agreed with a cursory glance, his own aquiline face not a million miles away when he looked about from his height. Inside was newness under endless contouring palm frond panels that diffused light from giant circular skylights, rising and falling over a forest of columns – and that was before the explosions of light and fashion of the designer shops.

Brightly coloured, diaphanous sheer fabrics modelled on vacant-eyed mannequins, jewellery in iridescence bursts, and handbags and shoes presented as pure objects of desire. For a moment, the garments and accessories on display in the mirrored glitz of the airport concourses had made her feel that her own creations were inadequate, these object d'art creations that shimmered in oases of fluorescent light. It was not ironic-peculiar, more beauty or as close to beauty as fashion without its wearer could be! The wearer was her thing: she always insisted on that. Nevertheless, the intoxicating scents of leather and newness had brought her back to her early ambitions to influence London, New York, and Paris with her creations. She needed that release again, statements full of innuendo, contradiction, and absolute daring that carried the wearer with the statement to an intimation of the sublime as well as innuendo. You had to '*live the life*', as Noel Gallagher of Oasis had said, and she had not since that time.

A sex-charged pair of red-soled Louboutin high heels sent a thrill through her. She always considered high heels a *mini-me* of legs and rear, the stiletto rising into the seat of the heel; it was how she picked shoes for her clients, not telling them this – and the less said about the insinuating redness of the sole, the better. Finally, she had made her purchases, a lycra swimsuit shoaled in colourful exotic fish displaying amongst coral reefs, an adventure planned for later in the trip. Yellow butterflyfish vibrated in coloured stripes amongst the coral and a large fish mooned. He made her smile, a red grouper with blue spots and a cocked eye – plus the Louboutin shoes that she simply could not resist!

Deciding to ignore Andy's suggestion to always 'eat in one of the health-conscious restaurants rather than *partake of junk food that sat in your stomach for the flight*', she had settled herself at a concourse bar that was a protected arbour under that roof, grabbing a spot beside a multi-national business type in the latest smart casual. A technology expert, sufficiently recognised to dress down, she thought – a named name in his field no doubt. He had a way of sharing an immediacy that opened between them, as he nevertheless frantically worked on a presentation. It was an energy solution with long, interconnected strings of logic and circuitry with coded shapes and arrows. She pretended to make out the logic and ask him about it before he excused himself after small talk with, *Needs must . . .* She completed the phrase to herself . . . *when the devil rides*. Well, another time.

Passengers had swirled around the restaurant island as throngs of humanity pressed through the adjacent walkways. Aviation fuel, earthy odours, and a perfusion of perfume auras had blended with the pungency of coffee. Her waiter had come and gone with that Middle Eastern warmth and curiosity: *Where you from? I have a girlfriend in Dublin* – that was a lie – and they then chatted back and forth about the new airport. They both agreed the control tower was a cobra despite it being named a tulip, and he had said that in the evening there was an intense red light that shone up its throat from the base that made it an avatar. She had gotten through her drinks a little faster than otherwise in the pleasantness of her coffee-brew cocoon, the relaxed surroundings, and the chat, almost floating. Hopper's paintings came to mind, more *Chop-Suey* tit-a-tat than solo *Automat* where a lone woman reads with avid interest in a public-private space. Was that the Hopper painting at the Chicago Institute, or was that another painting, *Nighthawks* that had an eerie feel – she had to go there. She hadn't once found it necessary to toy with her mobile while she sat.

However, she now tongued the aftertaste of three white wines along with the sharpness of the wasabi-coated peanuts that constituted her lunch. She wondered how soon the complimentary drinks would arrive to lift the throb of a headache that was threatening to settle in. The navy soft-leather seat was moulded to her – or vice versa – and she eased the seat backwards, not wanting to fully awaken from the dreamy airport experience. How had they gotten through it all? It was all behind at last and only the future ahead with white cushions on lapis lazuli through the window, as far as the eye could see, and her entrance would be along the plane's aisle bordered in aureoles like the runway of lights on a catwalk. Never mind the warning on the FCO website not to stray in Egypt because there was always a risk a bus could run you down as you crossed to the supermarket. Tourist areas were safe. A holiday of a lifetime that's what it was, well as far as Andy and Rick were concerned: Cairo and Luxor and then cruising up the Nile to Aswan and descending again, before off to the Red Sea for sun, sand and surf, and an amazing coral experience that she had missed the last time – James must be contactable!

She remembered their year, James's and hers, and what did anyone expect in a new millennium when they were just getting the first taste of bling and losing the plot big time? Ireland was coming out, centuries after the rest of the world and a whole Middle Ages of gloom just ending, and she was having the wildest, hyper-most first year in the College of Art and Design, into a new Millenium. Just out of the nineties that was more recovery than blow-out when the country had discovered a winning formula, and influx of migrants when the Irish were always emigrants everywhere else in the past. In the honeyed light of autumn that year there was a sense that it couldn't last, and grab it while you can, and James suddenly there to introduce her into his racing circle.

She loved race meetings, and James's betting on the horses based on how they moved from the rear, and then seeing they had an intelligent head to get an attitude – how he had picked her she suspected – and rushing through to see how they cantered to the start. Wads down and wait. His friend, Noel, leaving for a *slash* and saying he would be back for the *climax*, and James asking, *Whose?* Pointing her shoes and modelling high-fashion around the parade ring. Oh, the smell of money and horse dung and jangling hoofs and clinking champagne glasses bringing out the feckless in everyone. Taking a gamble with Lady Luck in the air, and not sure who or what was at stake.

The race, stupid, and stupid amounts of money, but serious intent in the white tents. Words whispered about developments and mega loan portfolios amidst the horseracing tips, though mostly kidding each other about the heli-purchases that had become the rage. Suited men strutting as modern tzars with hands in their pockets like they were in a Rolls Royce auction room kicking tyres, and beautiful women dressed in sheer, flowing dresses and fascinators, or floppy hat in her case, coping with the field conditions – the intensity of heat in the crush under the canvas. Got to be in a parade ring, show her class and hold her head, and James giving her a not too discreet nudge on the bum to point at his thoroughbred without taking his hands out of his pockets. Brat! Gave her that winner to lead-in and stood back, admiring them both from the rear. Brat again!

The helicopters landing on the helipad when they had stayed in dreamland castle-hotels where they had treated you as m'lord and m'lady in front of the large open mantlepieces with the ancestors looking down from above – *what would the helicopter pilot have for his meal?* James and she had drunk reserve whiskies in the bar starting at twenty-five a shot and then wandered the grounds to look at the moon dangling through bare branches.

What fun with his buck teeth and more of a guffaw horse laugh than braying was her James, and long and lean; and how did they make a person ridiculous and then he turned into a character who played it and it all worked; let's call him boldfaced or *bloody-minded direct* as he used to say and no problem getting into bed – *flesh in a flash* – any time of the day. Her term from back then was *scrunch* because she squeezed up her baby blue-greens to come in 'city central', her room at the top of the stairs. The owner had improvised it with frosted glass on each side when she had missed out on the other room-rentals, and not very private, only nobody had reason to come up. Decent to a fault James who always made sure she was good for everything, a student and all, and she only wasted it more and not cared; and he had found her weak spot that released all her inhibitions 'til sex was matter of fact – but as students, we all did these things.

She had also met Andy that year and could not dismiss him from her mind. It was right at the start during 'freshers' week' when he was working a political stand with blood-red-spattered captions on cartoon posters. She had thought she could do better posters and had told him so. Then, it transpired he was busy as a student leader making his speeches across the campuses and was the one on the news with long wild hair and Fu Manchu moustache. They had met again before Christmas when he had spoken at a mass rally in the college, and they had agreed to meet up. Between her own project deadline and the National Hunt Season on run up to Christmas, she didn't have a minute at the time, and then they had met again briefly just before breakup and agreed to get together the following term.

It was when he had organised a mechanical bucking bull to raise funds, and then had not been able to switch it on because of the insurance. That had been fun too, a different fun, because he had gone ahead and spun the bull with nobody on it and posted times and awards on the notice board. Everyone the next day had a story to tell of how they had fallen off the bucking bull and had their time in seconds for how long they were on that never happened. She agreed to go along to student marches and rallies that at the time were trying to get free third-level extended to all post-secondary, not simply university.

She had loved pouring herself into fatigues for the whole student protest thing, a little tighter than battle ready – for friendly fire maybe – and the buzz of the marches and all that pretend militancy, 'cause let's face it, they weren't going to get violent except for the few head-bangers, but that was the edge. She had dyed her hair a bright pink, and she had gotten matching bow tattoos – one on the back of each of her thighs long before body art was a thing – serious intent as well as pressie time. James had enjoyed the change too, gave him an arty girlfriend who was different and got him into the papers more, and that occasionally made her wonder was he using her.

On summer break, James worked non-stop on his new business – so completely drained when they met that he was hardly able to converse. Andy had volunteered overseas that took him to setting up accounts for a restaurant at the base of Kilimanjaro, and that included a hike to the top. She felt she was the boring one as she returned to living with her parents. It was a desultory, haphazard time when she helped at a wedding gown dressmaker – who called herself a nuptial designer and talked with a nasal intonation about structured designs, flowing effects, lighting lustre, and larger-than-life ballgowns – that initially bored her intensely. Until she got into materials and what they could do, that is, and that *marrying was not just about the groom, the dress should primarily express the woman and the relationship* – said with a slightly superior attitude by her boss. In no time she was the one dropping her fabric preferences for the bride to consider mikado, faille, or gazar, depending on budget; she retained slinky charmeuse that had a habit of clinging with an overveil of a plain weave batiste for herself when the time came.

In August, she and Ucind headed to Florence where they queued two hours in the heat for entrance to the Uffizi when pre-booked tickets proved unavailable. Her world opened to human beauty. Filippino Lippi's portraits, especially the gauche adolescent self-portrait looking for compassion that she could have cradled for an eternity, male beauty. Botticelli's *Birth of Venus* encapsulated female beauty for her, with red hair and blue-green eyes like her own, and with a figure not that dissimilar either – if she allowed for the painting obviously following a mannerist style from fifteenth-century Florence. In her eyes resided all those undefinable mysteries and qualities of womanhood. Botticelli had captured youthful tender and compassionate beauty upon which the world could only bestow its bounty and treat with all gentleness as she stepped ashore off a giant shell – perfection created.

Those paintings even affected Ucind, who was offhanded about art, as they both had tried to imagine how it was to move from the medieval two-dimensional religious art to rediscover classical human beauty. Another day they struggled through the thirty-degrees-plus heat to find David, a five-meter chunk of muscled marble that was more down Ucind's path, and who said that it made her want to suck one of those giant toes. Perspective adjustment for going on a twenty-meter column resulted in the statue having huge feet and hands – but a small willy that Ucind had said fairly destroyed the myth about big feet.

That summer, and especially seeing the *Birth of Venus*, had changed her and when she went back to college, she was much more her own person, assured of her qualities and more confident in their expression. Andy, whom she deliberately targeted déjà vu on the student representative stand during fresher's week, was much more substantive to her. There were his experiences from volunteering in Tanzania and his looks had changed to be more rugged, tanned, with stubble and the Fu Manchu gone. He had acquired a Red Yamaha motorbike that was the first of those racing bikes that became street bikes. That was not her thing, but she had gripped with all her might tucked in behind him and within touching the roadway taking a corner. Slipping between traffic and accelerating out of certain crashes, so fast that she had thought she couldn't hold on, and then braking and sending her splaying around him. The closest experience she had before that was on a spinning, gyrating ride at the RDS Funderland Christmas Carnival, that to be honest, was safe despite leaving her wobbly for hours. But this was real life with real dangers, as real as the magnified grit on the surface, and while it left her both exhilarated and breathless, it was not entirely enough to stop her seeing James. He still was not available that much, and she had become less taken in by his aura and the milieu in which he moved.

Then she was pregnant.

Finally, service was coming their way and the lads from the safety demo were back on the trolley service – that damn boring *boing* again and the fasten seat belt sign illuminated red with an X-rating. Trolley service was scurrying back up the aisle with a clinking of bottles and glasses that they couldn't have. A shudder through the fuselage, and she clicked her seatbelt buckle and sighed, rolling her eyes towards the adjacent couple. 'So much for being upgraded.'

The man commented amused: 'Grin and bear it; it is momentary twerbulence. They will take us out of it if it becomes worse.'

Oh, deep gravelly and very definitive, and big square head and mandatory bobbing Adam's apple and all-the-better-to-see-you-eyes – yes, Germanic rather than Eastern

European or Dutch. Dark and swarthy, not the straw hair and limpid blue, and authoritative advice – now she knew. 'Das-ist-Das' would be her name for him.

'Gin and bear it, more like.' That got a smile from him, but his girlfriend on the other side of him, none too pleased, eyed her suspiciously and prattled to him in German . . . and he had to give her lengthy explanations. They pointed back and forth to her – damsel in distress that she had not intended.

The plane climbed, banked, and settled into a new flight path, and then a surge passed through as the plane levelled off again.

'Wery responsive aeroplane?' he reassured her when he had finished the clarification to his girlfriend. More turbulence followed.

'Such muscular movement, is it extra?' She got another smile from him, but a glare from his girlfriend, who began rattling on again. She needed to make peace, as she could use the conversation.

'This is nichts,' he said, still smiling. 'I travel long haul to Singapore, and from Schiphol the route goes through stormy weather in winter. Otherwise, it is a good transit airport, very efficient.'

'A person I know travels to Singapore and is never sure which transit hub to take. I am travelling with my son over there, Rick.' She indicated him two rows ahead and then wondered why she specifically had not said husband, yet claimed her son? An empty fear pulled at her, as if her world were changing forever. She decided it was guilt for her disloyalty.

His girlfriend sought out Rick, and then peered over to Sara. 'So, you don't sit together.' She got back to her book, enough said, and took her focus off Sara. Where is your husband? What kind of mother are you?

Sara was going to explain. 'No,' she said quietly.

The German man answered Sara's earlier question as if the interruption had not happened: 'All the airlines out of Schiphol to Singapore fly the same geodesic down between the Black and Caspian Seas. It can be *twerbulent*. A different airport that flies more sideways. Munich, but can have snow disruption in winter? Frankfurt?'

She was going to explain that because they lived in Ireland, they had a choice of European hubs and only got as far as: 'We are Irish—'

'We are supporting your *backstup*!'

She heard that. 'Yes, we should hug every German.'

'Hug a German. We do not hear this every day. We will need to become accustomed,' he remarked, and they were both amused by this.

'I am Sara,' she introduced herself, taking advantage of the moment.

'I am Brigit-te. We should properly greet, but I don't think this is possible because you need to stretch across Gerhardt.'

He raised his eyebrow on her side.

She thought about mentioning that the name Brigitte might have originated from the Gaelic, Brigíd, an Irish saint at the conversion to Christianity who was credited with special powers, except lost in translation. Gerhardt though, a forthright male name, and as it happened the name that she gave to the Teutonic knight that hung above her bed in her student days. It was a copy she had done of an original stained-glass window from Oscar Wilde's house on Merrion Square, and in it he looked slightly blurred and stoned. James had said he didn't do defending after they had spent a night commingling beneath Gerhardt's gaze. She had replied then that he was her Hamlet, letting him sin while he waited for the perfect moment to strike. 'Heaven can wait,' he had dismissed, the only time James had let slip something of himself. Ironic-strange that she nevertheless knew everything about him.

Enough. She got back to her own thoughts – when did she ever have the time?

She looked out over the endless tufts of white, out to the faint blue horizon with its billowing clouds joining like soft stepping-stones. Look at things now? Nobody lost out, not even Andy who supported her, because otherwise it could have been tough all the time until Rick was adult himself. Of course, Andy need not have given up university and him that good academically and only a year to go; a part-time job with that auctioneering agency would have sufficed instead of taking on full time. They loved him there and would have gone along with part-time, and he'd have got to finish his degree in engineering, wouldn't he? Regrets it now deep down and him the student leader fighting to create an information age and not finishing himself.

Then, he wouldn't have had to make such a massive thing of getting his student-protest hair sheep shorn when he got into property for a time, and then maybe the sparkle wouldn't have gone out in his eyes, when he went all-conformist. And he might not have completely fallen out with his father, Henry, who was hoping that he would join the architectural practice that he and Andy's mother, Jenny, ran together. A sequence of blows for the father, his only son not following in his footsteps into architecture, and then Andy's involvement in student politics that his father called 'protest against anything' politics; and she the last in the chain leading to Andy not finishing – so he certainly could not lead the practice. But he and Jenny did come to the wedding breakfast that Andy wasn't sure, seeing as it was only a modest meal for a small grouping after signing in the registry office, because she and Andy had decided to postpone the church wedding until the furore had abated.

Her dream meringue of a wedding occasion was still waiting – now for a renewal of vows maybe. Depending?

At least Andy was in a multi-national technology company now and doing better than his previous classmates. Was it not finishing his degree? She wasn't sure anymore with how he was behaving lately with his reverting to his student causes and involvement in politics that was still possible – she dared not discuss.

Lucky with Rick though, fall-on-his-feet adorable, sensitive, and smart-as-can-be Rick, who has done all the growing up for them; a clock ticking a little a day – more a month – advancing through the seasons of the year and year into year without any hiccups – until last year! Seems good now, and no reaction to the paternity subpoena when Andy explained it to him. He made Andy focus, made a better person out of him doing bringing up in reverse. Men always stay boys and never have to grow up like a woman: only you'd have to love them when they get that light into their eyes like Andy during his anti-Iraqi war protests – carries you along. Giacometti's *Man Walking* that they saw at the Maeght on the first of their newfound holidays. He it was who also sculpted *Woman Standing. A woman has arrived and is not for turning,* as the saying goes; standing and walking these days has men totally confused. Poor men, not as perfect, they must make something of themselves, unless already made like James, who still had to make it again by the Red Sea after he parted from Ireland.

Andy was not right at the mo' as even took a note right in the middle of their lovemaking. Just held up, reached out to the locker, and noted his note and then kept on going – what was that, and where did he learn to multitask like that? Working late more than usual and Ucind said to look for a load of new dead-giveaway peccadillos in bed. Oh, she'd have loved more of those instead of straightforward missionary as a rule these days; but prefer more again if he just let himself go and not focused on her – could spend an age of angels on her thigh or her breast or another *sweet-spot* spellbound. More sensuous and she enjoyed not completely losing herself physically right off. She could dream about things until he got her arousal spread going. Back again for more next day, and nobody else had that kind of time. But sometimes she wished he would mushroom cloud her atomic as James did back then – but able to move Andy's fetish around and it need never stop when the littlest piece of her had that power to hold him . . .? However, no blinding light till she was out of her mind; yeah, more *voriations* though as in their student days when he had her tipping her toes on her side and then snuggle her warm in her purr. The doctor had said that's how they might have had Rick, assuming he is his . . .

He used to be fun too, called her bottom line a bottom smile and would they take it for a walk, her bottom? She always had a 'lazy-ass' despite good muscle tone and even when she was on the swimming team it had no effect – a woman didn't have to exercise as much 'cause the 'mones helped keep her toned latest science. Not like those keep-fit adrenaline junkies that came to her when she or her man got promoted glass ceiling and needed to attend this and that from restaurant to theatre; that was when she did personal shopping with them, often a whole week on their wardrobe – her the wild one with the crazy creations tamed. Yet she had a thriving business and her name had gotten about again after the recession; even getting lesser celebrity commissions again – not the heyday of Celtic Bling when there was no concern on the spend to create statement outfits and accessorise to the nines. Except she was always going to be the wild child from college who got pregnant and then tricked a student leader into marrying her only to ruin his degree – who might not now be the father!

In Egypt, she might produce that crazy fashion line from the past, a Cleopatra with snakes, not mentioning Cleo came to a bad end; only what fun on the way with two Roman General tick boxes, one an emperor; or just maybe using snake power with a Cleo Boo Asp that coiled in mood colours and knots. She could persuade Andy to go back and degree it courtesy of CB's bad vibe – or do whatever would bring back that light in his eye.

Whoosh! Flight was a bit bumpy again, *boing,* and get strapped in again; a *boing* was not necessary 'cause how was a flight smooth in the first place when they were moving through air and the clouds morphing and scudding about; she didn't get it – better do as they say and buckle back up though it had already stopped. Could study the clouds volumizing below?

A deep reassuring voice came from her right: 'Twerbulence is for a little time. Always when a plane travels over high mountains or from land to sea there are air ripples.'

Air ripples! Das-ist-Das! Such base tones, and now he had to explain to Brigitte the what and the how and the why – a tight leash for sure.

Before she had even thought about it, she had taken out her sketch pad and begun an off-the-shoulder, flowing white gown and then added Brigit-te's head, but wide-eyed and wild with OTT glowing liner.

Brigitte shot up from her reading to look. Sara held up her sketch and said to her across him: 'Glacier Lady?'

Brigitte beckoned, and Sara passed over the sketch for her to examine in more detail. 'So, this is what you do?'

'She is melting like ice cream,' Das-ist-Das commented.

More going on in the corners of that large cranium – men? 'I was thinking tragedy . . . glaciers are melting these days. This is a statement on tragedy, on life maybe,' she bluffed.

'Like an opera, Brünnhilde in the Wagnerian Ring Cycle, do you know it?' Das-ist-Das was suddenly excited, his dark eyes pointing. 'It is about the battle of beauty, love, and power?'

'Eternal battle cycle!' Sara said, that got a smile.

It was easy for men, but the wages of sin had come home to roost – good word – suddenly for her with Rick. Yes, a single event that spawned a whole sequence that took its course in an opera spiralling out from a crisis into a crescendo of arias – and the high drama of the time and everyone saying to not go through with the pregnancy. She had been able to hold onto Rick, for dear life Rick, and the smell of baby perfect that's moving, breathing, loving, and growing; and funny-peculiar when you are young, and you think that everything is going to come merry-go-round. It doesn't you know. Events such as births might happen only once – operas have got it right when they stop the action to sing endlessly. Not 'zactly true either as she didn't want another 'til they were out and lived a bit and only that now or nearly-not-quite; and time for another as her school friends were only starting now in their mid-thirties after years of good times and all in decent careers.

'Yes, Eternal.'

'Das-ist-Das.' She slipped in her name for him.

He smiled again.

'Thank you, she is too cold, perhaps dangerous.' Brigitte passed back the sketch, breaking into a long explanation of her opinion to Gerhardt.

Why was she bothering showing her work when there was no need? She turned towards the window, trying to pick out the dots of tiny crafts with white wakes on the blue coruscated surface of the Mediterranean below, all making for port. Which would get there first? What a joke, and that was gambling for sure. It wasn't about relationships, or love, or the right choice but the accidental whose sperm got there first. Would it ever let her go?

Oh, why was James back on the scene now claiming he was the father all over again, and looking for a paternity test out of the dim and distant? Rick was seventeen, almost grown. Well, he could be the father. She wouldn't bet: a betting person would call it a longshot, the way they say twenty or fifty-to-one bar these in one of his horse races. Was it simply a son or more? Her? He was her first real love, and she could easily have meant more to him than she had realised. Her suddenly getting married to Andy when he didn't come forward might have caught him off-guard – but these things can't wait.

Whatever about Rick's resemblance to Andy – James was a dead ringer for a donkey – and not her son. Just look at Rick there with Andy's mannerisms and gestures. He was still spending a long time replaying that same video. The truth is anyone not Andy was long odds and Andy was okay with that 'cause he accepted it as part of how things were with her, yet he still wanted her. This will strain what was a temporary *éloignement*, 'cause Andy's freaked out from James's solicitor's letter and thinking Rick is not his! What if James's sperm had romped home like one of his thoroughbred bets on a rear? Whose paternity would out during the holiday, gone legitimate or illegitimate-non-word, who is to say?

Thanks to Ucind that notice would come in five-star surroundings because been-everywhere, done-everything Ucind said they did not want to lose her to food poisoning or cholera or typhoid or one of those parasites that eats you from the inside; and even Andy, who never questioned, was going to go on about the cost until she said that it was 'Ucind said' and let him raid all his sweet-spots for a week – also Ucind's suggest. The announcement might carry a less favourable star rating.

'"Till or 'Tarkling. . . Madaam?'

The two had returned and were serving complimentary drinks in Dublinese sounds-like, popping up everywhere since the collapse as Andy says, and *Madaam* if you please – is this for real or a joke – play along? 'Tinkling.'

'Is that 'tinkling 'tarkling?' Baby faces the tall and the short. 'Or 'tinkling 'till?' Double act is very amusing guys. She hoped that Brigitte didn't twig the accent.

'"Tinkling 'tarkling, and hair of the dog G and T instead of prosecco?'

'Did you get that, TnT?' Tall fair-faced passing plastic cup of ice to smaller sallow; water hissy-fizzing, gurgling, guzzling, pouring, resealing and back and across for the hair of the dog and finally coming her way and then here's the 'tinkling 'tarkling.

'Thank you.' At last.

'And are you 'tinkling 'tarkling too, Tsir?' he next asked her neighbour.

Not amused: 'I would like a double Scotch on the rocks, please.'

''Tinkling Wouble Tcotch?' from the fair faced to his companion that didn't amuse. They got through the order, passing two individually sealed bottles of Scotch. Still not smiling is her neighbour but going through a lovely routine of opening each clear bottle and cascading it over the ice.

'Might be the last one for the holiday?' he said, tossing it back.

Oh, that's a hefty gulp for sure. 'Don't say that.'

'Egypt is much stricter these days.'

'It's a holiday of a lifetime for us.'

'Interesting? I am certain the better hotels will serve *liqweor*. It is Ramadan so who knows.'

Liqweor, great in translation – Das-ist-Das! 'We've have gone for the best hotels I could find.'

'Nothing to worry about. Drink your heart's contentment, yes?'

Brigitte took only water, 'tinking-'tarkling to her obvious annoyance. After the crew members had gone, she looked across to Sara remarking: 'They are your fellow country boys, yes?'

'Yes, very enthusiastic.' That fell dead. Sara suppressed a laugh. The first taste of gin settled nicely on her tongue with its herbs and juniper bite.

She got to excuse herself to go to the bathroom, squeezing through the space in front of Das-ist-Das and Brigitte. Out of the seat at last and adjusted and straightened and Das-ist-Das's all-the-better-to-see-you-eyes following, studying her. A sense of dread again overtook her as she smiled towards Rick as she passed. Was she on her way to losing them, her once wild student leader with his pillow-soft store of every scintilla of her, and her son of seventeen years?

Chapter 2,

Taxi to Tahrir

Andy

Andy ordered a hotel taxi, a request at whose insistence the dapper hotel concierge in an immaculate navy suit reacted with a grimace that creased his neatly groomed appearance. 'Tahrir Square during Jumu'ah prayers on the first Friday of Ramadan?' he replied, his words reverberating with the waterfall crashing in the high marble foyer. 'It is not safe for tourists!'

There were anxious glances from international tours clustered around their respective national flags held aloft for visits to the Great Pyramids and other attractions.

The concierge then translated into Arabic for the moustachioed hotel driver he beckoned from the entrance, and whose face likewise furrowed before he suddenly cheered into a broad smile that turned his expression to laughter.

'Abdul will drive you.' The concierge, composure restored, wrung his hands together in a washing motion.

Andy followed the tall, slim driver. As they neared the door, a uniformed security guard rose and, resting his hand on a revolver protruding from a holster on his hip, directed him through the metal detector through which he had come on his arrival the previous evening. He indicated that Andy should empty his pockets, and their contents went through a separate x-ray with an inordinate amount of time spent checking on the computer screen what was already visible to the naked eye. The rotund security man's deep eyes were the picture of cordial good humour, Andy thought, until he lifted the two mobiles from the tray to ask: 'Two, why two?' His driver repeated that the security guard needed to know why two phones. 'Terrorists have many phones,' he joked to Andy. The security guard gave no hint of amusement, and his eyes were steady black orbs.

He didn't react. He was an intrepid business traveller, hardened to the vagaries that international travel could throw his way, especially in recent years. Keep it simple, one easy explanation in as few words as possible, and stick to it.

'Buy . . . Local . . . SIM for this mobile,' he articulated, pointing. He always used broken English in a non-English-speaking country, mimicking back whatever version of pidgin English was used with him, and liberally throwing in international pop icons, designer labels, technological abbreviations, acronyms, and brand names that they might recognise.

The security guard understood but was not satisfied. Without dropping his gaze, he queried: 'Jumu'ah – no shops?' Then he and his driver conversed in Arabic, the latter running one hand through his curly dark head and looking perplexed.

After more discussion, the driver turned and summarised in a single phrase: 'He does not believe you!' Following this, the security guard held Andy in a constant stare, eyes that were now frozen in their focus and looked anything other than genial. He again moved his hand slowly and lodged it over the revolver.

The two phones were a long story: one he used for business and from which he had removed the work-*SIM* to allow him to buy a local-*SIM* – he didn't want an avalanche of urgent work emails coming his way. The other mobile was a private phone that, although a pay-as-you-go, was a backup from a different provider with cheaper roaming rates. He decided on a demonstration, asking if it was okay to take his work mobile and switch it on.

The security guard took his free hand and placed it over the mobiles, saying: 'Switch on? No!'

Abdul again intervened, and Andy was allowed to take the work mobile to switch it on.

He activated it, and the screen came up saying: *No SIM detected.*

He showed it to both men. 'I want to buy a local SIM,' he said slowly.

The security guard shook his head. 'No use today. I will keep for you. Shut it off.' He then nodded and smiled as if he had resolved a major situation.

Andy took only the backup phone with his other possessions.

They all stood. His driver confirmed: 'Only one mobile. Two is not permissible. Hotel will keep for you. First, you buy SIM, but not today . . . we will see.' He began rubbing his fingers, indicating money. 'Small notes or *wuros*. Extra problems for Sarim . . .'

Paying for the privilege of having his phone confiscated! He had local currency in large denominations that he had gotten at the airport. Instead, he passed a euro note to Abdul, who passed it to the security guard, who in turn examined it carefully and smiled when he recognised it. At prevailing exchange rates, this was a sizeable sum into hundreds of Egyptian pounds.

'Samir will keep your phone. Ask for him? If you have more *wuros*, he will be happy.'

It would cost him more to reclaim the mobile. He let it go.

When they had passed through the main entrance, the driver explained: 'Samir can send your mobile to the police for testing, but he says he will hold for you.'

Once in the taxi, Abdul began pressing Andy to go anywhere except Tahrir Square, perhaps the reason for his smile earlier when the concierge had called him. As they drove along the concrete motorway, speeding under an opaque blue void, his accented drawl began over his clicking worry beads. Once he found out which travel agent Andy used, Abdul had an in-depth knowledge of what was included in Andy's tour, the city's must-dos of pyramids, Egyptian Museum, and oldest bazaar, before the cruise up the Nile from Aswan to Luxor. 'You will fall in love.'

Andy supposed he meant the country, Egypt. Although his relationship with Sara was strained, the holiday when she and Rick arrived the following day would be an opportunity for a *rapprochement* between them. She presently described the state of their relationship as an *éloignement*, and not a *fracturation* as she had used the previous summer. That groundless subpoena by her ex-boyfriend was the cause of this *éloignement*. He had never gotten over being eclipsed by Andy, that simple . . . he smiled to himself that his driver might be advising him to move on.

Abdul then slowly laid out alternative offerings that might tempt Andy away from Tahrir Square: 'El Citadel –

afterwards Al Azhar Park beside with lots of people; Islamic Cairo; the Coptic Hanging Church on two Roman Towers; the City of the Dead,' – laughing when he related that the living also resided there. 'We can park the car and walk as you please, but later. Now we must drive . . .'

Andy had already visited the Hanging Church, and the City of the Dead held little interest, but El Citadel the following day, built by Saladin, was it not? Various other offerings came and went, even a drive to Alexandria, anything except his planned Tahrir Square. Andy rejected all. He was determined to get to Tahrir Square to walk down the revolution that had kicked off the Arab Spring in the expectation of a new dawn. It would bring him back to his student politics and those heady days protesting the drift into the second Iraqi War. He remembered that nobody had questioned his continued involvement in student politics while technically not a student back then. As far as anyone was concerned, he was taking a year out because of the birth of a child with his student wife that was then quite a novelty, but which break he knew was permanent.

That was the year when he had really lived, had arisen in the morning to plan protests for the Iraqi War, and had been one of those who travelled to the UK as part of a student deputation to take part in the protest marches and mass rallies there. The war had gone ahead regardless in March 2003, seeking out the imaginary Weapons of Mass

Destruction, the WMD three-letter acronym, under a rationale of unknown-knowns that became unknown-unknowns. When the anti-war campaign had failed, he felt a shared guilt at having let down the Middle East and when Arab Spring erupted in 2011, he had followed every newscast to witness a new beginning for the region. The walkdown would allow him to touch the bravery of the protesters and confirm that their hopes were not in vain. As people spilled out of the mosques after prayers, he could get a feel for the real mood of the country; he could see for himself that the revolution had been a new dawn. It mattered to him.

Abdul's modulated drone interrupted his thought train with a proposal of how they might break their impasse over his wanting to go to Tahrir Square. 'It is Jumu'ah Prayer, as you heard. Holy prayers for the first Friday in Ramadan. Nowhere is open until prayers are finished. Instead, I will drive for you to see the beautiful city of Cairo. It is my gift to you. A special service. Egypt welcomes travellers, Allah commands . . . Inshallagh.'

'Tahrir Square,' Andy instructed. He resigned himself to a special-service price tag for a detour that would be added, regardless. The comfortable hotel limousine eased over the motorway, turning misaligned slabs and patched road surface into rolling rhythms, and zipping past and around the few other cars. Their gleaming saloon was luxurious in comparison to some of the other vehicles that spluttered and lunged along in plumes of smoke with double-decked bouncing families gazing out through open windows. Women wore hijabs on their heads, he noted. That had not always been the case when they were last here.

He would much prefer to be like those families thumping along in a rusted tin can of a taxi that ramped each roadway slab, sweltering in the oppressive morning temperatures. That was the return that he and Sara had planned on their last visit when they were restricted to the standard tourist itinerary on account of Sara's pregnancy. The temperatures had been unbearable for her, but Egypt had nevertheless burst upon them in all its wonder. Even recently, when the return finally seemed a possibility, they had promised themselves in addition to the sightseeing, they would experience the people who claimed its ancient heritage.

The people, and the land itself with its fables and realities shimmering off the endless burning sand were the fascination. He remembered a random detail that their previous ebullient tour guide had imparted in a hushed voice: the ancient Egyptians had believed that the sky was in synchronisation with their lives, gods and goddesses moving in constellations through the annual cycle. They had been fascinated, and later Sara and he had studied the stars and constellations associated with gods who defined the flooding of the Nile, around which the Egyptian year had aligned. There were also gods that fought the nightly battle of good and chaos for the sun to rise, gods of love, of womanhood, of learning, of war, of the home, of the afterlife – all of life and death. He remembered them lying together on a woven rug in the fragrant wrap of night air and picking their own stars amongst the trajectories of the billion stars that were shaken from the desert skies, imagining their unknowable future.

Way back then, in their youthful optimism, he would never have thought that they would have to wait all this time to return, but here they were at last. This time it wasn't going to be coach tourism ticking the boxes on the holidaymaker trail: experience the real Egypt, or what was the point?

Only this was already a different holiday than they had intended. Instead of a traditional hotel with open courtyard weaving a magical spell of ornamentation, pattern, and light, they had ended up at a swish modern hotel, Pyramid Dream Palace. It was built so close to the Great Pyramids that they were a continuation of the slides, carousels, and colourful swings beside the giant plastic clown shower. It was a caricature of the culture they had previously embraced – the only remaining ancient wonder commercialised! No option on the hotel – Taafeef, their travel agent had told him, *they had been selected to be upgraded – the gods favoured them*. What also came with the package, he now learned, was one mobile and no walk-about during Jumu'ah prayers.

His mood brightened at the next sight. They passed another family, this time on a motorcycle puttering along the hard shoulder against a distant background of high-rise residential towers festooned in colour. There was a small child on adapted handlebars, father driving, mother side-saddle with an infant, and an older child balancing on the rack above the rear wheel. None of them showed the least concern, as if presenting a perfectly acceptable low-cost alternative for family travel. Cairo's ability to throw up the bizarre remained.

He remembered his own Yamaha R1 that he had acquired when he had returned from volunteering in Africa at the start of third-year engineering. Freshers' Week came, and then there was Sara, wandering over to him in a retro flower-power dress that she told him later was imitation Mary Quant. She was all over his time in Africa, especially the climb of Kilimanjaro, and they went to share a coffee and fruit scone in Bewley's Café, where she insisted they sit under Harry Clarke's stained-glass window. Four columns with different coloured flowers twists spiralling to the capitol where atop each was an urn of floral gems, surrounded by exotic birds, flowers, vines, and butterflies. Such vibrancy of colour, and Sara sitting colourfully beneath, excited to listen, agog to learn more about his climb. Words failed him and he found himself resorting to a chronology of the stages of the climb; what could be seen and heard from the different camps. Their first views had been the indomitable white peaks when they emerged out of the forest, with birdsong all about as the sky had parted; the stars had then rained down onto the peaks over meadow from their first camp; there were alien rocky landscapes with groundsels shaped like giant yuccas and other exotic plants while clouds amorphized beside them; when they had passed through the cloud line the peak looked to be a planet with the rings circling; at the crater camp he had seen the sheer walls of glacier icicles in the orange and purple sunrise over the other peaks, and finally he told her about holding on to get a photo under the sign on top as the weather changed.

He hadn't related how he had had altitude sickness with headaches and nausea and that he had just about made the summit, or that it wasn't just about the stages, or the views. When she asked about his most sublime memory, he initially denied one until having thought about it, it had to be those stars raining down, and of creation flooding out from this mother of Africa into the fecundity of a continent that he was somehow a part, a sense of the universal.

Then she was vivaciously relating her trip to Florence accompanied by Ucind, who wasn't half attractive either. They were never far apart, so if you got one you got them both – Ucind with her insinuations and innuendos pinched through pointed polished nails. It did not seem to have been a wild trip, though. Sara had spent a long time explaining about the reawakening of art to unadorned mortal beauty that had occurred during the Renaissance, which he had previously understood as the movement away from two-dimensional to three-dimensional. She had gone on to explain that it had somehow combined with the experience that she had gained with wedding dress designs, and that she was going to be a fashion designer – that totally stumped him. There was that completeness about her though, and an assurance to interrupt to simply contemplate. *One of her moments,* was how she had described them, a spaced detachment in her eyes that turned her eyes limpid blue rather than the blue-green. She was truly gorgeous.

However, their cosiness together nearly came unstruck when he told her about his new Yamaha R1 motorbike that didn't impress, and he had to quickly recover by telling her about the year of student representation coming up, and his need to be able to quickly travel between the campuses and venues if he was going to fit in his study. She came around then, and even took a ride on the passenger seat behind him in her tight Mary Quant dress and high boots when he dropped her back to her accommodation at the top of the stairs of her shared three-up-one-down red-brick. 'That bike goes with my sixties look,' she had dismissed. A coloured glow was rising at the end of the street and the tall, elegant windows were mirroring a golden sunset as she ascended the steps to the pilastered main entrance while he locked the bike in heavy, clumsy chains.

When they got inside, Ucind was there in the kitchen, and had begun to relate a story from the day that had happened to a trainee nurse, Nora, who shared. She had introduced it as worthy of a house party. At the hospital, Nora had been included on a consultant's rounds of patients, and nothing unusual had happened until they got to an old lady in her bed. The old lady had raised her head on the pillow and pointed at Nora. 'I know you?' And went on to say in a crackled voice, 'You're one of the girls in the house opposite me, the house with the tunnel.' When Nora had asked what tunnel, the old lady had replied: 'Yes, all these men go in, and none ever come out!'

Ucind and Sara had laughed to tears and Andy had thought nothing of it, but it was shortly after that he became one of those men who went into the house and did not come out. His life beat to the rhythms of the house's comings and goings, nine rooms rented and all intersecting in the kitchen and the glow of the study room that caught the evening sun through its bay window, revolving in cycles that never stopped.

One day after college some six weeks later, Sara insisted on walking him across the black Liffey in full ebb to a different Bewley's on Mary Street, apparently to sit under another famous stained-glass window, this time by Jim Fitzpatrick. It featured Cruithne, a famous character in Irish Mythology, who wore a gown of layered reds as she raised her arms and hands to frame her flowing hair. She was the mistress of Ireland's greatest Celtic warrior, Cuchulainn, who, when he died in battle, had strapped himself to a tree – none daring to approach until a bird landed on his shoulder to herald his death. It was a bit of a mystery art tour because she had shown him the bronze sculpture of the same Cuchulainn on display in the General Post Office on their way. Then she was joking about not all reds suiting her, her eyes yes, but any red needed to graduate with her auburn hair and skin tone. Did he agree that these reds in the stained-glass were a perfect match?

He agreed.

Then without warning, she said without losing the soft cadence in her voice, 'I am pregnant. Isn't it wonderful.'

He had spluttered and stuttered, congratulating, hugging, and asking how she was.

She was fine, but as she spoke, he realised that her 'Isn't it wonderful' wasn't a question. Crashing consequences came to mind along with his becoming a father – yes, a father. Like every man, he had rationalised in theory about having children early and what that might mean in a life plan, but while a student in college?

'How, when?' he asked; that amused her.

'How, the usual way I expect. When, maybe those new positions are more effective at getting past the contraception? It can happen, my doctor said. She was asking about your athleticism, and was the sex particularly vigorous? Oh, and were you extraordinarily active? I thought she was prurient until she explained that the contraception had been bypassed. When I had answered all her questions she put the pregnancy down to the new positions, conjuring exactly how that might have occurred – in details that you don't want to know.'

'You should have told her, "Heaven on earth!"'

'Ironic-descent. So quickly down to earth.'

Then, they sat quietly for a while, looking out on pet owners walking dogs in the little park beside the church on the corner. Well, here it was, fatherhood. He was proud, proud that he and Sara could create their own world. Thoughts came and went. Some people decide in a day to stay together, he rationalised, and he wouldn't have needed even that with Sara.

'Nobody wants me to have the baby,' she said then. 'Neither Dad nor Mam, not Ucind nor any of my friends. Offers of finances are coming flying from all directions, so it is not a question of affording a termination.'

'Termination?' His stomach went hollow.

'A baby would ruin my life is the consensus.'

Andy had thought he saw the beautiful features of Sara's face sadden. Sadness for her, it wasn't any one thing, it was that the life went out of everything about her. That liveliness of just a few moments earlier was vanishing. There was no doubting her desire. It was over to him. He knew he loved her, everything about her: there were never any filters between them as with other girls, where he could objectively evaluate. Nevertheless, he needed to think this through. 'A baby needn't change anything much study-wise for this academic year,' he had theoretically opined. 'Have we time to think through the options?' It was the first time he had thought 'we'.

'A little, maybe a week?'

His focus returned to the Cairo traffic that had intensified and slowed to a juddering crawl. 'Abdul, you should get a motorbike to cut through the traffic,' he remarked.

Abdul ignored his recommendation but explained: 'Each Friday they come back to Gamaliya . . . to pray in especially holy places . . . and to meet family – even if no food now until the sun has dipped behind the tall minarets and curved domes of Mohammad Ali and the songbirds sing the prayer of release for the taking of Iftar. Inshallagh!'

'Is night-time a reprieve from the fast? I have read more food was consumed in Egypt during Ramadan than in any other month.'

'Yes. Families will eat and talk throughout the night until the call to prayer again at first light. We fast to feel Allah in our hearts.' Abdul tapped his chest. 'Muslims are in especially good humour during Ramadan.'

Nevertheless, quite a feat to fast in these temperatures. 'Good humour, as you say?'

Abdul studied him in the rear-view before slowly breaking into a wizened smile, his bony face quizzically assessing him in the mirror. 'The President too, he sometimes goes to Gamaliya to pray—' he informed him.

'Tahrir—' Andy interrupted.

The worry beads clattered on the dash again.

'Tomorrow we will drive to Alexandria for a beautiful experience, the sea . . . much fresh air and sand.'

Alexandria again. Taafeef, his travel agent, when he picked him up to transfer him to the hotel, had proposed that same journey to Alexandria, while in a smooth coordinated action he had thrust his business card into Andy's hand. 'Sand! There is sand everywhere in Egypt.'

Abdul ignored his comment. 'Gold and silver sand shining and the blue sea, and cool from the Mediterranean. Sooo beautiful. No traffic.' He waved his worry beads scathingly at traffic billowing fumes all about.

Through the windows, the city had closed right up to the motorway in ten- and twelve-story-high tower blocks that abutted each other. He remembered the neighbourhoods that thronged on the streets below in what was an upside-down world of frenzy and chaos, with swirling music, aromas, and good-natured chatter. Here and there the towers separated for the tall, slender minarets of a mosque soaring, and occasionally a Coptic Church where the golden mosaics of bearded Messiahs smiled enigmatically. The city was more congested than he could have imagined on their last visit, when it was ringed in fields of crops interspersed with development, and the tower blocks were only beginning their encroachment. His guide from back then had waved an arm, pointing to the buildings beyond the fields of green, and dismissively said: 'All illegal.' Now there was hardly the width of an alley between the buildings everywhere. Abdul swung his worry beads along the dashboard announcing, 'New Construction since the revolution,' and speeded on without further clarification.

These towers did not look fully completed: blockwork infills between the grey concrete superstructures' skeleton was intermittent with patterns of missing blocks proceeding upwards haphazardly in a giant Jenga game to a line of rebar bristling into the sky at the top. An aberrant picture, and yet there were a few apartments that were plastered and painted, picturesque amongst the gaps and oozing facades of petrified mortar.

He asked Abdul how this was possible.

'An Egyptian home is never finished, always expanding, always changing. Buy one apartment for now and another for later . . . more children, a second wife perhaps – sometimes, yes, if one is very successful and no longer too busy – daughter-in-law maybe, more children. Finish one apartment, then start the second. Pay tax only when finished; families come and finish over many years.'

'I like to think instead that these are inverted worlds built in the hope of additional floors growing all the way to heaven, your Jannah.'

'Not that easy to get into Jannah.' Abdul's face became a laughing mask again. 'Tax not Allah!' The buildings crowded ever closer to the highway, bordering each other, and pressed onto the motorway. 'More important for now televisions and internet – later finish home. You see.' He pointed to the arrays of antenna and dishes rising along the height of the buildings. 'Netflix. Bollywood.'

'Is it true that soap operas have been banned during Ramadan?' he had asked Abdul.

The eyes in the mirror through which they were conversing startled. 'Yes, certain soap operas. It is a family time. How do you know this?' Abdul's expression tightened.

'I typed "Ramadan Egypt" into Google. Ramadan lanterns also came up.'

Abdul's laughing face returned. 'Fanoos! We can go to a square where they are made beside Sayeda Zeinab Mosque. The children will swing fanoos lanterns and sing songs to obtain gifts. It is a happy time. You will enjoy.'

'Tahrir Square,' Andy reminded him. 'What happened to the illegal buildings around the city? No permits when I was here last time?'

'Permission is not necessary, only registration. It is a blessing from the authorities.'

'A forgiveness?'

'To pay tax?' Abdul laughed. 'I will take you to such an area?'

'Tahrir Square,' Andy reminded him again.

'We will see the Cairo Tower and the Opera House. No argue? Beside Tahrir,' he added, anticipating Andy's refusal.

'A drive-by?' Andy used another of his trans-cultural terms, smiling at his own ingenuity.

'All-inclusive from Abdul at your service . . . enchanted to show . . .' His voice on this subject trailed away.

So many lives in the chaotic tumult unfolding outside the tinted windows reminded Andy of the circles spinning in Sara's rental house to which he had added when his Yamaha R1 had returned there some days after their café meeting on Mary Street, his mind racing faster than the screaming engine. What did it matter if Sara's pregnancy was planned or not, they would be starting their family early, that was all. These were optimistic times in Ireland with the Northern Ireland Peace Agreement holding and inward investment at its peak. If he had to drop out at the end of the year, he could find a way into one of the corporates, and that would define how his career developed. Instead of following on with a master's to specialise, he would move to engineering project management with the knowledge he had acquired to date. A general science degree that would be awarded for completing his three years was enough. Maybe that was him anyway? He was good at stepping back, holding up to take an objective look.

Except, of course, he had not been able to step back with Sara. She was beyond his dreams and her presence reduced him to charged emotions was the sum-total of what he could say, if asked. While with other girls, he could rhyme off a list of qualities and evaluate their suitability, nothing like that happened with Sara. Those things didn't seem to matter.

Sara's eyes were teary and red when she met him at the door and steered him away from the bustling activities of downstairs to her room at the top of the stairs. An art book was opened on the bed, and she explained that she had been studying Early German Expressionism, and that the sadness of Marc's and Macke's lives had made her cry. Both artists had been killed young in the First World War and she didn't know which artist's life was sadder. Macke, whose paintings in blocks of colour captured the mood of his subjects and their circumstances, had lost his life in the second month of the First World War. Her voice was breaking as Sara went on to tell him that Marc had begun coding colours through abstract stylisation of animals to discover something of the natural world's purity, truth, and beauty. Having painted the *Blue Horse* to capture its nobility, it was perhaps no surprise that he joined the cavalry when war broke out. He then became a painter of camouflage covers for troops – using other artists' works adapted to 'pointillism' – he was on a 'notable artists list' to be withdrawn from the front when he was killed at Verdun in 1916.

'War is such a waste,' he had responded.

She put her finger to his lips as the light flickering on the obscuring glass indicated that someone was coming from one of the rooms below. They waited until the stair had darkened below and they were left with only the skylight's fading red glow. Then she spoke: 'Life is precious, Andy. It can be gone in an instant. I am going to see the pregnancy through.'

He didn't have to come forward, but instead he launched into his prepared speech, going down on one knee, trying to capture in words his love for her, and how living without her was unimaginable. When he asked would she marry him, she had delayed her reply and he had feared losing her. The seconds had trickled past before she replied: 'Yes, and it's not ironic-anything.' One of *her moments*, he realised later.

When they emerged from the room to announce the news to their housemates, it had seemed for the first time like they were truly together, presenting themselves as a couple, an item was what her friend Ucind called it. Of course, pandemonium had broken out, champagne had appeared, and they had been toasted unreservedly. In the early hours, when he kicked the R1 into life and rode off into the night, headlights illuminating the route, he felt he had acquired an additional layer that was insulating him not alone from the late October cold, but from life's vicissitudes. It had never left him, not even when the subpoena had arrived.

The limousine had regained speed and was dipping beneath an overpass; it rose again parallel to a broad expanse of water that broke gilded around the point of an island. A luxury pleasure cruiser pushed its curved prow through the banded waters. There would be time for sightseeing later – they must be nearing Tahrir.

Next stop was when Abdul pulled alongside the latticed, climbing Cairo Tower, and announced: 'Nasser's Pineapple!'

Andy smiled at the solid column rising sheathed in a metal mesh that folded open near its pinnacle. 'Opera House, no argument?'

Andy had his own reasons for wanting to visit the Opera House: it was where the Egyptian revolution had started. The protesters had massed here for the push into Tahrir Square, joining a street battle with the police on Qasr-al-Nil Bridge. The car turned smoothly into the opera complex with its manicured gardens. It was a modern theatre retaining Islamic architectural influences that reminded Andy of the outline of the Mohammad Ali Mosque above the city, a place where perfect expression could occur. Here the Arab Spring had kicked off.

They sat soaking in the atmosphere. He knew despite the violence, the protesters had formed a human chain to protect this jewel of Egyptian culture, the more amazing when many of those protesting might never have been to a live concert here. But all would know of the great Egyptian singers whose statues in the gardens still sung interweaving arias with the river-song into the scented air. The ancient Egyptian goddess Sekhmet, seated leonine in a niche in the building, seemed appropriate for the revolutionary spirit that had been released here – the goddess of the hot desert sun, plague, chaos, war, juxtaposed with healing, and considered the goddess of solutions by the ancient Egyptians who whispered prayers in her ears.

They drove on and circled under the monument of Saad Zaghloul, leader of Egypt during the Egyptian rebellion against the British. He stood avuncular, impossibly balanced atop four fluted columns, and could be waving at the boats passing under the bridge.

As Abdul traversed the Qasr-al-Nil Bridge leading to Tahrir, the real Egypt panned in a panorama of sanitised technicolour from inside the tinted glass. 'Drop me here! Drop me here!' he told Abdul.

Abdul was incredulous. 'Here beside Tahrir Square during Jumu'ah prayers? The Army and Police will arrest you.' The wrinkles in his forehead returned and his brown eyes rounded in alarm. 'There is nobody . . .' He gestured through the window. 'The army is everywhere. What do you want to see?'

'Tahrir Square.'

Having hastily ejected him, the taxi took off in a screech of tyres without Abdul looking for his special service tip or arranging any of the tours that he had been pressuring him to take. Andy took no notice. The first thing, the most important priority, was to walk down the Revolution, and he was going to do that on this first Friday in Ramadan. He had had enough of being careful, always doing the responsible thing that had begun that fateful October evening.

Chapter 3,

Upgraded

Sara

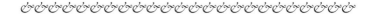

They walked from baggage claim, she and Rick, through a modern sleek terminal of steel and glass that could have been transported and dropped into position from another dimension, except that there was no mistaking this for anywhere other than the Middle East. Robed men and veiled women strolled – Arab men do not hurry, she recalled. She listened to the conversation she caught from the cacophony, how they held gushes of elided syllables cut off by hard consonants and glottal gasps, and she remembered. All of seventeen years ago, the same age as Rick beside her. The intervening years had been a blur, a mirage into which they had stepped, and were now emerging. She looked about, admiring the Arabic script on multi-lingual direction boards and over shops as she caught the wafting odours of spiced food. In open glass cabinets there were displays of mezzes, and behind kebabs on spits that oozed their spiced oils as they rotated. Pastries! She caught sight of a dessert that before she had found irresistible, Kadaifi, that the waiters had always mixed up with Knafeh. She had previously consumed excessively with the excuse of eating for two – its syrupy filo strings around soft Baladi cheese.

She stood to breathe in the aromas of an overpowering potpourri of herbs that curlicued towards her with the gentler floral scents worn. Were Egyptians the only ones who used spices to give a hint of the astringency on the palate as they combined east and west? Through the full-height glass, planes stood at gates identified as belonging to Egypt Air by a stylised falcon logo wrapped onto the fuselage: Falcon-headed Horus, Egyptian God of the air, if she recalled, and ancient protector of Egypt. Could be two birds, and she had come alone.

But in a strange way, she felt that she was coming home. This was the country James had adopted, or maybe the reverse, but amounting to the same thing. It was now a modernising country rather than a developing one, as it had been on their previous trip. Then an older terminal had been a crush of souls swirling around carousels in a Dante's inferno of heat, spilling disoriented into concourses. Their travel agent back then had steered her and Andy away through a labyrinth of passages and screened walkways that had finally brought them to a passport check. They had gotten through, if she remembered rightly, by their travel agent inserting currency notes into their passports as he handed them for inspection. Egypt had moved on since their last visit. She looked at her own Horus, Rick, towering beside her – he not yet born when she had perhaps been at this very spot.

At the exit from the baggage, there was a clamouring of waiting drivers and agents carrying clipboards with names. Waiting for Rick's sports rucksack had made them one of the last out, and she was afraid that their driver would be gone. Then they saw a placard for Laughing, a misspelling of her surname, Loughlin, and they identified themselves to a large moustachioed man to be welcomed profusely. He identified himself as Selim, bowing with the name placard, and added, 'Bey welcomes the Laughing family to his new country, his city, and his palace. He sends his blessings. Inshallagh!'

Sara was relieved when Rick smiled, amused, before replying deferentially for both with a hand on his arm: 'Please thank him on my behalf.' She whispered to Rick that she was playing along – these archaic greetings were probably Ucind's idea of a joke? But what if it really was James to whom the driver was referring? Did he already know she was here?

'I will be most happy to convey *Madaam's* thanks,' he replied, and then insisted on taking their baggage, loading both sets on a trolley that he pushed through arrivals. Sara had three large cases that he placed carefully, without commenting. Rick held onto his massive adventure rucksack and thanked Selim awkwardly. At an ATM, Selim asked if local currency was needed. While Sara rooted in her handbag for her purse and credit card, he had already inserted a card and at the amount's screen asking casually, 'How much does Madaam require?' She asked for and received ten thousand Egyptian pounds, about five hundred euros, adding that she might do a little shopping, and would need it to barter. 'For day-to-day,' she added, in case she was expected to appear wealthy. Was this a return to James providing for her as in her student days?

'What the hell?' Rick whispered to her.

She again had to put her hand on her son's arm to stop him from asking anything further. 'Definitely Ucind's doing? I have taken out local currency for you. It is very thoughtful, don't you think? No doubt it will be added to our bill.'

As they followed the burly driver outside, they were hit by a wall of heat, fumes, and noise, and they remained under the giant fuselage-shaped façade where atomisers sprayed cooling aerosols. He stopped at a monster carrier on enormous wheels with white and blue markings that sat blocking one lane of snarling traffic. The air-conditioning from the interior was a cool breath as she mounted the fold-down steps to the high cabin resting on the musculature of his proffered arm – *muscle mass* would have been Ucind's description. Then they were inside the cabin in a silence illuminated by a cockpit full of dashboard lights that gave them the feel of their own special world. The massive vehicle eased out, sailing above other traffic that moved aside when Selim flashed the headlights. He accompanied this with a broad-toothed smile beneath his dark moustache, after which his brown eyes would check them in the mirror.

Rick laughed and remarked, 'Like a computer game scrambling over other cars.'

They moved onto a congested motorway spaced with advertising billboards, and in the distance, skyscrapers amongst the minarets and domes looming through a yellowing afternoon haze.

'We ride above the city to let you see,' Selim announced.

'What is all this? We are celebs?' Rick asked.

'Ucind's doing. What a great skyline, golden domes glinting it the sunlight and spires and minarets soaring. Whose paintings does it remind you of?' She had been bringing him into art since he was little. Rick was older now though and she couldn't give him direct instruction, and instead she prompted connections that she hoped he had absorbed from before.

'Paintings of Venice by Turner or Canaletto,' he replied casually.

'I was thinking the same thing.' Sara smiled at a memory: 'Do you remember that you would not believe that the painter of canals was Canaletto?'

'It is still amusing.'

He had a real appreciation now. Superb at photography, and she noticed that he had opened the camera app on his mobile – probably too polite to ask if he could open a window to take photos.

'Selim, can Rick please open a window to take a photo?'

'Yes, I will slow more.'

As Rick pinched the window open, a barrage of noise and fumes rushed in from the four-lane motorway that in fact held six or seven lanes of choking traffic juddering forward. She watched as he snapped eagerly.

He adjusted the settings. 'Trying to get it to create rainbows with circles of colours?'

Selim turned back to point to landmarks, telling them about the area even as he negotiated clearances with other honking drivers. 'Very good areas, expensive. Look much green, sports clubs, leafy trees, not-high apartments, many schools, older areas . . . Baron Empain Palace like an Indian Temple.'

From close-up, the suburbs were neatly laid out and precise in every detail, exempt from the smoggy haze that deferentially held back at a distance. She did not reply but Selim nattered on once he had started: mosques, hospitals, landmark squares with famous restaurants, clubs, and colleges – many of which had a military connection and names relating to the 6th October War when Egypt had regained Sinai. He pointed excitedly at his latest landmark: 'Cairo International Stadium, where Egypt will win the Africa Cup. Very good Football Team. Name is "Pharaohs", yes? Never lost to Germany. Only African country to get to the World Cup until now.'

Selim got back to focusing on driving as he manoeuvred to take an exit, explaining that they would shortly look down on Tahrir Square and downtown and then travel over the Nile. This motorway was no less congested but moved faster, high above Islamic Cairo into what Selim called 'Egyptian Spaghetti Junction' with motorways rising and descending. She relaxed into the pleasantness of the journey, with the jovial driver's muscular free arm hanging freely over the back of the front seat, ready to direct their gazes.

'Tahrir,' he said and pointed to an open space between the tall buildings that shielded them from a clear view despite the road elevation.

What had happened to Andy? He had said little in his text, but she would hear the rest at the hotel once they arrived. She hoped he wasn't in trouble. They became part of the tangled stack of motorways peeling off.

Then Selim pointed out through the window to the expanse of water below. He announced, 'Nile!'

'It's a Tsunami,' Rick commented, taking a photo.

'Does it give you a queasy shifting feeling when you look down at it?'

'No, Mom. Paragliding?'

'Of course, no problem with heights.' The extent of the water enthralled her also; that sparkling emerald and silver surface that carried the sun towards their bridge in wavelets, lively and celebratory like a dance. She thought of the hypnotic chants of the White Nile all the way from Lake Victoria and the beating heart of the continent, combined with the wild deafening roars of the gorges of the Ethiopian highlands where the Blue Nile originated.

Rick opened the window fully to take a selfie and announced: 'Welcome to my country!'

'You are Irish, Rick,' she dismissed.

'I was born here on the Red Sea when you and Dad were on that last holiday.'

'You were premature, and we were Medevacked out. Oh, son of mine, you were born amongst the stars. In retrospect, it was not a place a pregnant woman should have come on holiday.'

'Egyptian, Mom. My passport says Hurghada as place of birth, and Dad says that's true.'

'You are Irish, and you live in Ireland. The timing was not quite perfect, that is all. Look at your passport – it says Irish. I wish Andy wouldn't go telling you things without discussing them with me. Why aren't you calling him Andy, as we agreed? It's good for your bonding, now that you are of an age.' Little twerp was right, of course: her stretching the pregnancy dates a mite and then he had the nerve to arrive early to compound matters. Could strangle Andy for registering Rick's birth in Egypt, but he had said the hotel would have done this, because to be truthful, Rick had been born in the Sunrise Palace Hotel on the Red Sea – that had another name now. Nearly-not-quite came unstuck with the post-partum complications, but all in the past. Near miss though.

'A young "Pharaoh",' Selim remarked, clearly buying into Rick being Egyptian. 'You are a star footballer?'

'I played soccer at my old school.' His eyes lit up for an instant. 'My new school plays a different sport, but I have to wait a year.'

There was silence, and she asked: 'What was that video you were replaying during the flight – to do with the pyramids?'

'Dawn over the pyramids, Mom.'

'There were people in the video?'

'Photographers.' He was suddenly straining to see the formidable fortifications and battlements of the Citadel in the distance. 'Saladin, who sent the crusaders packing.'

'Andy wants to go there. You two should head off together tomorrow if he hasn't already been. Might be interesting.'

'Mom? I'll see about tomorrow. Need to crash after travel. Might laze by the pool.'

'Have you heard from Andy?'

'Not on roaming. I have only texts – when there is a Wi-Fi hotspot at the hotel, I'll check.'

She looked at her own mobile. 'Oh, I have a WhatsApp . . . thought it was old. He is on his back-up mobile and already at the Citadel.'

Rick seemed relieved not to have to go.

Her son was doing all right, returning to himself after that school incident that was out of character. After years of being the perfect student, to have suddenly slipped; but that Cloe was trouble. The school was gutless, lumping them both in together for expulsion. Into the new school, just about, where they had insisted that he drop back to transition year because of *an obvious need to mature*. Poor Rick and him way ahead on his finals curriculum that he was now continuing by himself. His new friend Gareth was passing class notes to him.

'Gezira Island, with exceptional sister hotel,' Selim informed them. 'It is cool from the river . . . under palm trees . . . another day sip cocktails looking across to Tahrir, like Cleopatra and a young Pharaoh.' Sara saw that Selim was studying her in the mirror again. 'It is nearby. No alcohol until sunset. Instead, teas and splendid fruit juices in the shaded gardens or on the roof garden.'

Selim negotiated a route that took them through an affluent neighbourhood with gardens of tall palms and fountains that splashed dappled light in front of white marble apartment buildings. Behind bronze gates, women sat in groups conversing in the shade while curly haired children played boisterously dodging in and out of the sunlight. These held no resemblance to the crowded, chaotic centre through which they had just driven. How complete and nuanced these buildings were with golden pergolas surrounding balconies and with the pointed arches of fantasy stories over ornately carved doors, complete down to the calligraphic golden scripts on the gateposts. Rick was snapping furiously, and a soft mix of floral odours from the shaded gardens drifted through the open windows. The sky was open overhead with the ornate facades of these statement buildings rising on one side while on the other the intricacies of the treetops' patterns trimmed the edges of a lapis lazuli diorama.

'Of which artist does the scene under the trees remind you?' she asked.

'Mom, honestly? It has only been hanging in my room forever. Colour splotches like Macke's *Lady in Green Jacket*.'

Andy had gotten the picture along with Marc's The *Blue Horse* to mark the day they had gotten engaged, but they still brought a tear to her eyes because of the artists' sad lives.

They crossed to the west bank over the narrow branch of the Nile streaming the sun's energy between chunky high rises on the opposite side and riverboats moored with colourful bunting below. 'Many special birds, Egyptian birds, nowhere else. They are free to come and go from the zoo.' Selim swung his arm, indicating the landscaping of the zoo, with flocks of birds rising and circling before setting off in sorties.

Sara followed the flocks as they swooped over the roadway to arc into dives and skim along the water's surface to pass under the bridges, circling back again between the riverboats to travel parallel to the Nile's broad spangled back.

They were quiet then while their monster carrier eased away from the river to cut through the desert where construction was everywhere, rising from sandy sites in giant skeletons. Then there was only the hazy, windswept sandy road with its endless billboards blurring into the afternoon glare. It could have been an American freeway, advertisements with high-end products and company logos, and the incredibly beautiful eyes of Arab women mesmerising. They were heading towards that sunset.

Sara settled into her own thoughts. What had gotten into Andy lately? Perhaps, they could recover that freedom of spirit and togetherness of their last holiday here.

Despite their differences, they connected better than her own parents ever did. Her parents had lived a laissez-faire lifestyle on purpose, letting whatever happened happen, relating only when both their responses coincided. Given that her father, Frank, was an entrepreneur before his time, who would chase any government incentive scheme, and her mother, Maureen, was a secondary-school English teacher into her fiction, the likelihood of alignment had been remote. They had not been able to fully agree on her name even, Sara meaning princess, that her mother wanted, and Zeta that her father wanted. The last letter of the Greek alphabet, meaning spark of life, an apt name for the child of a middle-aged couple. Naturally, her mother got the final say, with what was altogether a classier name; however, that did not prevent her father occasionally reverting to Zeta whenever she 'sparked' about the place in his eyes.

Generally, she was expected to operate in the same offhanded manner, but as a child that was never going to happen. Somehow, she knew from an early age that it was she had to create those moments that might be of interest to both. That proved easier when she realised that she herself was their greatest fascination. Each had an insatiable appetite for whatever she said or did.

Her dad, always exhausted from his grant-aided schemes, tried to get at the rationale behind her words, often just giving up saying: 'Out of the mouths of babes'. Her mother thought that her daughter's innocent utterings were part of a new discovery for which humanity had yet to find a vocabulary. She maintained with her schoolteacher's confidence that artists' imaginings were decades ahead of technology that simply systemised for mass production. The real essence was in imagining and creating new insights, the colour of the sky, the breath of the wind, the texture and design of leaves that need never be the same, any new way of seeing the familiar.

She remembered a day at the beach when she was around seven. She had wandered back from a rock pool with a collection of shellfish of all colours and shapes in her plastic bucket, including a starfish. To Frank, the curiosity had been seeing how the pink spiny starfish was able to move, while with her mother, it had been to explore the creature's world. She had moved her hand over its eyes to make it move and to enthral both. To her dad she had gently held the starfish up to show its feet, and her mother, assuming the translucent crusty creature anthropomorphic, had gotten lost in what Sara now knew was a metaphysical imagining of it instinctively moving towards the light.

Selim commented again, squinting and pointing into the distance. 'Pyramids.'

They both leaned forward, picking out tiny triangles off on the horizon in the distance.

'Top of pyramid.'

'Thank heavens it's the top. It's a long way to come for a wonder that puny.'

Selim showed a toothed smile and his eyes twinkled in the rear-view.

The road ran in a line directly towards the triangles that slowly magnified to dominate the landscape; the side of the nearest one was eclipsing the sun. 'Gold and silver steps,' Rick remarked, reaching forward to take a photo through the windscreen.

As they approached the closest giant structure, it lost its magenta hue on the side facing and softened into different tones, drawing their carrier towards it. 'Five thousand years,' she commented to Rick. 'Make you feel insignificant?'

'The opposite . . . energised and challenged.'

'Very profound from my son.' She reached up and tapped his head. 'Yes, challenging you to be yourself, is it?'

'Excuse. I'll get another photo through the windscreen.'

Sara was still considering her son's answer when they pulled up in front of the hotel that was right under the nearest pyramid. Lost for a moment, she studied how it ran the light across the ledges that Rick had noticed until disappearing into the rays reflecting off the edges. The thumping of cases and Selim's voice as he instructed the concierge from the hotel on the luggage returned her. Selim came to the side door, unfolded the steps for her, and held out his arm to support her alighting. She raised her hand to indicate she needed a moment to compose herself. When she had gathered her things and replaced her floppy sunhat, she stood on the top of the steps and signalled, waiting until Selim came back to offer her his arm again.

He smiled. 'The pyramids are large enough for Madaam?'

'Yes.' Brat! 'More magical prisms than pyramids – the colours dissolving one into the other take my breath away.' She fanned her face with her loose hand.

'Mom, he hasn't a clue what you are saying.' Rick was there, interjecting.

'He knows exactly what I am saying.' Ironic-interpretative that, limited language and gets every intimation. Now fully recovered from one of her 'moments', she saw she was under a tall peristyle of golden slender columns that ran into decorative filigree arches floating in lace way above. There was an interplay of reflections of the prismatic pyramid and the peristyle on the veined white marble floor, the aura of the pyramid combining with the gold. It made her feel they were stepping into a fantasy world. 'Rick, I want Selim to take our photo together,' she called out to him a few steps ahead. Then, she handed her mobile to Selim, giving him instructions to take a picture at the entrance.

'Pyramid?' he questioned, smiling.

'Tomorrow,' she snapped. 'I need to send a "selfie" of reception to my friend who booked this hotel for me.'

'As Madaam wishes.' He took photos until Sara was pleased with the result: a photo of the floppy fashion hat drooping down over her face and Rick standing guard towering above her.

'Yes, he will be happy with that.' Selim smiled.

'She!' she corrected him. 'My old schoolfriend in Ireland.'

Selim smiled, conceding: 'As Madaam wishes.'

'Pyramid Dream Palace' was inscribed in gilt above the check-in, beneath Arabic script flowing one letter into the other from right to left, and its English translation below going in the other direction. Hard to believe that they were staying at such a hotel. She surveyed the colourful printed silks and lightest fabrics on the women seated sipping and discussing while the dapper hotel receptionist across from her at the desk checked her booking. He raised his head, fixing her with green eyes. 'I have followed traditional times. East is for the woman who naturally wants her children close by.' He pointed to a layout on the screen with adjoining rooms each side of a central seating area, *a majlis*. The receptionist explained: 'Mister Andy lives here. Then is the majlis. You are here and on the other side of you is Master Rick.'

Sara strained to hear his voice above the crescendo of noise reverberating around the marble foyer from a waterfall. 'All rooms connect along the veranda that is screened from the heat with a pergola: an Egyptian solution because of the intensity of the sun. It is necessary in summer I assure you, and when the sun is not high in autumn and spring it has privacy for sunbathing.' He continued in a more jovial tone: 'There will be no patterns on the skin from the screening. It will not be a comic book suntan.' He then rubbed his hands in a washing motion, breaking into a polite smile first and then a boyish laugh.

Those most incredible eyes!

'Madaam is happy with our proposals in these matters? It is no problem to change the rooms. You face south onto the Greatest of the Pyramids – it is a spectacular view. It crumbles in the sunlight before your eyes, as you have seen at the entrance?'

'I was spellbound at the entrance.' He had to be artistically sensitive, too. 'I am an artist, well in fashion design now,' she found herself saying. 'I look forward to falling asleep under its aura. I used to put a pyramid tray under my pillow when I was growing up to help me sleep.' She flapped her hand to indicate how the real pyramids had affected her. 'Whew!' She had leaned across the desk to make her point and, having arrived at that posture, chose to stay.

'Yes, the spell – usually it does not affect guests this quickly. Only when they are leaving do they notice that they will miss the pyramids forever. Many moods: you can enjoy the view in privacy from your veranda. However, Madaam, you cannot put these pyramids under your pillow!' He smiled broadly and the speckled gems in his eyes livened.

Brat! Not slow on the uptake here, the littlest flirtation . . . and Ucind had to let slip about their soft skin.

The receptionist continued to hold her glance, and it was a moment before it registered that she had been asked a question on the room arrangements. She knew a little about Arab customs, and that male children transferred to the male wing at puberty. 'Excuse me, Master Rick is Mister Rick?' She pointed to her son of over six feet, who was walking about scrutinising the decor while checking out those in the coffee area.

The receptionist smiled. 'Of course. Madaam is so young, it is easy to think of a younger child.'

How could such emerald eyes be combined with a deferential manner towards women? That was simply unfair.

As he studied the rooms, going between the layout and a computer screen, Sara noticed the framed portrait of a man in Arab regalia on the wall behind his desk. A style between Lawrence of Arabia and Yasser Arafat with a check keffiyeh that wrapped around his face and with blue eyes that followed you? He looked familiar.

'Peter O'Toole?' she asked, gesturing toward the striking man in the picture.

The receptionist caught where she was looking. 'No. That is our pasha – he is not from Egypt – big baaša. Egypt is used to foreigners – they all fall under the spell of the pyramids and our beautiful women. He stays here when he visits his contracts in New Cairo. Big Baaša.'

'Contracts in New Cairo?'

He considered her for a minute, as if evaluating before continuing, ignoring her question. 'Alright, no east wing because no children. You need to make more children before you can have an east wing.' He smiled again. 'I have moved Mister Rick to here, the opposite side of Mister Andy. You are beside Mister Andy and the lounge will be yours to invite. The room beside the lounge will be locked . . . another guest or a lounge. Perhaps our pasha?' He hesitated, watching her. 'The door along the veranda will also be locked from both sides. Only the screens over the garden cannot be opened?'

'All very discreet?'

'We will need thirty minutes to rearrange the rooms.'

She answered, 'Yes', her focus returning to the portrait. Ucind? She asked if she could take a photo of the portrait, and then if she could include him in it. She sent it to Ucind with the message: *When you stop drooling over the receptionist, let me know if you recognise the person in the picture behind him?* 'Has Mister Andy been in contact?' she then asked the receptionist.

'Ustaz Andy has returned from sightseeing. The hotel taxi driver and the security guard brought him to the Citadel and other famous sights. Yesterday, trouble for the travel agent when he went on his own. He is resting in his room. I can let him know that you have arrived.'

'No. That won't be necessary. We will surprise him?'

'It will be a very pleasant surprise, I am sure.' He smiled at her and waited for Sara to acknowledge his smile with her smile.

With that, a notification buzzed. It was Ucind back to her. *What, you don't recognise him with his clothes on? It's James Al Bahr Al Ahmar Bey.*

Then she turned and Andy was standing beside. He must have sidled up the way he did and waited for her to notice him. He tried to give her a hug while she rested her hands on his chest and reaching up proffered her cheek to be kissed formally: she could feel the laser green eyes of the receptionist on her back.

Andy kissed the proffered cheek. 'They kiss on both cheeks here in Egypt.'

She slipped out of his embrace.

'Where's Rick?'

'He was here a moment ago. He is somewhere about, probably the pool. The hotel does have an air of dreaminess – probably the diffused lighting effects in the foyer from the pyramid so close, and the waterfall hypnotic? What do you think of her arrangements? I have sent Ucind a photo of the entrance canopy.'

'We have been upgraded, according to our tour guide. This hotel is luxurious. We are part of an international tour judging by the names with a good mix of nationalities.'

'Not Ucind then?'

'VIPs – a suite, four rooms?'

'I had to rearrange the order of the rooms. You are in the same room, and I am in the next room now. Rick is reallocated to the other side of your room. Apparently, I must have more children to earn an east wing to myself, so we are adjoining.'

'The rooms are a monstrous size – plenty of room for two!'

'Adjoining rooms, like the aristocracy.' The weight of the world! Poor Andy. You are never going to be that student leader who threw caution to the wind and challenged every convention.

'You may not get a lot of sleep. There is all night feasting during Ramadan and then you will have the joy of being welcomed into the new day at four when every muezzin in the city breaks into chant, accompanied by a dawn chorus of birds. The chanting is quite relaxing though – that might be my cue to take the great haul back?'

She raised an eyebrow. 'Let's not plan – takes the fun away. Rick is up to something I am certain. He kept replaying that same video on the plane, but I couldn't see what it was. See if you can get it out of him. Oh, he was hoping to go to the Citadel with you tomorrow, but I expect he will be happy to stay by the pool, acclimatise, the Bazaar later?'

'We can visit the Citadel again if he wants.'

'Let's discuss over a coffee outside.'

The receptionist overhearing her commented: 'It is pleasing to sit in the shade while listening to the water fountains and the many birds. The hotel is very proud of the garden's design in imitation of paradise and with many red flamboyant trees, our pasha's favourite.'

'I will follow you out,' she said letting him go ahead.

She rummaged in her bag until he was gone. Then she rechecked the message from Ucind: James Al Bahr Al Ahmar Bey had found her, was her host. As she walked across the polished marble foyer, she enjoyed the timed clicks of her heels synchronising with the surges of the crashing waterfall, as peripherally she saw all heads turning to follow her movements. She supposed that she must look exotic to Egyptians in the same way they were exotic to her. What will James make of her after all these years in comparison with the classical features of these women, soft in their finest flowing garments and with those glittering attractive eyes?

Chapter 4,

Revolution Walkdown

Andy

 festfestfestfestfestfestfestfestfestfestfestfestfestfest

On Qasr-al-Nil Bridge, the blazing sun beat down on him even as he felt himself the centre of the Nile's great span between downtown and Gezira Island. A slight river breeze cooled sufficiently to focus. Upriver through the metal trellis, a mass of water was advancing tumultuously in vast currents as it diverted around Gezira. It contorted and flexed in rebellion, tearing at the granite rocks along the embankment that protected the downtown before moving on. This much water on the move was a malleable force, a leviathan swelling to occupy the broadest widths of the channel.

The churning water below him had forgotten none of its ancient freedoms. Continuously twisting, deforming, and reforming, it still searched out every crack and fissure, roiling, twisting, and prising to test its limits. It sought out its furthermost expansion, to curl its flows through the land, to flood vast undulating plains of burning sand with the fertility of its quenching salve. Tamed with dams, it nevertheless continued to bring life to the desert, for a thousand miles from the southern border where Ramesses II had built his boundary temple at Abu Simbel and sat godlike protecting his people to where the Mediterranean crashed onto the northern shores of Africa.

His thoughts turned to the battle for the Qasr-al-Nil Bridge during the revolution that had surged from the Opera House to be fought fiercely on this very spot high above the violent waters. A sense of the intensity of the revolution was all about, wave after wave of protesters hurtling themselves from out the masses at the police lines with the Great River's tenacity. They had eventually prevailed to spill through the police lines and flood Tahrir Square. It must have been a ferocious, ecstatic moment. An unstoppable force!

His and Sara's own unstoppable force had not yet fully unravelled. Begun so innocently with a pleasant doorbell chime as they enjoyed breakfast in the newly installed kitchen of their 'doer-upper' and looked out onto the wilderness of a garden through the flaking paint on the French doors. When he went to answer, the craggy-faced postman, whom he had not met before, held the letter out and looked for a signature on a tablet. 'It's for you, your first registered letter in the new home. Hope it's good news!'

'No doubt it's not,' he had replied, amused that the postman remembered this despite their having moved in over six months earlier. He signed with his finger on a touchscreen tablet.

'You'll get an email confirmation before you get back to the kitchen.'

Knows what they had for breakfast, that guy. Probably noticed that Rick was eating alone in the front window as he waited for Lucia to lead her pooch past the gate. When he did get back to the kitchen, Sara was aglow in sunlight at the new island, the light on her satin dressing gown outlining her figure and the darkened hollows in her cheeks making her looks more artistic. Lucky him! She raised her eyes inquiring as he approached, and he slid the envelope across the table to her. 'Here, you open it! Our first registered letter, according to our ever-knowledgeable postman.'

Her blue-green eyes smiled while she tossed her auburn hair gold-tipped to take the letter. 'Looks official?' she mused as the knife cut through the crayon cross. 'Cross your heart officialdom, *mmmm*?' Her expression had then frozen.

'Well?'

'That's the limit. From James D Sullivan, after all these years, a subpoena challenging your paternity of Rick. It's a joke!'

But it wasn't a joke when he contacted Moriarty, their solicitor, later that day, and everything became frantic and complicated with tests and affidavits – and then he had to bring Rick into the picture. Egypt would be a healing distraction, a chance to leave it all behind. It was where their life together had truly begun, after all.

He walked past the black lions that had flashed across news screens with protesters clinging to the manes of these great symbols of Egypt's ancient history, waving the red, white, and black of Egypt, the red of blood, life, the black of the afterlife, and white for peace between them. This was hallowed ground. Forward, he closed on the green spaces around the centre that he recognised as the encampment from the protests, and where Cairo opened under an immense powder-blue canopy to the intensity of the sun. He took shade in the narrow noon shadow under the statue of Umar Makram preaching and pointing upwards. His mosque behind stepped its increasingly slender minaret impossibly high into the haze of the communing sky. The monument commemorated a leader who, after having been instrumental in replacing Ottoman rule, was himself exiled when he objected to an Abyssinian ruling Egypt. A Muslim God and an Egyptian soul. That wasn't true either – wasn't it the Copts who were the true descendants of ancient Egypt, and they were Orthodox Christian? Egypt was a land of contradictions with a rich history, and he looked forward to their exploring it properly this time.

Prayers broke over the square, insistent and amplified. He breathed the incantations suffusing the air with esoteric messages and stepped out again into the cauldron of heat. The sun extracted a dryness from the very slabs under his feet, releasing their history. He could feel the heave of crowds in the kenopsia of the square, the throb of the people, the sacrifices on the front line in the intense heat, the suffocation of the social media organised swarm that compelled a regime to leave office, a new way of enforcing a contract between people and their leadership. The start of the Arab Spring.

What had he ever done in comparison with what they had achieved here? This was the real deal, not the safe, well-constructed letters he had penned to hand in at various embassies during his years of student protest, and not the messages of encouragement that they had sent political prisoners – and him thinking himself part of little victories when they were released. This was the front line that made what he did well-meaning but safe, like everything he had done.

Was he a fraud? Worse? Was he the interloper on what his solicitor euphemistically referred to as the substantive issue of Rick's paternity? Sara being pregnant with Rick had now become another unknown-known, or possibly an unknown-unknown. Sara had said he was Rick's father, and he should not doubt her. He reminded himself of his arrogance leaving university at the completion of third year. That had been a success, at least. After that short period with the auctioneers – that was the easiest money that he had ever made with the housing boom – he had side-stepped into projects' management at a multi-national and quickly developed his career in management to where he was hiring his old classmates. However, it still rankled him that he had sold out, not as an engineer, but rather on his student politics trajectory. University was not so much about the piece of parchment at the end, it was as much about who and what you became during those years. There was consolation in that he had set himself up as the social conscience of the multi-national subsidiary and was able to influence significant decision-making in a corporate with the global turnover of a medium country.

He became aware for the first time that he, as Abdul had warned, was the only one on Tahrir apart from military personnel. Machine guns mounted on half-tracks trained onto him. Was trouble expected? Other military vehicles were sitting in silence and *mariahs* were queued on the feeder streets. He remembered from their last visit seeing handcuffed hands through the bars on the vents – a disconcerting sight. He ignored their presence, making his way through the heat pouring down and intensified off the yellow monolith building to his right with its arrays of blank windows.

Three soldiers detached themselves from a group conversing beside a parked jeep and approached him, two in black berets either side of a senior officer with epaulettes and a crimson beret. They came to a halt in front of him, blocking his path, and then the sinewy soldier to Andy's right with an angular face stepped forward.

Without an introduction, he demanded: 'What are you doing here? Where are you from? England? Germany? Turkey? Where?'

'Ireland. I am a tourist,' he replied with as much false enthusiasm as he could muster.

'We will decide if you are a tourist as you say. Why are you here on Tahrir Square during Friday prayers?'

'I thought it would not be busy. I could avoid the crowds later,' he replied. The image of handcuffed hands through the bars on the vents of a *mariah* persisted.

'Why are you here? What are you doing?' came again. The lines on the soldier's forehead had become more pronounced and his manner more abrupt.

'Sightseeing. Qasr-Al-Nil Street. The financial district.' Andy knew that Qasr-Al-Nil where the front line of the revolution has become focused was a busy shopping street, and that it was the part of the Cairo that was built along the Paris model in the nineteenth century.

'Why? Everywhere is closed. Why are you here?' At the again-repeated question, the third soldier raised a machine gun to point it at him.

'The architecture of the buildings and layout was modelled on Paris?' He answered with what he thought was enough information.

Instead, the soldier countered with another question. 'When were you in Paris?'

'Not for several years,' he replied, thinking that was the end of it. He had no idea where this was going.

Another question came. 'How do you remember what Paris is like? Did you live there?'

'No. I visited. It is a popular tourist destination for Irish people.'

'When? When were you there?' The soldier snapped back at him.

He should have known better than to complicate his answer. Paris was about art, and love, and joie de vivre – and chic now that they could afford it. Sara had insisted that they begin her global art odyssey there. 'Two thousand and fifteen?'

'What month? It was popular with a lot of people at that time. Yes?'

He racked his brain trying to figure out where this was going, concluding that maybe he needed to give more detail to authenticate his story. 'It was a beautiful month in Paris in 2015. My wife and I sat along the brick wall of the

Tuileries on the foldable chairs soaking up the last of the heat as the sun descended over Place de La Concorde. There is an Egyptian pylon on the roundabout in the centre from the Temple of Luxor. The Seine and D'Orsay Museum were shadowing beyond, and we sat until the Eiffel Tower was illuminated in coloured lights in the distance.' He remembered that they had gone to the Rodin Museum earlier in the day and seen both his *Kiss* and his *Thinker* before returning to their sunset. Sara had explained that Rodin's *Kiss* was to show a woman's equality in the ardour of lovemaking. While he, to be honest, was focused on imagination and its possibilities that were evoked by the *Thinker*. It must have been June because the heat had returned. 'June,' he added.

'June, two thousand and fifteen years, Paris?' the questioning officer repeated. He seemed to have gotten what he wanted. 'Many people were in Paris at this time – there were preparations to be made.' Throughout, the senior officer in the crimson beret stood motionless, looking through him with grey eyes. Andy had never experienced such a blood-curdling stare, a cold ruthlessness. He suddenly realised what the soldier was implying: it was the year of the Paris atrocities. How had he jumped to that inference? This was no routine check.

'Your passport and visa!' his interrogator ordered.

He didn't have them with him. Taafeef had said that he should not bring them. 'There is nothing that you will need that requires your passport. Take a copy at hotel reception,' he had advised in that polished English accent. He saw the second soldier slip the safety catch off the machine gun as he rummaged to get the copy in his money wallet. He feared those unmoving eyes more.

When he handed the paper copies over to his inquisitor, the soldier held them up by two fingers, letting them flutter. 'What are these? Where is your passport and visa? Have you authorisation to be in Egypt?'

'At my hotel – I took a copy.' He braced himself for a reaction. The sun was burning his shoulders and back, and yet all stood immobile.

'This is not okay, I assure you.' He turned to speak to the senior officer, who nodded when he had finished talking. Andy was left with the others guarding him while the first went to a jeep, where he handed the copies to another soldier inside. They both studied a laptop screen, discussing intently. The sun railed down relentlessly: the water he sipped had no effect. The soldier returned, tapping the folded copies against the holster on his hip as the black ribbon on his beret flapped in the breeze.

He stepped close enough for Andy to smell the laundered khaki tainted with the pungency of the soldier's sweat. Another time, he might have made a joke to himself. Instead, he froze to the spot as the lined face and piercing brown eyes looked directly through him. With that same smug manner that he had used when announcing the timing of Andy's trip, he asked: 'Why you missed your connecting flight in Istanbul?'

Had they traced his flight itinerary, the delayed flight from Ireland, his connecting flight to Cairo? He resisted an immediate reply. They would know that he had arrived in Cairo on the original booking probably; they presumably also knew that the flight from Dublin to Istanbul had been delayed. In truth, he had made his connection in Istanbul, but how to explain what had really happened. When the delayed flight from Ireland had landed, he had pushed forward on the plane, waving his boarding pass for the connecting flight. The other passengers had allowed him through until a man solidly blocked his path. When he had raised his voice to announce his connecting flight, the man had turned. 'We are connecting also. Wait and follow!' He had had no option.

The man had exited. He had hurried to tag along as the man ambled with the other disembarking passengers to where ground staff directed the line of arriving passengers into the main shopping concourse. The man had stopped, showed the uniformed woman his boarding pass, and she had allowed him to go directly ahead along a rising corridor. Andy similarly had flashed his boarding pass and had been allowed through. Further along the corridor, the man had turned right through a single leaf doorway, holding it for Andy to grab before it fully closed. Pulling it open, he had found he was at the departure gates with the update departures screen ahead of him – five minutes' brisk walking brought him to his gate just before it closed. He would not be relaying that explanation: *How do you know the secret corridors in Istanbul Airport? It is a new airport, how you know?*

'I ran. Just in time!' He had the feeling that the yellowing buildings of the open and deserted square were dispassionately witnessing just another incident.

'It is not possible! You are lying! I do not believe you. You arrived in Istanbul on an earlier flight.'

The handcuffs wrapped around the barred vents in a *mariah* again came to mind. 'I have my boarding passes at the hotel!' He didn't know that they would still be there.

'What can that tell us? Anyone can print boarding passes. They are of no use!'

His mind focused. Taafeef's business card. 'My travel agent picked me up,' he stammered. 'I have his business card. We can phone him.'

The mood changed.

'Which travel agent?' the officer asked, annoyed.

Andy was careful travelling: when he was given a business card, he had a deliberate routine for slowly storing it safely in his wallet, and that wallet was secreted in the money bag around his waist. He rooted agitatedly for the card, laying on the difficulty finding it. Producing the card, he held it aloft like a trophy, and then before anything else could happen, he tucked it into the cover of the backup mobile and began dialling. He hoped Taafeef would answer. Dialling tones came up after what seemed an eternity – probably routed halfway around the world. Then the call went dead. The mobile left him and his interrogator ridiculously staring at it, a useless piece of modern technology. The display activated, an automatic text message in Arabic script. He quickly showed it to his interrogator.

Unexpectedly, he heard: 'He will call. We will wait.'

Andy studied the tough features of the face that had been menacing him – it was as unflinching as the officer's. He took in his environs: the burning slabs reflected an extreme heat – it must be close to forty degrees. The red-bereted officer had not moved a muscle. The echoing from the mosques over the square had become more concentrated, he noticed, probably into the sermon because there was an insistence to the words. He had no way of knowing whether it was radical agitation or extolling the hadiths. Fire and brimstone equivalent, anyway. He finished the last of his water bottle.

Finally, the mobile rang and when he answered, he recognised Taafeef's clipped accent: he had been at prayers when he had gotten Andy's call. Andy explained the modified version of the story, the one he had told the soldier. Taafeef asked to speak to the soldier. An intense discussion ensued. He waited, listening to one side hardened in consonants, truncated vowels, and rushed pauses. The mobile was handed back.

He raised the mobile to his ear. 'Okay, Andrew, are you there? This is not good. You should not be on Tahrir Square. They could arrest you, but for me they will allow you to pay a fine. You have Egyptian money from the airport, right? The fine is fourteen hundred Egyptian pounds, right?'

'Yes.'

'On the spot fine is very generous for what would be called suspicious activity in Ireland.'

'I have the money.'

'They will allow you to sightsee until I pick you up. You need to leave Tahrir Square now and to stick to the financial district.'

'Okay.'

'I will collect you later because I am at prayers and then work. Al Horreya Park entrance at the Saad Zalgoul Statue at the Qasr-al-Nil Bridge. Do you know this place?'

'Yes.'

'Four p.m., alright.'

'Yes.'

'Please hand the mobile back to the soldier. I need to explain.'

The call ended. Andy paid the fine as quickly as he could and made to leave.

The officer held him there to look at mugshots in a folder. Most looked educated, unassuming men and a few women, but with the occasional bearded warrior slung with shoulder ammunition belts. He could feel eyes studying his reaction to each, and he shook his head exaggeratedly, not yet entirely sure that he would be allowed to go. When he had gone through the pack, his interrogator returned them to the folder.

He spoke to the senior officer and then returned. 'You may go for now.' Both soldiers saluted the officer and all three turned in unison.

He was quaking, his muscles trembled, and his lips were parched. Moving quickly to leave the square, he decided that he should follow Talaat Harb Street that would bring him to the financial district. He passed the American University, locked and bolted, where a soldier eyed him through the wire netting and high spiked railings. Despite the soldier's attention, he took a quick selfie in front of the entrance. He would finish his walkabout and photograph his progress, but needed to remain within the financial district for consistency if he was stopped again.

Using Colonel Saunder's avuncular face over the KFC that he had often seen on news flashes as a landmark, he turned onto the Talaat Harb Street with its ornate facades and lolling palms on sheltered side streets. On the open square, the founder of the first Egyptian-owned bank stepped off a pedestal on high – a black larger-than-life figure with traditional fez, the statue holding a scroll whose significance eluded him. The area around was a thriving business area renovated with nineteenth-century streetlamps and having flower boxes and greenery in profusion. The facades overhead did speak of Belle Époque Paris, and the multiple roads that intersected radiated elegantly outward to connect the city. He walked on towards the Central Bank where prestige buildings vied with each other to make statements, and where a diminutive figure of Mustafa Kamel, a famous Egyptian nationalist, stood central on a plaza bearing his name. Carved in black granite he rested one hand on the head of a pharaoh and the other pointed downward in yet another puzzling gesture – as it happened to an unkempt person who looked destitute sitting below. He gave the man Egyptian pounds, but his state was such that he hardly registered the notes. Perhaps the revolution had not trickled down to all as Abdul had suggested.

Andy turned back onto Qasr-Al-Nil, where shops were a collection of high-street multiples and local fashion shops. Any number of mannequins modelling clothes complete with hijab and niqab in display windows were protected by what Andy would have called Lucozade paper in his childhood. But each store also had what he guessed was a fanoos in the window, a large lantern with dazzling designs on printed glass inlays.

He found no evidence of the revolution, the last front line where a wall had been built at the end of Qasr-Al-Nil to contain the protesters. There was no pockmarking on the buildings and the pavements were not broken up from the rocks and missiles that were reported to have been dropped from overhead. More importantly, no memorial existed to the revolution's fallen. He gave himself a moment's silence to acknowledge the sacrifice of those who had bravely fallen. The colourful fanoos lanterns in each of the shopfront windows, outdoing each other with more fantastical images, were memorial enough. The first of the cars were beginning to appear as he retraced his steps to a Costa Coffee he had spotted earlier. He would have preferred a visit to Richie's where he had read many of the revolutionary leaders had been, but demurred.

Once he had rehydrated, he re-joined the streets that had become thronged with families meeting up after prayers, smiles and chatter all under a merciless sun that was now at its most severe. How could anyone survive in these temperatures without food or drink until the feast at sunset? Yet, here were families in colourful garb shopping and going about their business, oblivious to temperatures amid the noise of streets festooned in bunting that were chaotic drowned in the continuous honking and roar of engines. He spotted an old thin man in impeccable grey sultan selling bags of lemons, while he effortlessly balanced a sack of sweet potatoes on his head. He pushed

Egyptian money towards him – Ramadan – and then made his way through Tahrir Square towards his meeting point. It now buzzed with traffic and was thronged with pedestrians, and the military presence had drawn back except for the strategically located armoured personnel carriers.

He made his way across it back towards the bridge and his meeting point, past the mauve Egyptian Museum where its symmetric domes contentedly sat amongst the palms spilling silver sunshine. In the distance he recognised the top floors of the Hilton, a vantage point from which Western journalists observed – and occasionally ventured out onto the Square. Looking back onto the Square, it created a picturesque vista emitting and absorbing colourful processions of people in waves of humanity. Having seen first-hand where the Egyptian revolution had happened, he felt somewhat absolved of his protest movement's failure to stop the Iraqi War. Life had moved on in Egypt: a regime change had happened even if he understood little about it. He would record the moment with a selfie at the two Qasr-Al-Nil lions above which protesters had waved Egyptian flags during the revolution.

As he was taking his photo, a western-dressed Egyptian came across to him and politely offered to take his selfie. Why not? Andy would not stop trusting others just because of his questioning earlier. The man took Andy's photo and handed back the mobile. Then he explained that he had a papyrus store nearby and insisted Andy accompany him to view the merchandise – *no pressure to buy*. It was his family's shop that had stayed open during the revolution. Yes, he saw all the revolution, and could discuss with Andy over delicious herbal teas. It was a happy time for his family. A sister would get married the following day. 'It is a lucky time. Inshallagh!'

Andy's curiosity to learn more about the revolution made him follow. Once inside, he looked at the well-carved statues of the gods in cabinets and was brought to a little alcove. It would be quite a coup to get to discuss with a witness of the revolution – and in these surroundings.

'Yes, my friend . . .?'

'Andy.'

'I am Rashid, meaning the high-one,' and extending a hand he introduced a young woman who was close by in a long, embroidered robe, 'and this sister is Safiya, meaning the pure one. She will serve us tea shortly. Yes, my friend, the revolution took place around the corner on Tahrir Square. Protesters broke through the police lines on the Qasr-Al-Nil Bridge overhead to occupy the square. Thuds of rubber bullets, pieces of pavement thrown, tear gas, smoke, baton charges, chanting, sirens, noise – cries of injured protesters. Do you know the chants? "Freedom, Justice, Bread?"'

'"Freedom, Justice, Bread,"' Andy repeated. 'Why Bread?'

'Egyptians eat more bread than anyone else in the world. The price is important to all people, especially to those who are poor. Lots of poor people joined the revolution. Justice for all – social justice – a chance to work like now. You have seen much construction. People no longer sit idle, but instead work to earn a living. Freedoms also, yes freedom to speak out, to protest, also freedom for education, for work, many freedoms needed.'

There was further confirmation of the qualified success of the revolution. 'How violent was the revolution?' he asked

'At times, extremely! When the police charged or when the protesters pushed against the police lines trying to keep them back. Little skirmishes and fights broke out all the time with agent-provocateurs making trouble or police snatching a person to make an arrest. Always there was chanting, day and night. "Semeyya, Semeyya", peaceful, peaceful. I continue to hear it in my head every day. A peaceful revolution, and yet more than four thousand dead in all of Egypt. The army refused to take part: they stood back when the protesters chanted, "The army, the people, one hand!"'

Rashid continued: 'It is not as you imagine a revolution to be. On this side of the square, women brought food and supplies, especially medical supplies for those injured. The soldiers do not stop them. Women walk in! We give what we can from a table at the door – no looting by the protesters.'

Safiya reappeared carrying a bronze serving tray, engraved in geometrical arabesques upon which sat a porcelain tea service: it was composed of a gilt tea service. She set out a small inlaid table with hand swirls and arcs that necessitated continuously readjusting the metallic bangles on her wrists. Then with long jets of hot tea she poured from the teapot held high into the gilded interiors of the delicate cups. Finally, she swung away, completing a circle, and stood nearby, still holding the gold teapot on which was a golden pharaoh making an offering to Isis.

Mesmerised, Andy felt he should comment. 'Do you ever miss?'

She smiled. 'If I intend.' She broke her silence and laughed playfully

Rashid quickly enthused: 'The tea set is a copy of the one Napoleon bought for Josephine after their divorce had come through. Both Egypt and Josephine were failed campaigns for Napoleon.'

Would this be him, remaining on good terms and sending Sara gifts for birthdays and occasions? He asked the young woman serving: 'Are you married?'

She cast her eyes to her brother.

'Safiya wants to meet a European man because she says she will never marry an Egyptian. Now, she is nearly too old for marriage in Egypt. Many suitable men have been fascinated and pledged themselves.'

Safiya blushed. 'I want to leave Egypt,' she disclosed, and continued, 'It is too hot! I am young for Europe.' That lyrical, girlish laugh followed, and a question was returned: 'Are you married?'

Who knew how things would go between Sara and him? 'My wife and I are on holiday to try to patch up our relationship.' He was being truthful: Sara's 'éloignement' could so easily turn to 'fracture'?

A heavyset, sallow-faced man approached the table and embraced Rashid and Safiya. 'This brother is Hamid, meaning the praised one. He has a store in Aswan and has returned to Cairo for the festivities.'

'We travel to Aswan and spend three days there.'

The brother produced a business card and passed it to him. 'In the old market – I will find you whatever you want. Another store, I will get you a special price. Look for me.' He snuck a petit four. 'I am travelling today.'

Andy wasn't paying attention when the owner asked his children's names, and while Andy explained he had one, Rick, the name went onto one of the better papyri.

Rashid produced a small papyrus: 'Cleopatra!'

'From the tomb of Nefertari,' Andy corrected. Painted on a wall in a tomb that could have led to their undoing in the Valley of the Queens. Sara had gotten pains after climbing down the steps and Andy had had to carry her out. 'My son, Rick, might prefer a male god.'

Impressed, Safiya asked: 'Which country are you from? Sweden, Germany, England?'

In her order of preference, no doubt? 'Ireland. Egypt turns the pyramids green for our St. Patrick's Day.'

'It is the colour of Allah here.' Safiya seemed satisfied with his answer. 'Is Ireland part of the EU?'

'Yes. Many opportunities in Ireland, and it is very attractive to live and easy to travel. The American multi-nationals call us one of the "islands" – Ireland, Singapore, and Puerto Rico. You would enjoy it there. There is a restaurant run by Egyptians in my neighbourhood. I keep asking for knafeh, but nobody has a good recipe.'

She was evaluating him with her eyes then, he could see. Could it all be that simple: an exchanged look and a resonance of attraction that would build throughout their lives? A single instant? Love at first sight? Their eyes had met during her swirl – a stolen, darting glance, no more? *Only if I intend.* He felt a connection and thought he already knew her. Was he still that person who could take that risk, his old student self, a headlong leap like when he had proposed to Sara?

Safiya had a basket with an embroidered kerchief that she had left on the table for tips. Instead of putting an amount in it, he took money from his wallet and let her choose what she thought was appropriate. 'I want all,' she said, raising her eyes from an inclined head, but then taking only two notes, she added with a teasing smile: 'For now.'

The owner began pulling papyrus after papyrus out of drawers to show him – the quality of these were poor compared with the two windscreen-sized ones they had brought home from the last holiday here, but Andy did not want to appear mean. He picked a small one with Ramesses II in his charging chariot and did not haggle about the price.

When he left, Safiya looked back over her shoulder with an interested smile.

He returned to the bridge, and he again looked down into the Nile's glassy green depths, listening to the noises where it broke around the hydrodynamic footings and raced through their length impossibly fast. It was a river spirit that gave of itself the great gift of life. It had not changed its life-giving role over the millennia despite the Aswan Dam and the canals that now controlled and drained its flow and held it waiting to spill through sluice gates and channels. It nevertheless invaded the very soils that it had once ravaged at will with its black fertile earth and that was celebrated by a panoply of gods in the stars.

He admired the tenacity of its now more subtle conquests, continuing to live by its own rules despite appearances. Even here, at this late stage of its journey, it was swift and furious, the last stage before turning chameleon-like to steely blue further downriver where it divided amongst the tributaries of the delta – to eventually slip away beneath the waves of the blue sea without changing its nature. Had he done as much? Was he the one who sparked the seeds of life in Rick? Unlike the Nile that proudly flowed beneath proclaiming its progeny, might he have been the sap? Whatever the case, he had as a student representative worked on just causes, and on this day had paid respects to those who had been on the front line in this country. He could not go back – that chapter had closed, but he could start to decide upon his future based on this truth.

Cars behind him began honking in concert. He turned around to see traffic backed up behind a car directly beside him and recognised Taafeef's rounded Egyptian looks. He got into the passenger seat beside him.

Hassled, Taafeef asked: 'Al Horreya Park, why are you not there? Why did you come to Tahrir during prayers? Where is Fami, the tour security guard? He is to accompany you to all places. What were you thinking?'

Andy answered the last question. 'It is innocent, I assure you.'

'Egyptian security does not think so. Egyptian plotters are in Istanbul. Turkey writes you a visa at the airport, you know. The soldiers think that is what happened.'

'What?'

'That is what they said, yes! I need to know exactly what happened, and to see your boarding passes, your passport, and your visa to vouch for you to security. They have intelligence that there is a terrorist attack coming. You will not go out without Fami again. I phoned the hotel: they gave you a driver?'

'Yes, I asked him to let me out at Qasr-Al-Nil Bridge. I did not miss my flight. You picked me up. I can show you my boarding passes at the hotel.' Andy's whole body tightened at the thought of another interrogation leading to arrest. He then told Taafeef about following the passenger along the rising corridor to the departure gates.

'Okay. Have you a boarding pass for both flights? I know the flight into Cairo because I picked you up, but the flight from Ireland . . . You did right to not mention the short-cut to departure gates.'

'I expect the passes are in the room unless it has been cleaned.'

'No cleaning on Friday. Also, your passport and visa – get them for me when we arrive. Fami will accompany you. He is waiting. I will talk to security. They have been following you since you talked to them. Did you see them?'

'No?'

Taafeef phoned, one hand to his ear while at the same time he negotiated with other hooting drivers converging on intersections, and with pedestrians timing their crossings between the advancing cars. Andy realised that there were no traffic lights outside the centre, and no cross-walks, so that cars inched forward like a push-penny arcade game and pedestrians simply zig-zagged through the chaotic traffic. He wondered would this be his last sight prior to handcuffing in a *mariah*.

Taafeef came off the phone just as they reached the hotel. At the hotel barrier, the sniffer dog checked around the car and mirrors were used to examine the underside that he did not remember from their arrival. The hound settled back in his kennel behind the high wall that fronted the hotel. He could see Fami in his perfect Armani and dark shades at the entrance.

Taafeef pulled over and cut the engine, allowing a silence to settle. He sighed and said: 'Fami will go with you to get your passport and tourist visa – and most important your boarding passes. Bring them only to me.'

Fami led the way. At the metal detector again, there was only a hardness to Samir's eyes, and he treated the contents of Andy's pocket as evidence, not touching anything and confining his examination to on-screen. He made Andy leave all the contents except the room card. They went on, between two full-size copies of Tutankhamun's Ka's from his tomb, past the shoeshine station with its throne and array of polishes in antique pots, and the shop with lines of souvenir gods and animals, to the elevator and hence to his room. The bed remained tossed, and he found the passport with the visa folded inside the safe. Sure enough, there were the two boarding passes sitting in the waste bin. He waited while Fami checked that the fixed balcony screens had not been loosened, and then as he looked through to check out the area beneath and the hotel's back gate in the high wall.

When they returned outside, he handed the documents over to Taafeef, who examined them and photographed the relevant pages. His travel agent sighed in relief. 'I will keep the boarding passes. We still need to talk,' he said to Andy, and directed him inside.

Samir released his contents in an official manner, making him sign. There was no mention of the work mobile Samir was holding. They found a quiet spot near the coffee dock, Fami standing behind him while Taafeef talked.

'You should not have gone out without Fami today. Tomorrow, no excuses. Fami will go with you. Tonight, do not leave the hotel. There is a traditional Egyptian group playing in the bar beside the pool.'

Andy nodded, agreeing.

As they shared a coffee, Taafeef continued to quiz him about the day and particularly about Andy's last visit to Egypt. He explained about Sara's pregnancy and Rick's premature birth in Hurghada and the Medevac home.

Taafeef laughed. 'This time, we need to make sure you go home on your scheduled flight. Security, they are on edge because of the terrorist threat. Hand me this mobile:

I need to give it to the police. You will need to get back your work phone from Samir.'

He nodded – resigning himself to the endless work emails on his work phone when it was returned by Samir.

Taafeef hesitated and then said: 'There is another, more delicate, security matter.' 'They have had a tip off – maybe a security check – that you were once a student radical.'

'Hardly. I was a student representative and took part in the anti-Iraqi war movement. Who didn't? These were large demonstrations worldwide. My protests went no further than Ireland and the UK. Perhaps it was because I was one of those who spoke.' Then he decided to add that word from Rashid. 'Semeyya,' Andy said, and immediately regretted it.

Taafeef eyed him suspiciously and said, 'Be careful, my friend. If there is a terrorist incident, security will interview you again.' A few moments later, he rose to leave. 'Listen to the traditional group in the bar tonight.'

Andy tipped Taafeef generously for his efforts, giving him the Egyptian equivalent of what would be an acceptable tip back home – a month's salary here given the exchange rate – baksheesh.

Some hours later, when he had replayed the sequence of events multiple times, he was certain there was nothing upon which he could be pursued. He was an entirely innocent tourist, and since his walk-down, he was more optimistic on all fronts. As he lay down resting, exhausted after the walk-down, he felt more optimistic about his relationship with Sara. After all, there was a synergy between them in no small way, evidenced by bringing up a son together. A holiday to reignite their passions and recreate that easy reciprocity that was there in the beginning. What had happened, had happened, and he would operate as Rick's father as Sara maintained unless proven otherwise. For the first time in months, he allowed his eyes to close, and then he drifted off into a deep, restful sleep, anticipating Sara's arrival.

Chapter 5,

Sirius Star

Sara

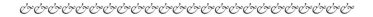

The Great Pyramid pulsing in sunlight that close to the veranda – the speed of happenings in the universe, Andy had said. Having suggested he join her in her room for his opinion on which dress to wear, she now saw Andy exiting the shower in record time. She felt she had been dismissive of him earlier when she had maybe burst his bubble on the room's nocturnal meanderings, and to make up she had proposed something that they she had not done in a long while, bounce outfits off him, teasing them against her body and seeing the effects on him. He had good taste – but, more importantly, it allowed her to get him focused on a chosen aspect of her. She had already decided on the rose tattoo on the left where her bust rose: it was solely Andy's having arrived later than the bows on her thighs.

As she returned to her room, Andy came through the adjoining arched door on cue in cotton shirt and chinos, carrying a blue linen sports jacket, fashionably crumpled for later. She liked the care that he took – brushing shoulders with multi-national professionals in their endless 'smart-casual'. She made up her mind there and then that she would make mental notes of what she found attractive in him – it would create a better atmosphere between them. She had no illusions; it would not completely smooth that elusive *rapprochement*. That would need more than 'likes'.

'You look remarkably refreshed for all the hassle of missed flights,' he complimented.

Another 'like'! 'Nothing to it. We transferred to a hotel when the flights didn't connect. Cheese roll fritter for breakfast, another titbit to add to our middle eastern pastry collection. Oh, there were the most tempting kadaifi and knafeh in the airport – I thought we had eaten all of them last time.'

'Don't know how you do it. How is Rick, do you think?'

'Rick is fine. He could not believe the size of his room, and then within five minutes, he was asking about room service options. Have you talked to him about that video he keeps replaying – it shows people climbing the pyramid?'

'Not yet. There hasn't been a chance. I'll try to catch him before we go downstairs, otherwise over dinner?'

Then spontaneously she asked if the rose tattoo was fading, which caused him to kiss the tenderness of the skin that she swore if he left a hickey the rose was out of bounds for the holiday. She played around with different necklines with the rose, upsetting his advice on the type of dress, one-shoulder or boring elegant A-line – that he of course had chosen first. She had already decided on which dress, and it was more a question of getting him on board with her selection. 'Might need a looser plunge,' she suggested, 'if we are not to hide the rose.' He agreed after analysis, and she teased a few more dresses with the rose tattoo for the fun, before insisting on her selection.

She asked would the rose become inflamed in the Egyptian sun, had it already become inflamed – she presented her chest and the rose so he could see it better? Did he think the petals on the rose were still unfolding correctly and holding their shape, weren't blurring at the edges – she knew they weren't – was it appropriate to show it, a woman her age and all?

Then as she dressed, she outlined each characteristic of the dress she had chosen, starting with the correct name of the asymmetric one-shoulder sheath dress. It had pieces of equestrian tack printed on white, gold chains, links and bits, and inter-connecting blue reins – that was classy – and even a rope knot that could be an old Celtic motive, all stabilized with a halter-neck complete with a gold ring that was her addition.

'Printed sheer dress? OTT for a first evening?' Andy commented. 'It is more what you would have worn to a racing paddock back in the day, but what man would not want to be accompanied by you?'

'It's all for your rose,' she assured him. As she was applying eyeshadow two toned, blue into purple, she changed the subject and asked what the trouble was the previous day – the receptionist had mentioned to her that the travel agent had to bring him back to the hotel.

'A misunderstanding. I was crossing Tahrir Square and there was a small army there and I was stopped and asked for identification – apparently, they can do that here. They made a big thing out of me having only copies of my passport and visa. I was just following instructions not to bring the originals. Did Taafeef pick you up from the airport?'

'No, a driver called Selim. Then there is nothing to be concerned about with the military, Andy?' She enunciated as she did with a serious question.

'No, I phoned Taafeef there and then, and he spoke to the soldier, and then he came to collect me later. The centre of Cairo was designed as a copy of your favourite city, Paris, the financial district at least. I walked there from the Qasr-Al-Nil Bridge, you know, with the black lions, across Tahrir Square, past the outside of the Egyptian Museum that is part of the tour. The heat, though, was as intense as the Valley of the Queens last time. Do you remember?'

'Did you get to walk down the Revolution as you planned?' She tried sounding her most casual.

'There was no walking down. It was a small area, and cleaned up. I know there were a few improvised shrines about, but after being stopped, I did not want to draw more attention to myself by looking for them. Oh, I like that look, now,' he said, referring to how her outfit came together. Then he came over and kissed the nape of her neck while she made the final touches in the mirror. There was an excitement in her eyes, she thought, that showed even in the reflection in the mirror, like she was that woman rushing to an assignation.

Andy interrupted: 'I do understand that I can't roll back the clock and be that student leader again, but I had to do the walk-down to get over that campaign failure. Sorry, but I didn't know until afterwards.'

She acknowledged with a sympathetic look.

He teased a tress of her auburn hair. 'Safe is not the worst thing in the world, and we have come through the difficult years, and doing all right. I just need to think about how best to proceed from here . . . rely on your advice?'

'Of course! No need to ask. We should go!' She looked at him in the mirror as she dusted her exposed top before lowering the dress to create a clear soft line with his rose, and then she clasped her embroidered clutch closed.

It was sunset when Andy, Rick, and she got to the outdoor restaurant. An orange afterglow was rising behind the pyramids and transitioning through turquoise into a band of daylight blue holding back the night. The twilight in the garden caused hair to glisten, eyes to glow, and skin to gleam in lambent clothes, evoking memories of evenings spent dancing, last to leave the racecourse. No wonder sunset was a time for lovers to seal their unions. Sara could not immediately think of a painter who had truly captured this transitory effect of which she herself had been aware in her fabric selection since her days as a *nuptial designer* – those pearl studded gossamer gauzes that radiated opalescent and for a fleeting instant created an ethereal softening.

Andy being so attentive, as only he could be, had restored him into her good books – those kisses on the nape of her neck and the rose that now sat blushing above her dress-line. It hadn't led to anything more but that was due to time pressure, but there was always later. Besides, she always felt it was a dead giveaway of guilty pleasure to arrive in a bother. Neither had the 'substantive issue' of Rick's paternity arisen. She was glad that she had started him on the rose tattoo though; that if they did resume later was one of her own sensitive on-buttons that would not be an eternity to the promised land.

She guessed their tour from the etiolated faces of those at a scattering of tables around the travel agents' flag of black, red, and yellow. Andy excused their way into a circle, insisting on introductions to those at their table – another 'like' that he didn't see why he wasn't everyone's equal. There was a Russian family of parents, young son, and daughter; and then a woman who sat by herself with her two hands arced around an opened bottle of red wine as if it were the treasure of her life – no comment there. The Russian names could be from an Olympic team: Svetlana, Boris, Karolina, and Aleksandr – parents and children. Boris was a heavy-set man with a grey-flecked beard and bemused smile, had good English and was clearly relieved that they were not also Germanic. Upon hearing that they were Irish, he welcomed them to Krautsville, explaining that they had gotten the hotel wrong. Svetlana, petite and perfect, sitting on the edge of her seat, was silently beautiful.

The woman on her own was German, it transpired, or rather Germanic, being from Austria, and after introducing herself as Kirsten, she spelled her name and then gave it its correct pronunciation. Her ruddy complexion, she explained, was windburn from recent storms at a ski lodge that she ran in Innsbruck in the Alps with her husband. He was a well-known downhill skiing champion, Michael Muller, whose name they may have heard. Because he was the champion, he got to give the skiing lessons, while she did the rest. Upcoming male skiers wanted lessons with the multi-Olympic gold and multi-world championship winner, and especially because he had World Cup race victories in different classes. But all wanted him because he was famous for the aggressive lines that no one else dared. 'Young women?' She sighed. Many young women skiers wrote personal letters, stacks daily that she had given up reading because they were all the same. 'Could he lead them down a daredevil run? They were good skiers and were sure they could follow him, but if that were not possible then just to see him take one of these runs, and then getting his autograph was enough. Of course, each encloses a photo.'

She mused that she was no better. She kept the chalet because she adored him and had willingly enslaved herself for him. What woman got to marry a famous athlete who was top-notch physically? Whenever he cast a testosterone-charged glance in her direction, she would weaken – it was living with a god. 'It is a void inside me when I miss his presence,' she elaborated. She then disclosed that this April had seen late snow that with the partial melt earlier had made skiing treacherous. She could no longer stand by as he took on dangerous runs at crazy speeds to impress 'gushes' of 'gosh' groupies. She had simply taken off on this holiday with the last six bottles of 'WeineStadt' (Wine in the city) that was only available locally near where they lived.

What a sympathy story – and Andy swallowing it and reaching out with his empathetic round-eyed look. He was such a sop for any woman's tale of woe, which was strange as he was analytical generally – he just seemed to switch off any filters. When she had challenged him about it once, he had said all men responded to 'damsels in distress' – it was archetypical and captured in all fairy tales. Or was it that men were sympathetic only when attracted to her girlish allure and a sporty build? Rapunzel in her lonely tower with trailing hair tresses and 'wines in the city'?

Boris jovially cheered the air: 'You will want to share the wine with the suppliers of your country's energy in the interests of continued supply.'

Kirsten thought about it, before replying, 'It seems a fair exchange if you can guarantee my gas supply next winter?'

'Your personal supply, no? You must pay your bill . . . for once!' he joked.

A fanfare of loud music broke from speakers, and a procession of waiters tapping riqs led a man in gold dress with a pharaoh's veil in royal blue and gold fanning out to the side of his head. He had kohl lined around his eyes to give an eternal gaze like the Tutankhamun mask that they would visit. A gold tunic came forward in a triangular skirt that formed a stiffened apron that bobbed in front as he walked – almost fancy dress. Andy was mentioning its Egyptian name, shendyt, and that it could be used as a board to assist writing in the field that interested Kirsten. The pair were chatting like new friends who had suddenly clicked, she noticed, as the procession wound between the fountains to a raised podium where the mock-pharaoh ascended to make an announcement.

'I am Ramesses II, the greatest of the Egyptian Pharaohs.' He then smiled and said: 'No, I am called after the Egyptian Pharaoh, Ramesses II. I am Rami, your humble tour guide and Egyptologist first class honours, American University of Cairo. Rami is easy to remember. Our security guard for the tour is Fami. So, Rami and Fami. Fami is standing below me, and he will be always with us – if you notice anything suspicious, tell Fami or myself, Rami, immediately.' A spotlight focused on the suited figure of Fami staring down the audience with dark glasses. 'Fami, please smile.' When he did not smile Rami continued: 'Fami does not smile, that is okay. You can smile. I can smile. Fami does not smile. He has night vision in his glasses to see the beautiful ladies, but he does not smile.'

'Fami is guaranteed to be military or ex-military,' Andy said, returning his conversation to include her. 'Did you notice hotel security scattered throughout the garden from the veranda?'

'Rebels about,' she joked. 'I had a boyfriend that was a rebel student leader. He had a Fu Manchu and zero-blade, and I had pink stand-up pigtails, and I remember he always looked at me when he spoke at rallies – my very own demagogue. Maybe he has gone undercover.'

'A speaker is supposed to look just over the heads and everyone in turn thinks you are talking to just them.'

'He wasn't looking at me!' she said to everyone.

'I could always pick out your stand-up pigtails, and I carried you with me – amour.'

Redeemed. Always going on about how her amour gave him a layer of armour, playing with the sounds. She enjoyed when they did this coded semi-public exchange – that wasn't half obvious. *TMI*, because Rick shushed them, suddenly wanting to better hear Rami instead of his texting.

Rami was drawing attention to the pyramids behind him lined in laser light, their magenta evening cloaks under-lit in unearthly colours. 'Are these babies not magnificent? They are only young. Only 4,700 years old. The pyramids are the only remaining wonder of the ancient world that even today we are only guessing at their construction. You will hear all of that later during the spectacular laser light show, because this hotel that I, Ramesses II, have chosen for your ultimate comfort and enjoyment, is close enough to see the show and to hear the commentary.'

Sara contented herself with listening. Who'd have imagined she'd be sitting in a fragrant water garden of trickling marble canals and fountains, with the fronds on the palm trees whispering into the close evening air. James was doing well to own a luxury hotel such as this – even if

Boris had called it Krautsville – and not alone one but a sister hotel on Gezira according to Selim, and perhaps a whole chain. Rick's father, as he had always claimed?

Rami was continuing: 'I, Ramesses II, will now reveal their real purpose.

'Each one is a mausoleum, for the body of a god and a goddess, a tomb where the occupants are mummified for eternity. There are three for the three successive rulers of the Fourth Dynasty of Egypt. The nearest and the highest is Khufu's, and the next with the ice cream on top is Khafre's, and the third – you can just see the tip – is Menkaure's.'

Rami continued: 'To understand more, we must imagine the pyramids in their original form. Instead of the chunky rows that mute the light of the sun, they were covered in purest smooth white marble with a tip of gold, real gold that would reflect a blazing radiance – bright enough to blind! The Ancient Egyptians thought that the pyramids connected the energy of the Sun-God, Ra, to earth without which there would not be life. And each allowed its God Pharaoh and his Queen to commune back and forth with their place in the cosmos. Yes, my friends, the pyramids are portals to the afterlife. Amazing idea, don't you think? Stargate SG-1, eat your heart out. Egyptians had this series five millennia before Netflix.'

'Rick, are you taking this in?'

Rick raised his head from his mobile. 'I am listening, just posting. Getting 90 percent "likes".'

'You up to something?' Andy questioned, and Rick raised his baseball cap, continuing to text furiously on his mobile.

'Nothing! Posting.'

'It's not home, you know. It's Sharia law here. At fifteen here youth status applies, with the same penalties as an adult. You pull something like your school break-in, and it won't just be expulsion or a flight home.'

Rick smiled. 'It wasn't that bad. I was studying late. Cloe was helping me.'

'We are worse for practically rewarding you. "School's out for summer" and hardly into May.'

'We didn't do any damage. If the smoke alarm hadn't gone off when Cloe wanted to smoke?'

It wasn't the time for this, but Sara did not want to interrupt Andy, as she had been the one to ask him to speak to Rick. She decided this type of opportunism was another of his good qualities, a spontaneity of sorts. It was honest rather than calculated.

'The fire service and the police and an ambulance! You were there under the desk for three hours according to the security reruns, and when they reviewed the video archive, you and she were going at it, on camera?'

'Cloe and me went everywhere together, and besides, you couldn't see anything 'cause we were under my desk.'

Boris broke into deep throated laughter. 'In Russia, you would get the Order of Lenin for services over and above the call of duty.'

'If you were allowed wine, I would offer you a taste,' Kirsten added. 'I have a soft spot for men who dare, as I said earlier.'

Andy did a second take at Kirsten's words.

'I don't drink, thank you,' Rick responded in all seriousness, as if there was nothing funny.

Boris held his glass out, which Kirsten filled.

There was a fuss by staff to lead an entourage to a screened-off area, and Rami stopped for a moment while they seated themselves. 'Welcome, honoured guests. You are most welcome.' He did not elaborate, and it was not possible to see who it was. A murmur ran through the group that it might be a famous Egyptian celebrity or a soap opera star.

Sara tried to get a better view: there was a fit-looking trim man dressed in smart casual. She remembered earlier that the receptionist – while she had lost herself in his diamond studded eyes – had said that James would stay at the hotel. An air of anticipation was creeping over her that she could not explain. She would have to get a closer look once Rami had concluded his mythology that he was recommencing.

'The Egyptians believed that their lives were reflected in the skies, aligned with the actions of gods in the cosmos.

Does anyone know why the Egyptians thought this? There is one special reason?'

There were answers shouted, before Kirsten, after holding up her hand classroom-style, called out: 'It is because the annual flooding of the Nile was predicted in the skies.'

Rami repeated: 'It is because the annual flooding of the Nile was predicted in the skies. All because one special star foretold of the flooding of the Nile.'

'It is the star Sirius, the brightest in the heavens, and it is already shining through the half-light.' He pointed to it. 'It is to see this star descending that I have called you here early. To understand why the star is important, we need only look upon the snaking ribbon of the Nile. You will see that it vibrates in colourful light through this most verdant valley to which it has been a source of sustenance and renewal. Each year the Nile enlarged, and its waters broke their banks and brought life-giving black earth to the lands of the pharaohs abounding.'

The Sirius star to which he pointed was scintillating in sapphire blue as it dipped southwest over the inky pyramids, clearer than any other and with an aura that dimmed surrounding stars. Rami became silent and studied the star for a moment. 'Imagine the effect of this majestic star when it reappeared in the pre-dawn morning predicting the flooding of the Nile?

'My friends, the sun has now set, and we will break our Ramadan fast and embrace each other to offer special Ramadan greetings. I have asked the circle at this first table to break the fast with me this evening – it is called, "taking Iftar", and it is a special blessing to receive this. There is a special prayer that I will recite to bless my companions. Do not worry, there is a full month of "Iftars" and I will be able to join each of you in turn. You will each receive the benefit of my special prayer.'

Sara excused herself as Rami descended from the podium: it was time to check out the mysterious VIP! 'Anyone know the hieroglyphic for *ladies' room*?' A giddiness was coming over her.

'Not hieroglyphics: there is a pharaoh on the door of the *Mens'* along the corridor, maybe Cleopatra or Nefertari – with vulture headdress?' Andy replied.

'A queen with a vulture headdress?'

'Yes, it was all the rage back then,' he joked.

Showing off to Kirsten, Andy?

Kirsten took the bait. 'Yes, you are correct, Andy. I remember the film with Elizabeth Taylor as Cleopatra. I will open my second bottle to offer you a glass.'

Sara went towards the door to the foyer they had come through, her stilettos pinging staccato off the marble paving. As she distanced herself from the buzz of conversation and eating, she enjoyed her body swaying to the slow rhythmic double-beat of her heels. Must be in the air – she hadn't touched the apéritif from earlier. She noted that there was another door further along, nearer the screened-off area where the 'honoured guests' had gone.

Emerging past the vulture headdress, she strolled across the now-silent foyer, and through the second exit that the night receptionist, a military man, identified for her. Containing her sense of excitement, she passed the VIP area at as leisurely a pace as she dared. There was a group of six gathered around a low-level table discussing maps laid out on the table – including an attractive-looking Egyptian woman who cast gleaming eyes towards Sara. She caught a glance askance of the man sitting with his back to her, recognising him immediately as the portrait pasha – her James! There he was in real life, after a twelve-year-exile! He had that same curved aquiline nose, was more tanned, and wore a loose local kaftan embroidered in writing over his physique – gold and white writing that could be read all over instead of black and white and read in the newspapers during the 'crash'. He was different: his buck teeth that had been his signature feature were gone, and then she heard that guffaw, more of neigh than a hee-haw – James, her James of old.

He looked to be a very affluent man in his forties, and his tan had a depth from unhurried exposure to the sun, the sort of person who could well have his own island. He continued to hold his head jutting forward enthusiastically, and it was he who was leading the discourse while others listened. When she had glanced over his shoulder through the screen, they were rearranging a massive city map by moving play-blocks about. It must have been the size of downtown Dublin that they were simply shuffling about. They built big in Egypt, taking a cue from those immense triangular outlines against the backdrop of stars. As she idled past, a security guard in Arab robes standing at one corner of the VIP area had eyed her through the screen and nodded towards the seated man – signalling she was passing?

Did the big baaša just nod, as if to say he had noticed? Using his security to scout her out after all the trouble he had caused her. Had he deliberately brought her into his orbit? She certainly was not going to give him the satisfaction of acknowledging his presence. She clanked on, pretending not to have noticed, nevertheless slinking into each steel stiletto, and baring the red soles as she lifted each foot to place it overlapping, following an imaginary line to the tables. Oh, she was a brat, about to make love to her husband, and still testing old territory.

Andy, who was studying her deliberate saunter, smiled as she reached the table. 'Your best catwalk-catwalk?' he joked.

'And which modelling school did you go to?' She did an imaginary curl of hair over one of her ears with her finger and then poked her cheek. A funny-peculiar mood, a high rather than a specific funny. They settled into their food. Rick agreed to put his phone to vibrate, where it continued to pulse on the table beside him.

Everyone was making small talk, Boris and Kirsten in the way that adversaries can respect each other's opinions – and Andy following every word; he always appreciated a woman who had opinions of her own. Kirsten shared her wine 'in the interest of winter heat', and Andy, with an unexpected sophistication, aerated each first sip of wine in his mouth to fully appreciate its nuances, leading into a conversation of fine wine tastes, where Kirsten talked at length about the WeineStadt and tried to get them pronouncing the German correctly. 'There is satisfaction watching next year's vintage ripening before your eyes as you savour the previous year. It makes a continuity.'

'Same time next year,' Andy joked, that, of course, Kirsten thought was hilarious. She looked towards Andy. After his quip, he was continuing to contribute to the discussion on wines, which completely surprised her, but then he was travelling that much. Apparently, grape variety was his map to taste; he tried to get a feel for what each country did differently using the same grape exampling pinot noir. He was quite at home comparing Californian and French, the main difference being that the French Pinot had a lower percentage of companion grapes and better balance. He preferred the more rounded Californian because they were not as predictable.

'You will spend a long time in Germany and Austria, I think,' Kirsten said. 'You need to taste a variety of terroirs and styles, maybe over a hundred with a range of tastes. Pinot from limestone is much more fruit focused and has a silkier mouthfeel, and balanced with acidity that is close to a French Pinot that you don't like. But there are hedonistic Pinots – lush and sensual, I think you would say. There is hearty, rustic, Pinot with cloying tannins, and all that long journey to the aromatic and ethereal.'

Did she know everything, and there was Andy again hanging off her every utterance? Sara wanted to break up that cosy little tête-à-tête – *no one getting a word in between them now*. She had never considered that Andy might be attractive to another woman, and after she was the one arranged the holiday, here he was pairing up with Kirsten. Maybe he could move on more quickly than her that she had not considered – she would have to force an indulgent smile if Kirsten looked in her direction.

'From silkiness to floating like an angel on the tongue. Which is your favourite German pinot?' Andy asked, him now the schoolboy impressing his heroine – *give her patience!*

'Except my favourite German wine is not a pinot,' Kirsten replied. 'It is a Grüner Veltliner, an Austrian grape. After the skiing season, when we were both exhausted competing, we would go high into the Alps. We spent days lying under an open cloudless sky in an Alpine meadow recovering on beds of wildflowers with only the sights and sounds of nature. You have seen this portrayed by Klimt.'

We get the idea!

'Walt Whitman's poem from school,' Andy responded. '*Give me the Splendid Silent Sun*, where he asks for nature until he is ready for the intensity of the city, and then the city until he is ready for nature.'

Andy, the Brat, ignoring her blushing rose.

'I will note down the name of the poem. Not the same, I think, but I must read it. For me, Grüner Veltliner wine holds the fragrances and organics of an Alpine meadow. If we need to relax and recharge at another time of the year, we can drink this wonderful wine and remember how we were restored by the Alpine meadow.'

'Are you a downhill skier also?' Sara asked Kirsten, thinking that this tied in with Kirsten's athletic build.

'Yes, downhill. That was how I met Michael.'

'Did you win any of the World Cup Races?'

'Yes, two races, nothing compared to Michael.'

'Andy, Sunday afternoon Alpine skiing on Eurosport? You may have been watching Kirsten.' Then she disclosed: 'He always had that programme on silent in the background. Isn't that a coincidence?'

Boris and Svetlana laughed.

'Guilty as charged. I have been known to be fascinated by fast women at breakneck speeds in the downhill. Were you one?' Andy tried to fob it off.

'Which, a fast woman or a woman at breakneck speed in the downhill?' Kirsten asked.

'I'll take all-in-one. I found it incredible that legs could crouch that low and take that level of vibration and gyration. It must have been hard on your knees. I was simply mesmerised by having that skill . . . and bravery, I suppose.' Andy tried to wriggle out of it.

'Andy, admit it: you enjoy the sight of athletic women manoeuvring with long poles in aerodynamic ski suits, streaking in colour on soft snow-white blankets,' Sara teased, rubbing it in. 'Remember, you would have a favourite, Andy, and delight when your choice took a position on the leaders' seat and removed her helmet. You waved back when she shook her little mittened hands . . . and even *awed* when she was demoted down the order.'

'Thank you, Sara. Everyone, I was just making fun. I listen to music and read the papers on a Sunday afternoon and need a background that is too demanding.'

Sara stopped teasing – she did not want Kirsten to avoid her husband thinking him pervy: an idea had occurred to her that she might need her for a 'loan-to' to keep him occupied while she caught up with a certain *honoured guest*. She looked down to check the rose tattoo that she had touched up a mite in the Cleopatra's.

Kirsten looked pleased, smiling at Andy.

Rami was back on the podium. 'Here is the Goddess of the Egyptian New Year: look how she swirls her veils and dances in ecstasy, a dance that will all too soon exhaust her. You can see Orion with her in the heavens. Look and you will see him, with an outstretched arm holding a bow, and an arrow over his head protecting her in her descent.'

'Sirius is exhausted in the evening, exhausted in the morning . . . always exhausted.' Andy was messing now.

'Men can be exhausting,' Kirsten replied, giggling.

'This very evening may be the night when she disappears from the skies for eighty days. When she returns, she will outshine the dawn with her sparkling presence in the east, and in ancient times this favourable event happened with the summer solstice and foretold of the great flooding of the Nile in July, as my learned friend has said. In the very first dynasty, over five thousand years ago, it was said that "Sirius, the star of the goddess Aset, coaxes out the Nile and causes it to swell".' Rami stopped for effect before adding, 'Yes, it has many meanings from the many parallels between gods and men.'

There was an exchange of smiles among the tour members. Kirsten commented: 'This explains why she is tired.' Andy laughed.

'Before she decides to go, I have one more secret to tell you. The shaft from the queen's chamber of the Great Pyramid of Khufu, the greatest of the Egyptian pyramids, aligns with Sirius to allow the soul of the Queen Henutsen to connect with the Sirius star in the afterlife. A similar shaft in the king's chamber aligns with a star on Orion's belt. Orion has now gone below the horizon and is waiting for her to follow him.

'What a beautiful star? Do you think lovely ladies of the tour, that this pyramid should carry only the name of Khufu?' He looked about before announcing: 'I, Ramesses II, will give the Greatest Pyramid its new name for all conversations, Khufu-Sirius.' There was a gentle applause.

'Now I have a surprise: the good news is that it is possible to take a tour inside the Pyramid of Khufu-Sirius and see these chambers for yourself. You can purchase tickets from me when I descend to walk amongst the tables: what a lovely experience to see the dawn and then go inside the Pyramid of Khufu.'

'Longest sales pitch ever. Is everything to the satisfaction of our royal God-child?' Andy asked Rick.

'Inside the pyramid sounds *Kool*. Not tomorrow morning, Dad.'

'Our last morning here then; we can rest on the flight to Luxor after. I will check. Does the Royal Prince agree?'

Rick nodded.

'The light show will now commence, and you can relax, look, and listen. You have seen the real light show in the sky and understand the secrets of the pyramids. My advice is to wait and enjoy the spectacle of the lasers and listen to the history. But this is a free country and if you wish, of course, stroll to get a closer view of these mythical monuments from the pyramids' car park. While you are there, enjoy the constellation that descends from the sky to become Cairo in these early hours. For like your happy homes far away, the lights will come on for the baking of bread. In Cairo, many people bake a special nutritious and tasty bread – it is called Aish Baladi.'

'Count me in on a walk to take in the view,' Boris remarked.

'Dad, Mom, would it be okay to go to the pyramid car park for the walk later?'

Rami explained: 'Twenty minutes walking will bring you to the car park and it is cordoned off to traffic at night. I must tell you that the lights on the Great Pyramids will be extinguished after the laser show, and it will be dark until Ra has ascended. If you still wish, then ask one of my friends here to go with you.' His arm swept wide to include, to their amazement, a circle of black-bereted security in white uniforms, armed but smiling beneath heavy dark moustaches. 'He will wait with you, all night if you want, until the first rays of light spread across the pyramid valley and awaken the Sphinx. The hotel will give you "Eastern delights" most delicious, in sealed hygienic snack packs.

'My friends, pick a star and sleep happy dreams. I wish this for you.'

He got down off his podium and then stopped to point out the different stars to a table as he sold them tickets.

Sara whispered to Andy, 'Sirius is my star, don't you think?'

'Many parallels?' Andy answered, not elaborating.

'Boris – can Rick go with you to the car park when you are going later?'

'Yes, I will take a short nap first. We can go from here one thirty or so, Rick?'

'Yep. I will take a nap also. Need my energy,' Rick replied.

A woman close by had asked about a string of stars dropping from the belt of Orion.

Rami began speaking to the group again. 'This lovely lady has asked about the string of stars that hang below the waistline of Orion. Did you notice these earlier?' A ripple of laughter ran through the crowd. 'It is okay. In Egypt, we are not shy about these things. The two brightest stars are the Nebulae Orionis and the lowest, Iota Orionis.' A louder peal of laughter interrupted.

He continued, 'No, I hate to disappoint. They are not representing his manhood.' More laughter ensued. 'It is his dagger, I assure you.'

Kirsten then asked Rami when he came by selling tickets: 'Why does Aset only get a star in a constellation called Ursa Canis, Big Dog?' She thought this was amusingly clever.

'The brightest star in the heaven and the heart of the Top Dog.' Rami brushed his hands, dismissing her.

'Sirius is a poodle, I think, following Orion over the horizon. Does he not chase the six remaining six sisters of the Pleiades?' She laughed again. 'He is similar to my husband.'

Rami dismissed her again. 'That is a Greek story – not Egyptian.'

'How do you find time to learn all these facts when you are slaving away all the time?' Boris asked.

'I hear them while I work; factual programmes turned up very loud.'

'The guests are very informed when they leave, I'm sure.'

Andy bought two tickets for the early morning tour inside Khufu, that he passed to Rick for safekeeping.

A short while later, they excused themselves from the table, and went together clattering over the marble, Andy's focus having returned to her, and Rick still texting madly behind them. She looked towards the VIP guest area. It was empty.

'It is sad to see a young woman alone with her wine,' Andy said. When she did not respond, he clarified: 'Kirsten. She deserves a more caring husband.'

'Yes,' she replied. Despite her newfound ease with Andy, she felt only emptiness inside her – James?

Chapter 6,

Khufu-Sirius

Rick

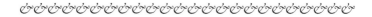

Rick pressed the mobile, and the display told him the time, one fifteen, in an instant lighting up the Moorish mirrors and reflecting off the bulbous brass lampshades in his room. He knocked it off and listened. There was only the hum of activities in the distance, broken by those moving about below. He was feeling recovered after the snooze, alert and clear-headed. Through the screen to the garden, there still were a smattering of people coming and going, and those security guards in white uniforms dotted about the compound. A few linked couples stepped carefully along the palm-lined paths to the rear gates, where they added to a string of lights that wound its way along the streets and up the incline. All were heading to take in the constellation that was Cairo, as Rami said they must. He could see the huddled crowd high above, dwarfed by the blackened triangles of the pyramids.

He took a few deep breaths on the veranda. The air was thick and heavy and carried the smells of the city, redolent odours laced with the day's traffic fumes, and the sprinkled earth that now gave up a sweetly pungent earthiness. He breathed in its heady mixture in the dew-laden air and remembered the expression 'the smell of napalm' from *Apocalypse Now*. Palm trees were giant look-out towers overseeing everything above the real-life security guards below. He was sweating through as much as earlier. Were two bottles of water enough? After finding a litre bottle from the room bar, he gulped it down for extra reserve. His rucksack was fully checked, and his camera was well protected at the bottom – his partners in crime. He needed to be there well before sunrise. Would she be there to fulfil the photo op on the summit of Khufu? Just wait until he posted that to his new school classmates. Route fully memorised and Rami's snack packs tucked inside the rucksack – they would share them while the sun crept in cinnabars and reds over the endless desert sand to galvanise the Sphinx.

No noise from his parents. Texts were sent for when they awoke. He had not been lying when he said he was going to see the morning sunrise from the pyramids. They had seemed a happy item earlier – his father had said there was no truth in the paternity suit. Oh, there was his mother's sketch pad on the seat where she had drawn a model with Svetlana's head in a short slave-girl dress. Orion warriors looking more like cupids all over it, a massive belt with the three stars from Orion's belt and a string of stars hanging, a star on the off-the-shoulder strap, and of course Rami's flat sandals with thongs crisscrossed to the knee. She had captured it all! Hilarious! If you can't have a constellation, then wear one circling on a dress – subversion by his own mother! Even her little trademark rose tattoo – with such upbringing, your honour, how could he be anything other than wild?

He picked Boris out alone at their table below where he was waiting – he wouldn't look out of place with him. Him going to the car park was a break he hadn't expected. Shush! Careful, careful. He reversed back into his room, closing the sliding door. See you tomorrow, today actually. In his room, Rick switched the mobile to silent, photoflash off, flight mode – not powered off just in case he needed it for real. Careful placement in the mobile pocket of his zippie, Velcro closed and double-checked. *K.* A brown sports hoodie of the Boston Bruins, of whom he wasn't particularly a fan: its colour would offer the best camouflage against the rock and sand.

It would be less conspicuous if he carried the massive brown rucksack, he decided, and he pulled the baseball cap right down over his eyes. He wanted this gear to be remembered, not him; he had packed Raiders' gear for his return. There was no skin visible except in the shadow of his face, and that he would disguise with eye-black closer to the pyramids. 'Base camp' was beside the smaller Queen Meritetis' pyramid, in front of the largest of the three gigantic pyramids, his climbing challenge. Khufu, the Greatest Pyramid! *Khufu-Sirius*, Rami had called it in deference to the ladies. Lady Luck would be on his side.

It was eerily quiet as he exited the lift to slip as quietly as he could through the foyer without the noise of the torrential waterfall cascading down the wall. His climbing boots reverberating round the empty space were the loudest sounds, enough that the security guard on the reception desk beneath the time-zone clocks raised his head to peer at him as he walked towards the garden. From the doorway, he caught sight of Rami's security friends spotted in groups throughout the garden. What the hell, a small army, and not looking too friendly. Lot of muscle. Nothing wrong with a wave though – holy crap, forced smiles of death.

Boris saw him, and he waved and walked briskly towards him. The big man hoisted himself slowly to his feet, perhaps regretting his earlier decision. He mentioned immediately about his family having gone for their beauty sleep without him. He laughed at either the waste of beauty sleep on him or his need for sleep as they proceeded together towards the roadway. Boris suggested he take the rucksack from him, and it did not look out of place when he effortlessly slung it over one shoulder. No security bothered to offer to protect the bulk of Boris and him as expected, and once on the street, they simply joined the trail of tourists going to take a view of the city. Lighting was poor and the pavement was badly cut up and they, copying others, turned on mobile phone torches to see their way and add to the procession of lights. Boris was sweating in the heat and laboured in large slow strides, deceptively fast causing Rick to scramble to keep up – the big steps of a giant man and his gangly companion.

A few moments into the walk, Boris turned to ask, as if it were the most ordinary thing in the world: 'How long do you think the climb will take?'

He must have guessed, but Rick trusted him and replied matter-of-factly, 'From the base the climb route itself is two-fifty metres, sloped and stepped. With clambering over the larger blocks lower down and easier near the top I have allowed forty minutes to get to the top. I have been in training.'

'You are taking it on alone?'

'Yes, but I may not be alone at the top. I was part of a blog where we discussed the best climbing routes and shared previous videos for a climb tonight. A few weeks back it was suddenly shut down. They were interested in the position of the planets and the dawn light at this time of year for a photo opp.' It took a weight off him to be able to talk openly.

'With a girl involved, I am guessing?'

'All my dreams, AKA Venus. She had an email address that linked to a modelling website.'

'Sorry I can't join you. I'll give you my WhatsApp in a minute and you can send me photos from the top. Yes?'

'Yes?' he replied hesitantly.

Boris explained: 'It is insurance for you. Lately, Egyptian security has begun strictly enforcing the ban on climbs and will delete all photos if they catch you. The last to try were treated quite badly when they were caught. They were in prison for months. No photos to show.' He laughed, a deep rumble that the thick air muted. 'No problem when you are back in the hotel – no one will suspect you there.'

Upon reaching the car park at the top of the ridge, they followed others to the low stone wall looking out over the city as would be expected. It was the sight Rami had promised: the Nile was a stippled serpentine carrying its braided light into the intensity of Cairo. Neighbourhoods glowed alive in lights amidst endless tower block and illuminated domes and towers competing with the minarets banded in rings of colour. He would get a better view from the top of the pyramid.

A ruddy-faced Boris good-humoured commented, 'Millions of souls feasting makes more lighting displays than baking bread, I think. Ramadan after all.' He then asked: 'What time do you need to be there?'

'Before three. I want to see the night sky change over the city and then gradually lighten into dawn. It should be a sight.'

They swapped WhatsApp numbers and connected. 'Hey, I appreciate it. It's better than nothing if I am caught. I'll take a few panoramas on the mobile and send them to you.'

'You had better go.' Boris checked about. 'No one is looking. Go! I will call them to help me with my bad knee in a minute.' Rick carefully put his phone away again.

'We will celebrate by the pool when you return. Don't get caught.' He winked, returning his gaze to the river gifting its gold and silver to the city.

Rick slipped back across the car park. The wall that ran from a small hut gave him cover from the security police and he hid in its outline until the road curved around left and turned uphill. Veering away from the footpath, he found cover on the opposite side in the shadow of the higher terrain. The lights were out on the pyramids, and only their brooding triangular shapes guided his way. Sirius had long descended following Orion into the arms of night. He took a pathway running beside the roadway to the top of the hill where he could break off to cross to the three small hillock pyramids: base camp. Headlights appeared on the road coming towards him. He pulled back and froze into a sandy bank. Two security men in a jeep.

He was up and off again panting already from carrying the heavy rucksack and in a welter of sweat; he could hear his footsteps grating on the loose stone, the swish of his clothes, and a clumping noise from the rucksack. A risky stretch was coming up where his outline would be clear along the city skyline. He held up to see if he could find little outcrops to run between. The incline was a lot steeper than on 'street-view'. Poking his head as high as he dared, he could just make out the three small block pyramid mounds over the umber and purple contours. They were under the massive shadow of Khufu-Sirius that looked indomitable in the night, and he had to remind himself again that it was a straightforward climbing exercise, ledge by stepped ledge.

He got back to the task at hand. The only concealment he saw was in a dip that ran in a line along the top of the hill. Cowering as low as he could, he moved across the rise and took cover in the first hollow, and then turned to listen. Nothing except the city's frenzy in the distance. The moisture drew odours from the earth, the deep chalky sour smells of millennia. No snakes or scorpions, he hoped. He was out and shuffling forward again, working along the little hillocks until he was amidst the crumbing mounds of the three smaller pyramids.

Closer now, Khufu-Sirius changed, and he could feel the draw of the mountainous structure. Strangely, it was losing its intimidation and again challenging him as when he had first seen it. He reflected that this silent sentinel had connected man's achievements with their reflections in the eternal cosmos for nearly five thousand years according to Rami. Alexander the Great, Julius Caesar and Mark Anthony, Augustus, Napoleon – they had all come to register their presence.

His own motivation was trivial in comparison to such iconic leaders: he wasn't measuring himself against history. He needed to complete a dare posted to Facebook to become accepted in his new school. Then, if suddenly he acquired single-parent status, hfs, he would already have his circle. It had been a solitary existence since Christmas when he had changed schools. His father had pressed him to hang in there, telling him that these new contacts would be his for life. But they were all a year younger, with more privileged backgrounds than his family had. However, he was athletic and worked hard at the new sport of rugby, hoping to impress – only to be politely ignored. The coach had demoted him to the thirds, despite him being the speediest winger – telling him that the next year he would be ready when he had learned their systems better.

What the hell! His climb had already become the center of attention and would mean that transition year classmates would accept him as their year's legend that they would have to include. They were already taking those six-meter dives off the pier into the black waters of the harbour. It was the school's summer rite of passage, postings of smiling faces with glistening bodies under the 'No Diving' sign. Those who had been in rugby training had six packs and posed like gods. He, if he took it on with his extra year and height, would look ridiculous, an overgrown wannabe part of the lads. His challenge was Khufu – he needed this breakthrough.

The prizes were there. All winter curious classmates had jogged past his house, leggings with bobtails swinging, which he had taken as an indication of interest, because it necessitated a detour off the park and promenade route up the long hill. Lucia in his year brought her pooch for a stroll past his house every morning, and that really was devotion to duty. Lucia of the sallow looks from her part Italian heritage that Gareth, his only new friend, was able to confirm was the case. Her dog was a playful, adorable little bundle of fluff that she smothered and pampered when she had to carry it, and that was *kk* too. He had identified the breed from the internet in case they got to talking. But as the bobtails and leggings became Michaela buns for the dives and running gear morphed into bikinis, it was as if he had grown Monkey Puzzle spines like the tree outside his new house.

Would AKA Venus be at the summit? She had said to be here tonight when he had told her about his interest in photography and sent her those sample photographs. She needed him to help take shots – *kk*. It was worth the dare! All his dreams, what the hell. He could do it! He took a few deep breaths, and his courage echoed above the frantic pounding of his heart. The pyramid, although worn and molested by time, was inviting him. Those exposed mighty blocks made it pliable, playful, tempting him into how easy the climb would be. It was a contradiction: daunting in its overall scale yet surmountable by clambering up the exposed ledges, ledge upon ledge the routines he had practised. Forget him being legend forever. Would she be there?

Strapping up, he checked and double-checked knee pads, elbow pads, and his pack. He tied a bandana and camouflaged his face in eye-black, leaving a circle on his forehead for a 'C' and a 'V', cobra and vulture like a pharaoh. Then he decided against these – it might look foolish or boyish to AKA Venus. He smiled in satisfaction despite a dread that tasted metallic in his mouth. He edged down to his point of attack to lie in the shadow of rocks. From here, he examined the route ahead, and once he got there and looked up at the enormity of slab upon slab narrowing into the chasm of the night, a wave of fear ran through him again. Its outer layer showed only endurance and strength, a mass of massive rocks receding and tapering ever upward to its narrow apex.

Khafre, with its sugar-topped cap catching a greenish aberrant moonlight, was the jealous sister watching with contempt, and Cinderella-sister Menkaure off in the distance, inky-blue sky against the deepest shade of magenta, ignored his attempt. He made fun of his challenge. Khufu-Sirius – stairway to heaven. No turning back. A little rougher round the edges than he'd expected, but no more difficult a challenge all the same. That did not sound too intimidating. Why take its size seriously?

A deep breath and he darted across the open area and up the two levels of steps and began his scramble upward. He was at the tenth level and cut back to within five metres from the taper. The stone was slippery with a heavy dew that he had not anticipated. He inhaled, looked up over the never-ending ledges – a clear line to the starry splashes overhead. Cracked, worn, and chipped, the slabs this far out on the pyramid were intact and clear of rubble. He ran his fingers over the soft and slippery smooth surfaces: it was alive and sweating into the night, treating him as a human insect on its massive bulk.

There was a knack to this. The combined routine was between hurdles and the double bars, as he had practiced: leg up, bring up the other, position, alternative leg up over the next ledge. Carefully rotating, he checked for patrols, and saw it was all clear. He scampered up about twenty meters, adjusted the rucksack and then lost himself in the activity. Focusing on testing his body and feeling its performance under pressure, the weight of the rucksack bearing down on his shoulders a comforting reassurance. He enjoyed his rhythmic breathing, his heart thumping solidly, and he felt the fitness of his muscles tackle each ledge. His training was paying off. Then he coasted for several levels, barely aware of touching the blocks as he moved. 'Emerging ahead of his accomplishments' – Macken, his new English teacher, would be proud of him remembering that key line from Steinbeck at this moment. He was equal to the challenge.

Further up the steps would be shallower, and he would gain time. There were headlights on the road below. He froze, becoming part of the monolith until they had passed. The slightest whisper of a soft breeze curled around, wafting up into his face – it had not turned to the offshore north wind yet. Then he returned to the rhythm of the ascent, hands exploring, and legs moving in synch in a prehensile scramble ever upwards. They were part of the same stuff, this Great Pyramid and him. It was pulling him into itself to allow the thermals and eddies swirl over them both, pressing them tightly together.

'I am legend! AKA Venus!' He cast his voice about into the void and was surprised that it came back to him in a deeper echo. He was defying gravity, floating on the warm currents as he glanced back to the dark mantle of the eastern sky where he could pluck spangled stars with his hands. They were still partying below in Cairo in the distance, the concentrations of lights amidst the domes and minarets! The Nile was shooting into the heart of the city before spreading its silver tentacles out on its way to the coast. Push on. Push on.

He was doing a steady pace, but the going was now tougher than expected. As the ledges went higher and became smaller, his grips began to slip, and he had a sense that he could be shaken off. He was two-thirds of the way up. Was he large enough to be visible from below? Over the ledges to the ground, no one could be seen. He looked upwards and was disappointed not to see activity. It would be him alone and Khufu-Sirius sharing the dawn together, another solo experience. What the hell? He needed to stay focused. He couldn't get careless or complacent and be encouraged into a false sense of security, become elated and giddy thinking he had conquered it. On the videos, everyone got spotted near the summit or on the way down. There was no option except to walk straight into police custody. Fatal Error! His father's warning about youth status – thanks, but no thanks. He would not be taken in such a facile manner. *Nfw!*

His plan would work. Once he took a 'selfie' looking to each of the points of the compass in turn with the radiant wings of the sun circling the horizon in its morning embrace, he would abandon his conquest. To escape, he would paraglide in triumph off the north face and be hidden from view within minutes. The tours would not have started. He could quickly change into his Raiders gear amongst the pyramid workers' ruins before Rami's security friends arrived. Ruthlessly sticking to the plan, he would not get excited into false security. Unless AKA Venus, for which he had no plan.

He pressed on. The climbing was easier towards the top as he had expected, yet Rick found that despite his months of training, he had the occasional spasm in his leg muscles, and his rucksack now pressed crushingly into his shoulders. The pyramid was narrowing to its apex and there was a wind whipping around him trying to dislodge him. Suddenly, he was out there on all sides . . . Hey, it was an apex of a once sublime perfect form that reflected the sun, and maybe that swirl was the wind beginning to turn north? He reviewed the last few levels to the flat top where the pyramidion was missing. Stopping his ascent, he took a few deep breaths to steady. He would not look back down or try to glimpse the sky until he was settled on the top. If he moved ledge to ledge, step by step, he would surmount the apex. The laws of physics had not changed, and those winds were softening finally, whispering gently to the dawn – they were turning.

He made progress again, one grasping limb at a time, completing its basic movements over the last remaining ledges. When he could almost see over, Rick stopped to catch his breath. He felt about for a grip without raising his head. When he caught a fixed object, he raised his head slowly to look directly ahead into the darkness retreating over the endless shaded undulations of the dunes in magenta, violet, and amethyst and with a silver glow on the horizon – the distant sea. He had made it!

Then his view was obstructed – two pairs of heavy boots were directly ahead of him. He allowed his eyes to adjust upwards. Two men were holding onto the sides of a frame single handed and extending their free hands. What the hell was next?

As he rose to try to secure himself within the frame, a heavily accented voice met him. 'Come on up,' it welcomed.

And another voice joined: 'Yes, come and join us, why don't you?'

It was a moment before he registered that they were not security. When he did, it was such a release he froze. Then, holding onto the frame, he moved to sit in its centre where he would not be seen. This was not in the plan. 'Wazzup?' he jested, taking in the suspicious looks of his two companions. The smaller had a strong muscular build with tight wiry hair and the taller, leaner man had a ponytail and an earring. The latter studied Rick while he checked the view through a camera mounted to the frame, and whispered to the shorter, broader guy whom he referred to as Roman.

Roman then spoke to him: 'First, we are taking long-exposure photographs of the city. It will be spectacular with the energy of twenty million lives and the stars moving in light-arcs. A modern *Starry Night*.' Then, kneeling on his hunkers inches from Rick's face, he disclosed: 'When Venus rises, we will do a photoshoot of our Venus with her planet. Then we will capture her when the sunrise creates a red aura above the city, and then we will, as you English say, "bluff our way out". While we descend, sample photos will go viral, more famous than Marilyn Monroe's red satin pose.'

The other smirked.

They would all be caught. Two idiots who think they will bluff their way out of this. He had gone to all that trouble to stay concealed, and they stand on top with mirrors and reflectors, and cameras flashing? But did they say, 'their Venus'? Her statement poses from her website came to mind.

Roman's companion returned to the equipment and a harness that he was tethering to the frame at the top to allow him to swing back and forth between different faces.

'We will set up a site to sell the remainder for an Aladdin's fortune. Our Venus will be a famous model and we will be her personal photographers. Open Sesame to the wealth of the world.'

There, *Venus* again? Why were they telling him all this?

'It is best we do not tell each other anything else,' Rick said, 'in case any of us are caught.' There was quite a lot he could say about them already. They were Eastern

European from their accents, and one was called Roman. What's more, they had almost certainly been spotted – the security police would have seen the light flashes, and the props they had assembled must be visible from below. Would they be able to recognise him again without his camouflage, identify his accent? They must not know he would paraglide off, but that took away any idea he had of leaving quickly.

A young woman who must have been sitting on a lower ledge raised her head to rise out of the cascading sand dunes. Roman, who had been mulling over his answer, introduced her. 'Say hello to our Venus?'

It was she, that face from the website, an attractive remoteness, but one that he thought could so easily break into a smile – and that genie top knot swinging as she busied herself. He hoped that she was only a year older than him. 'Hi, AKA Venus.'

'AKA Peg'sus?' She stopped applying her cosmetics. 'You have made it? Roman, André, Peg'sus is here to help with the photoshoot.'

Chapter 7,

Hello, James!

Sara

ஐ ஐ

Sara came out on the veranda and stood beneath the towering black mountain of Khufu. There was a deafening chorus of cicadas. They were everywhere in Egypt: it was coming back to her in dribs and drabs. What a coincidence, cicadas have a cycle of seventeen years Andy had said, and these could be the same cicadas that had gone to burrow underground the last time they were in Egypt. All those males clamouring for a mate, one last hurrah after the long years under the soil, and the cycle renews. Andy had called her 'his little cicada' back then, and here they were back to the start of the cycle. She felt optimistic. There had been sex after they had gotten to their room. Seventeen years completed and perhaps another seventeen years about to start – she would put that out of her mind for now.

The sex was different than usual. It wasn't just the red rose where she had been trying to focus his attention all evening that had captured him and where he would normally have stayed, allowing her own sensuality to spread into an all-over pleasure as he obsessed. It was more that he was unfolding her like the rose, appreciative of each delicate petal, tentative and sensitive-tender and not just pressie time. Just how many buttons did she have available to press anyway – and then emotions to take her there as well? Ucind would again no doubt have chalked it down to his peccadillos, but was this one?

It hadn't seemed like that. It was as soft and close as the night that now wrapped her on the veranda, like it was saying, 'let's be gentle' – perhaps after all they have been through. What happened was neither intended nor planned, but they had come through and could get through the rest.

She went back in and sat beside Andy, unsure about waking him. He was snoring lightly – waiting for the call to prayer for the long haul back in his mind. He moved when she told him about the cicadas coming out to welcome them. She thought he didn't hear, but he smiled, and she guessed he had at some level. She hadn't mentioned about him calling her his little cicada the last time – one step at a time: they were getting on. She needed to work on his silence though, not major sound effects but enough that she was reassured that he was completely involved, and not just pleasing her – but he wouldn't be coming back that often if he wasn't enjoying.

Thanks for reminding her, little fellows, that everything advances in cycles and nothing good, or bad, lasts forever. Two giant rooms, where would they be going? She laughed to herself. Should she wake him? No, leave him for now. Wonder how Rick was getting on? Through the open door, a chain of lights still wound down from the escarpment as people returned from viewing the city. She hadn't seen Rick amongst those who occasionally split off to come through the hotel's back entrance. The drone of the cicadas was softening. She got up and walked along the veranda to double-check Rick's room – the sumptuous bed was deserted hardly disturbed. Imagine the little twerp living in such luxury.

As she returned, she thought she saw a flash of light from the top of Khufu and checked her mobile. A text from Rick to say he had gone to view the dawn from the pyramids. She peered more closely into the dark density of the night. There was another flash and then a continuous spread of light flooded down over the top ledges, briefly turning them a lurid yellow. The lights could be filming. Rick would be closer – he would be able to tell her in the morning. She hoped he had not become involved in anything. Then she recalled the rucksack that went as extra baggage, and the pyramid video that he was replaying – of course! She returned to his room and searched for the rucksack to put her mind at ease. It was nowhere.

These days, Andy awoke snapping into life with the day planned. His work required him to sleep on long-haul flights when he went straight into meetings upon arrival. Following the same pattern, he had taken to waking in the early hours, doing his preparation for the day ahead and then falling back into second deeper sleep. When Sara shook him out of his light sleep this time, he was immediately alert as she told him: Rick missing, lights on the pyramid, and rucksack gone.

He sat on the edge of the bed. 'He's smart enough not to get caught again after the school catastrophe.'

'That video he was replaying on the plane was of a group ascending the pyramids.'

'He was with Boris?'

'Rick's mobile is saying *Not currently available*. His last text said he would be back in the morning after sunrise.'

'Can you text back to say I'll join him.' Andy was already dressing. 'Might be nothing: texts blocked by the shadow of the pyramid.' He looked up to see the lights pinging from the top of the pyramid through the humid night. 'No guessing what is happening up there. Let's not assume Rick is involved, but no harm to link up with him.' He placed a reassuring arm around her shoulder. How quickly he had recovered his touches. His hand fell away, and he moved towards the door and was slipping through into the corridor before it registered that he was going. 'I'll check with Boris and let you know,' she called after him.

It took security on reception some time to identify Boris's room and put her through after initially refusing to give her his room number, asking her directly how did they know that she was not a loose woman chasing an older, richer man? Boris's room phone rang without answer and then cut out, and she had to repeat the procedure through reception again, only for the same result. She went back out onto the veranda to peer through the lattice at the mammoth dark mass shutting out the stars. It was less active, with only series of flashes occasionally. She texted Andy: he replied that he was at the car park and neither Andy nor Boris was there. He was taking the route to the Pyramid of Khufu. She would dress and go to reception and insist they give her Boris's room number. She would bang his bloody door down till he answered. It was her son.

'Is everything alright?' A male voice coming from the next suite along the veranda startled her. It had an English-speaking origin but with each word enunciated from living abroad and adopting local rhythms. He sounded genuine in his concern though, and in any case, there was that locked screen between them. She walked towards its source, trying to get a better view through the light escaping from the garden below but keeping her distance.

'There are lights at the top of the pyramid and our teenage son hasn't returned. A text to say he was waiting to view the dawn,' she confided, thinking what was there to lose?

'Your son! What time did he go?' He was immediately concerned.

'He went to the pyramid car park with an older Russian man from our tour about one. He sent a text to say he was going to wait for sunrise, but his mobile is not responding since. My husband has gone to the pyramid.'

'It's coming up to four now. Can I phone reception for you? I speak Arabic.'

She felt she could trust the soft, measured voice. 'Boris is the Russian man's name, wife is Svetlana, and they have two kids. My son is Rick, Rick Loughlin-Sexton.'

Her neighbour was on his mobile in an instant, shouting down into it in rushed phrases. He was certainly fluent! She smiled at the irony of having this stranger raising hell for her despite her not moving. Ucind would be impressed.

'Reception is going to Boris's room. I will make another call.'

'Sure.'

He paced up and down in front of his room as he made the second call: it was again in Arabic, and this time, it was even more imperative. A similar call back home would be considered loud and aggressive, but was that how things were done here? She wasn't sure anymore that she had done right in involving him. She could feel his eyes on her through the screen, and realising she was still in the hotel dressing gown when it began flapping around her knees in the light breeze, she indicated to him she was going into her room to dress.

When she came back out, her neighbour was off the phone and had moved closer to the screen. His voice began, this time more resonant and somehow familiar. 'There is good and bad news. Boris has been back from the walk to the car park since three. Reception asked him about Rick, and he said that Rick has gone on to the pyramid to watch the sunrise from there. We don't know that he climbed it, but the lights are from the top of the pyramid?'

'It could be a photoshoot, bursts of light, screens, and reflectors. There they are again.'

Both peered into the darkness. 'Hard to see exactly. I will phone a contact.' He was on the mobile in a moment, and this time it was deferential in tone. She could hear the voice on the other end, deep and authoritative. The call went on and then he made another call, back to his earlier manner. She noticed movement through the garden: the robed man whom she had seen with the VIP group earlier and another hurried towards the back gate and got into a white land-rover. It took off in the direction of the car park and then she saw its beams continue beyond the car park before it fell out of view. Her neighbour came off the phone.

'Look, thank you for all the calls you are making. I am sure it will have a simple explanation.'

'Perhaps? I can update you on my other calls. The police have no special alert relating to the area around the pyramids – I couched it in concern about my staying at the hotel. Provided Rick is not at the peak when the police arrive, there will be no issue for him. Have you had any more contact?'

'I'll try again, but his phone was still not picking up while I was changing.'

Sara phoned again and received the same message. 'Not currently available. I'll send a text to tell him to get off the pyramid,' she relayed to the man.

'Okay, I asked about having a helicopter come to the hotel, but there is a "no-fly" situation in Cairo for anyone other than military, because of this terrorist security alert. I will be honest, this is worrying. I have sent my two security guards to the pyramids, and we will see what they find. Just in case he is involved, they can smooth any *misunderstanding* the police might have on Rick's involvement. It can be sorted out very quickly early on. Now we wait.'

'Was that them going through the garden to the white land-rover?'

'Yes.'

'Hello, James! It's been a while! You can show yourself.' She hoped he would get the tone in her voice.

He came closer to the screen. 'Hello, Sara. So, you recognised me?'

'The portrait in reception had a likeness. I sent a copy to Ucind, and between us, we figured it to be you despite the different look. Your aquiline nose and light blues gave you away.' She didn't mention the teeth. 'We live opposite now.'

'Closer than ever?'

'Yes, like old times since we moved in at Christmas. Our tour guide announced you as a *most important guest* earlier. Reception referred to you as the big-baaša. And I noticed the hotel logo was an upended horseshoe with a coiled snake. Is this hotel yours?'

'Yes. My lucky horseshoe might have been why I got to build in the shadow of these. Makes rezoning back home look small scale: the revolution freed up land for construction throughout the city. Not everyone is in favour of building this close to these ancient wonders, but there are always objectors.'

He wasn't that different with that casual confidence about him, she supposed. 'I'm impressed. It's a beautiful hotel; who came up with the concept?'

'The concept is nothing special internally, multiple standard rooms around an atrium, each convertible. It gives flexibility and allows families to be together. But I tried to incorporate Arabic elements: majilis, furniture, and the screening that creates privacy?'

She remembered the eyes of the bemused receptionist as he explained the room-screens and the layout arrangement. 'Yes, the screen adds a certain intrigue as people pass. Valley of the peeping windows.'

'Discreet, and practical too. Absolutely necessary during the warmer months, creates security and deflects noise.'

'Absolutely,' she repeated, the way a Dublin person would say it. 'You have held onto one expression from home. Your receptionist already explained the screening and the practicalities of the East wing for Mama bear and baby bears. He had to move Rick when he saw he was an adult bear, so there could be more baby-making with Hubbie bear!' She wanted him to know that Andy and she were still together despite his challenge.

He ignored the implication, and clearly wanting to keep her in conversation, began a different train. 'The entrance and the garden are the real homage to Arabic culture. Did you ever get to see the Alhambra on your Spanish hols as a kid?' Not waiting for a reply, he continued, 'Water flows magically through lush gardens and courtyards, channels mimicking those from Muslim paradise. We took certain features to create a space that is cool from the evaporative cooling and relaxing from the sounds of babbling water under the canopy of trees and loggias. Even at forty degrees outside, it is pleasant to sit in the shade with the fountains talking back and forth to each other. The installer spent months adjusting flows to get the sounds correct, would you credit that?' He smiled, but it wasn't the same smile, not the toothy madman smile of old. His pursed lips too had been sculpted into form, and his expression was frozen in a decadent golden mask from behind which those old forlorn eyes looked out. She nearly laughed at the comicality of a hangdog look with perfectly sensuous lips.

'It's a beautiful place. A long way from Ireland.'

He didn't respond or even acknowledge. 'You know, it's not that we thought too small back in Ireland: we didn't think big enough. Here is the home of the mega-project. El-Sisi city, as they call it here, will eventually stretch all the way from Old Cairo to the Red Sea. Recently, I took over a bunch of construction contracts there when a developer fell out with the regime. It was part of getting into the inner circle here. It suits me.'

'Suit you it might, James, but it must carry risk – a disaffected developer?'

'Ah, he is continuing a media campaign from abroad, but Government sources assure me that he is under continuous surveillance, and for me not to be concerned.'

Was he trying to impress? 'A mite ironic-peculiar,' she commented, giving one of her looks that he always ignored in the past. 'Your mini-projects cost our taxpayers two billion euros.'

'Just bad timing. Credit dried up globally with the financial crisis. Saving all the banks was what brought the country down – fear of the bondholders. Hell of a thing for a republic to do, sell out its own to foreign capital.' His face profiled as it tightened in a wince, unable to form into the lines that previously gave it character. 'Such a cumbersome way to get to the same outcome.'

It must have taken its toll. She felt for him despite the carnage that he had wreaked. '"Blunt instrument", you called it in the papers. We were all rooting for you, ironic-peculiar that was more strange-perverted.'

This time, James did laugh in guffaw horse laughs like of old. 'You're still using those expressions – and if I haven't said so, you are beautiful, beautiful as ever. They always catch me off guard.'

She wasn't going to allow him to slip in a compliment to charm her. 'You got to keep all the viable companies, didn't you?'

'I was allowed to buy them back at par once I established their viability. My family members manage them.'

He had done all right. 'So, you'll be coming back home?'

'No. Cost the taxpayer a couple of billion, as you say. You never know how things will turn: it could all change in the morning – someone saving their own neck by implicating you. Nothing to go back to except you and

Rick. Janis divorced me, as you probably know. I offended her sensibilities and lifestyle. Do you know her friends wouldn't meet her in public? Eventually, her family pressured her into leaving me. I don't blame her: even my own family don't want me back.'

'Pride of a respectable line of publicans turned horse-trainers?' she replied.

There was silence then for the first time, the closeness of the night broken by wafting air movements and the drone of a frenetic city way off in the distance. 'Look at these.' James spoke into the night, pointing at the dominant triangular structures against the night sky. 'They are from pre-history, hardly out of the Stone Age and the first thing they do is build the mightiest structures, wonders not matched for thousands of years. We think we have funerals covered in Ireland? Feast your eyes on what funerals are about, celebrating a person forever.'

'The nearest pyramid was iridescent in colours when I arrived, and the canopy floated in beautiful golden details high above the entrance. Your receptionist thought I had lost it when I was trying to explain it to him.' She had shared an appreciation that she had not intended.

'The entrance is also influenced by the Alambra, I'm afraid. Still the same Sara, opening your artistic sensitivity to everyone and trusting that the world will respond. I have missed you. Are you not going to invite me in? It's feels like I am in a confessional.'

A tear formed in her eye at what might have been between them, and she had to immediately remind herself to refocus. Not that she was not as fascinated as ever with a sudden energy surging through her body. His leathery perfume filled her nostrils every time he came near the screen. When they had been together, he had showered with strongly scented soap to mask it; he was doing similar with local essences, but she could nevertheless catch a hint of his odour. 'How are Rick and Andy would be appropriate.'

He asked again: 'Can I come in to explain?'

'Mine to lock and control and the lounge mine to invite, your receptionist said?' That would be crossing a line, and she could not entirely trust herself. His looks may have altered, even his expressions, but he had always kept himself. While he was not the muscle and bone country boy she had known – more filled out – he had retained his ruggedness, and a sense that he could be dangerous. 'Was our hotel upgrade yours?'

He nodded.

'I am grateful, as I have always been grateful.' That was another thing she always ended up being the grateful one for his generosity.

'Didn't want you slumming it.'

'We would have been quite content in the other hotel. Rick might have found friends, and we weren't slumming it. Ucind always selects a suitable hotel on the upmarket side.' She was suddenly annoyed with him.

'To answer the question about how Rick and Andy are, that you still haven't asked about. Well, they are awful. That was the shittiest, lousiest thing that you could do to a decent person like Andy. When you and your line would not have anything to do with me – bit on the side of your grand ambitions – Andy was the only one who came to my assistance. He married me, gave up his degree, and has never stopped putting us first. He is not you, not the highflier or mover-and-shaker, and there are none of the wild sparks or chemistry there were between us. But he adores the ground I walk on, and yes, we are reasonably happy, or were until your subpoena dropped. You know where he was yesterday? He was walking down the revolution to recover his student rebel self-belief. He nearly got himself arrested – reading between the lines. You know where he is now? He has gone to protect the young man he believes to be his son. Incidentally, Rick too has gone completely off the rails, thrown out of one school, and has hardly left the house since we moved him to the new school, and who may at this very moment be pulling a devil-may-care stunt to ingratiate himself with his new classmates. What if he gets into trouble here?'

He interrupted her outpouring. 'Sara, I am sorry. I am truly sorry.'

The words hung resonating in the air for a long time before dissolving in its currents. She looked at him through the screen. She would never have let him get his teeth done. It took away from his old country gobshite look that made his face long, thin and forlorn, going with his stringy body, muscle and bone, the sanguine complexion and the tight receding hairline that completed the picture. What was he now submerged behind that rounded, frozen face and the treatments that had locked it? She focused on his eyes that continued to be shaped down – that was totally ridiculous – and that hook nose, as he began to speak.

'Sara, please. When you are the one who dreams the dream, grasps its possibilities, its existence even, persuades others and gets them to back it, you are the boxer in the ring, the one taking the blows, the hits. When it goes wrong, all the false camaraderie and back-slapping is shown up; the bed-mates, corrupt and smiling and really angling for a better slice, walk away for you to take the knock-out punch. I am not excusing myself, but deep inside, it hardens you to find out that you are completely alone.'

'James, believe me, I could be sympathetic under other circumstances, but you are destroying my life, such as it is.'

James deliberated for a moment before replying. 'I had time to think before I got going here, that as you know, I don't usually do. I don't regret anything bar one thing:

that I deserted you and Rick. I want you and me and Rick to be together as it should have been.'

'Only give your heart once, James? It's not like that Janis Joplin song, where you can take *Another Piece of my Heart, baby*. The whole goes, even if I was only your bit on the side to you.'

'Sorry. I will make it up to you and Rick. Nothing has been right since we split.'

But there it was again, she and Rick. 'James, you are getting ahead of yourself. Why aren't you the one out there finding your son? I am not opening the door or screen or whatever. I have never said this to you – No! Now find your son if you believe he is yours!'

His mobile rang, and he excused himself to take it. 'Akar?' He walked along the veranda and she felt he was walking out of her life again rather than getting an update on her son's whereabouts. When he returned, she had drawn back the screen.

Surprised, he stood gaping down at her – at least that ridiculous expression had not changed. 'Akar thinks that Rick might be one of those on the pyramid just below the top. He has seen four of them on night vision, thinks he is the younger. There is a photoshoot going on, all right. Get this. It is it of a semi-naked woman modelling with veils.'

'Is Rick safe?' She went forward and crossed an imaginary line she had drawn between them. His rangy body of old reached forward about her to comfort her, and she let it happen to feel the power of his embrace before she backed out from his now more muscular and padded frame.

He looked over her at the pyramid. 'My call was to a contact to make sure Rick would not be arrested. But if he is a part of the shoot, it will be different. He is safe for now, Sara, but this will be a police matter and the consequences for all of them are serious. It is lucky that there is a no-fly situation, or the media might be all over this. All news leaks in Egypt.'

'Please get him down safely.'

'Masood, who is with Akar, has begun climbing and will try to get Rick out of danger. What were they thinking, and in the middle of Ramadan? He is as mad as me! Akar will drop back for me, and we can wait in the car pending developments. Are you coming?'

'I can hardly take a lift. Andy?' For the second time, she was left out. Rick was her son. Ironic-peculiar, or what?

'Here, let me have your mobile number and I will keep you updated.'

Then he dialled her number, and her phone lit seconds later with that old-fashioned phone ring she kept. She answered it briefly, even though James was standing beside her.

'Probably connects all round the world and then back to you. I'll connect you on Bluetooth also, in case there is no reception, and we are close by.'

Then she saw the Bluetooth request: it held that old schoolgirl thrill. She pressed *Yes* on the pop-up. 'Like next door?'

He was hesitant then, looking indecisive like he hadn't earlier. He stood as she smiled at the predicament she had provoked.

Then, collecting himself, he vanished through the door of the lounge into the corridor. 'The sooner we extract Rick, the easier it will be to sort.'

She was never going to be able to decipher the intricacies of the schemes that were continuously circulating in his mind, but she knew at any instant how he was feeling and where she stood with him. He had no secret agendas with her, a naivety that made him vulnerable. He was all action, *bloody-minded direct,* full of bluster when it came down to it, but she had missed that excitement.

Sara returned to looking at the pyramid where the more persistent flashes exploded violently, fireworks crowning the peak and spotlights that strobed the sky. How could she face Andy in the company of James? She would phone Andy to say . . . she didn't know what, but she needed to talk to him.

Chapter 8,

AKA Venus

Rick

❧❧❧❧❧❧❧❧❧❧❧❧❧❧❧❧❧❧❧❧❧❧❧❧❧❧❧

'What is this?' Roman addressed Venus. 'I pay the expenses for this trip, clothing, the photographer, and lug your portable dresser up this pyramid, and you have been scheming on the internet all the time?'

'No scheming. I was learning about the climb. Peg'sus had his own plans to climb, and he takes good photographs. I shut the blog two weeks ago. Besides, you just said that you will make a fortune.'

'We will all make a small fortune if you do what I have asked.'

'I get the original memory discs from the camera.' She reminded him of an arrangement they had.

'As agreed.'

Rick was certain he saw a glance exchanged between Roman and the photographer, who was checking the cameras that were focused downtown.

'You have one follower already,' Roman remarked sardonically to Venus, before turning and standing threateningly over him. 'You, move off the top, now.'

'Roman, the shoot will take too long if André arranges me. You cannot arrange me. If you want a successful shoot, leave me Peg'sus. I will give him tests and if he passes, then he can stay.'

'How old are you?' Roman then demanded of Rick.

'Eighteen.' Rick added a year, and even so, he thought Venus might be older again.

Roman continued to stand aggressively over him and pushed Rick's shoulder a few times for him to move. Rick chose a space below Venus on the west face away from the city and access to the pyramids where he would be least noticeable from below. Energetic, excited, and busy, she bobbed about applying cosmetics while continuing to chat. 'What is your zodiac sign? Peg'sus is not a sign.' She had a pink multi-level elaborate portable dresser opened out in front of her while applying her cosmetics.

'My sign, Aries!' he answered, as she was about to repeat the question.

'Your sign is open-minded: mine is a rebel sign, Aqu'r'us. It explains why I am here at the top of the greatest pyramid for, as you have heard, a professional photoshoot.'

While Rick was pulling out the breakfast packs that had been provided by the hotel to lay them out beside him picnic style, he saw her eye them. 'Fruit juice?' he asked as casually as he could manage, holding up the clear sealed container and offering it to her.

She accepted it and asked, 'Now you have none?'

The silk wrap hanging off one shoulder failed to completely conceal her beautiful figure. 'There are two packs.'

'Is there an energy bar?'

'Be prepared!' He held up the scout sign.

'You Anglos, always with your funny formalities?' She smiled, but not as she had earlier.

Clearly, the wrong thing to say – what was he thinking – he may as well have produced the scout penknife. Quickly, he decided to confess his nationality to distract her from focusing on his real age.

'I am from Ireland, a country of rebels.' He passed the energy bar. He was certain now she had little on under the printed silk.

'Thank you, Irish Rebel.' Leaning over, she took the bar. 'A photoshoot is more exhausting than you think. Roman brings only equipment, lots of equipment. He is a camel who climbs pyramids, and he thinks we are all camels who climb.'

He examined the contents of the snack pack. 'A breakfast roll – most delicious meat?' After his offer to her was turned down, he passed the second pack to Roman and the photographer. He himself chewed gluttonously, gulped, and then took another bite until his was gone. 'Most tasty bread – someone must have been baking really early.'

This last remark got strange looks from the two men, who were re-tightening the frame onto the top and continuing to do macho swings out over the sides.

Venus had finished her make-up. 'Now, I need to test you to see if you can position me during the photoshoot to have me soar through the heavens. There are three parts to the test. If you get them right, you can be a part of the photoshoot. Otherwise, Roman is right and I am sorry – we are not that familiar and you cannot be the audience.'

His heart was pounding faster than at any time during the climb. He inhaled the floral notes of her perfume that layered into deeper essences as she moved closer. Looking into that smiling face, her brown eyes lined into wingtips like an ancient Egyptian, he could not interpret the least thing about her. All he knew was that there was not the slightest blemish on the soft tones shadowing her face, and that he was in no way in control of the situation. She, behind the brown whorls that carried intent, was directing procedures and he was her apprentice.

She rearranged the silk print, allowing the scene of herons and tall grasses to loosen. He was that mesmerised that he was only aware that her lips were moving when his mind registered that he had been given his first task: he must point to Aqu'r'us in the sky.

'I know this. Aquarius is beside Pegasus, my favourite, and my internet name.'

She laughed. 'Where? Beside your favourite Peg'sus? That is not enough, AKA Peg'sus.'

He played for time while he found her constellation. 'The problem with most constellations is that what they represent is mainly imagined. Pegasus had three arms coming off a square, well head and two forelegs. The wings and his hind legs are imagined. He pointed east not high above the horizon, where, sure enough, Pegasus was galloping towards the zenith. 'To the right of Pegasus's head star is Aquarius.'

'Go on.' She gave nothing away.

Identifying her constellation was difficult with the glow of the city below, although Cairo, apart from the motorway arteries and the illuminated centre, held only those random domes of neighbourhoods alive to Ramadan feasting. He traced out a cluster of stars that forked into three branches and pointed. 'There! Aquarius is still rising to clear the horizon.'

'You are right. One down. Now, tell me the zodiac symbol of Aqu'r'us,' she said as she stood up about to climb the last ledges to the top.

'I know this too. It is the water carrier, a woman with a water jug, who is normally portrayed kneeling, pouring water.'

'Bright Boy! Two down. Now, you must tell me how you can arrange my constellation about me. I do not want all my zodiac's stars in the water flowing from the water jug, that is everywhere. Do you have many girlfriends?'

'Not since last year. My last girlfriend and I were expelled from my previous school for going back into the school late and setting off the alarms. We were caught on video under my desk.' He shrugged.

She laughed. 'Where is your girlfriend now?'

'I moved to a new house across the city with my family last December, and we have lost contact, except for texting.' He tried not to appear sheepish about it.

'So fickle?'

How did she twist that? 'No, not fickle. It's just how it worked out.'

'Keep in the back pocket,' she concluded. 'No new girlfriends at your new school to help you with your studies in the evening?'

'I am just trying to get to know everyone at my new school. It is not easy because my new school held me back a year, and that makes me at least a year older than anyone else. They are diving off the pier in the local harbour as a rite of passage. It is juvenile. This will go on all summer to the shrieks of the girls completing their dives and the horseplay of the guys, and I will be expected to complete mine. I prefer to climb a pyramid.' He thought this sounded pretty *Kool*.

'You do not need a rite of passage because you have already completed a rite of passage with the girlfriend that you dumped. You are familiar with a woman's body, I think. My third question: can you position me within my constellation?'

With that, the printed wrap dropped to her waist, and she stood statuesque swimming against the black star-studded night. There was no comparison with the slim models from his mother's fashion magazines. She was a modern Venus, a woman whose perfectly toned figure ruled the sky, destiny awaiting her constellation as she moved amongst a myriad scintillating stars. Completely overcome, surges of desire cascaded through him, his breathing had quickened, and his heart palpitated. He wanted to scream into the infinite universe proclaiming what was theirs together.

She was coolly checking herself, quickly rubbing in a cream with her hand that made her skin gleam. 'No goosebumps.' She laughed. 'Have you solved my positioning?'

He pulled himself together. He would have to find a new way of presenting her within the stars of her zodiac, or he would be banned from her presence – over before it had begun.

Roman had come by to hold a mirror as she tossed the reflecting tresses lightly onto her clavicles and softly around her shoulders. Then coolly, as she focused her eyes on him, she asked: 'Well, how do I look?'

'Roman is skimping on the clothes budget.'

'Now you make me smile. Roman, are you pleased I do not frown?'

Rick caught her laughter as it came to him and floated a little with its rhythms; however, the presence of Roman, hovering near his Venus, was breaking the enthrallment – him thinking that she was his alone. He looked despondently at the outline of Aquarius that was clearing the line of the horizon and stood on two of its branches while the third branch shot off, rising to the left. It was easy to see how he could make it into Aquarius kneeling looking towards her right with the stars mainly in the water flowing from an urn. She was correct. It made no statement and could be accessed under standard images of her zodiac on any internet search. There was no stamp of them upon the scene to capture her.

He retraced the outline of Aquarius fully risen and now floating clear into the deep magentas amidst a glitter of multicolour stars. He studied the constellation, focusing on the stars formed by the descending branches that would leave her facing to the right. But now that the constellation had fully risen, he could see that the outline of the stars connected differently could be a woman looking left. Yes, standing in a questioning pose, looking left. Uncannily, the constellation could be an outline of the Venus de Milo pose – with a few stars left to sprinkle in the water flowing from an urn on her right shoulder. Caught mid-activity? He was convinced that no one had ever imagined this before. It was theirs.

'Time is up,' she stated impatiently, satisfied with her preparations. 'Do you position me?'

'Of course. I have been waiting.'

'Venus de Milo pose,' he announced.

Merely its mention was enough for her to adopt the pose. 'It is on display in the Louvre. Man's earliest known appreciation of a woman's beauty.'

Of course: Parisian, he knew from the internet. 'In Dublin, we call the pose: "You want what?"'

'You must position me exactly.'

'During the shoot. We don't have much time before your constellation is too high.'

In an instant, she was ready, and the shoot could finally begin. She broke into that smile that she could not suppress as she turned to pose aligned with her constellation. Taking long diaphanous scarfs from Roman she wrapped these around herself, using the breeze to trail these behind her. Then, it was her, telling Rick exactly where she wanted each star, and he modifying her poses in minutiae with hinted hand movements. When she was perfectly positioned, he signalled to the photographer, who swung wildly back and forth in sibilant arcs.

'We will photoshop the urn into position later.' Roman was pleased, as André's camera continued to shutter. She cast Roman a look when he interrupted, and Rick could see that they were not on good terms.

There were endless poses, where Rick continued to be allocated the task of nuancing her body, following her clear visual images to create both a pose and an attitude. She moved his attention to each part of her in turn while he tried to focus. Sometimes, she was Manet's *Olympia* reborn and asking her observer to explain himself, and at others simply soaring in completeness, he fine tuning every perfect part of her in silence. She responded intuitively to each of his gestures, knowing to what each referred, taking immense pleasure in discussing which part of her body to move until he lost all discomfort, her body lustrous within her constellation and the scarfs flying madly into the breeze. He wondered was she deliberately making him familiar with each part of her wondrous physique? He imagined them hurtling through space together.

Roman was becoming increasingly annoyed with their dallying, but André reviewing the photos kept giving thumbs up and smiles. Finally, the photoshoot organiser had had enough. 'Venus is rising and then there is the sunrise to come, and we will need to take serious photos now until the colours disappear from the dawn. We need quiet.' He turned and snapped at André to adjust lights, mirrors, and reflective screens for the main shoot.

Then the shooting commenced in earnest as Venus itself rose for her to eclipse as it as it arched. Every now and then she smiled at him and immediately there was a burst of shots from André. However, there were further sharp words between her and Roman, after which he ordered: 'Absolute quiet, or you go!'

'Only silhouettes,' Venus reminded, as she lost the trailing scarves for the next poses. While he was intoxicated with desire, to lose all sense of himself in her, his fear of being barred from her presence for the shoot made him look away breaking his enthrallment and finding it replaced by concern about their predicament.

The ante had been raised: he was sure that they had crossed a line by filming semi-naked, now in naked-silhouette, on the top of Egypt's most famous monument. As if to confirm his concerns, the morning call to prayer came in echoing incantations from all over the city, pure and haunting harmonies that blended into an eternal voice and enveloped even the peak of this tallest pyramid. With them came the strict rules on modesty, unchanged for over a millennium in an empire that once extended from Istanbul to France. Their photoshoot would not end well for any of them. Thinking that they could bluff their way out was foolhardy at best – the stakes could hardly be higher.

He felt for the security of the paraglider in the rucksack, its soft folds that could inflate into a comforting canopy to effortlessly lift off the pyramid. His plan was still intact, but that would leave Venus to an uncertain fate. He raised his hand to check the wind. That breeze had turned, driven by offshore winds coming from that faraway coast. It had strengthened. He would not have to rely on the ridge effect alone to rise off the pyramid, but it would nevertheless be a dangerous buffeting. The sky above was clearing as the velvet cloak of night retreated over the desert leaving lingering stars to be gathered by the dawn in her innocent blues.

He wasn't leaving Venus to a fate dictated by Roman and André. They were going to escape from this together or not at all. She had teased a little of herself at a time, the only girl who had ever gone to the trouble of making him totally comfortable with her physically, allowing that intimacy to create its own connections with a power over him. He resigned himself: his mind resonated in her presence: his body pulsated to her heartbeats.

An idea occurred to him. He checked in his mobile that the two tickets for the visit inside the pyramid were still there. He signalled to Roman that he wanted to talk, and who then slipped away from the shoot to tower over him. Rick tapped the place on the ledge beside him for Roman to sit down. They looked out together over the desert extending into the distance, mauve and magenta streaked with glittering golds and reds from the early light. 'It is spectacular, don't you think?' Rick said to disarm him.

'We don't have time!' Roman was impatient. 'What is it you want to say?'

'We have been spotted for sure.' He opened his hands feigning an experienced negotiator acting with confidence. 'Who knows what has been seen, but this is a Muslim country with Sharia law. If Venus goes with you, two things: your bluff will not work, and everyone could be charged with blasphemy or worse. This will be serious for Venus but you too as the organiser could be subjected to worse penalties.' He was laying it on a bit, but it was having the desired effect on Roman, whose face lost its lustre, the whites of his dark eyes shifting nervously.

Rick gestured again. 'Venus, if she agrees, can descend with me on the opposite face. Then your plan to bluff your way out will work.' He showed him the two tickets for the pyramid tour that he did not intend to use.

Roman mulled over the offer, thinking aloud: 'It might work. I will be saving the camera's discs to the cloud. Venus will be taking the discs because she wants the originals, and we will have, how do you say, no incriminating evidence about us. There will only be photographs of downtown to show. If they are deleted, it does not matter.' He shrugged. 'Venus and the original discs can go with you. We won't need either.'

Rick could barely stop himself. This guy would shop his mother. 'Could we take the harness and the ropes?' He needed the cameraman's harness and ropes, assuming Venus could be persuaded to paraglide off.

Roman shrugged again. 'Less to carry. Sure. You must take her Pandora's Box also.' He pointed to the portable dressing table. 'We would have to explain it.'

'K.' He had no intention of doing so.

Now all he had to do was ask Venus. Roman looked back up towards where she and the photographer were filming and remarked, 'It was worth lugging up the frame; we have the greatest iconic images ever seen.'

Rick turned his head and was both awestruck and alarmed at what he saw. Venus, naked, was silhouetted in profile against the early sky that still held stars in the rising red dawn. She was leaning onto the frame stretching into the heaven a leg curled back so she stood one footed in a body curve that, he presumed, was a take on the Marylin Monroe pose. She proclaimed perfection gently reaching into the embrace of the day, an image, with its myriad resonances in his mind, that would intoxicate his senses forever. He was no longer the gauche schoolboy who had climbed the pyramid to be a legend some hours earlier. Her silhouette caught the sunrise blazing into blood reds that clung to her amidst the city skyline of clustered buildings, broken only for the points of minarets communing and the domes of mosques that glinted as their sickles cut into the shifting, burning, morning mists.

He was certain they had crossed a line.

The poses continued, and Roman called to him laughing. 'Hey, Irish harp!' Venus was leaning out, supported by the frame from behind.

Rick indulged him, but thinking he had to convince her to leave with him.

As she finished, Roman called to the cameraman to begin saving the camera to the cloud, and André began loading the tiny discs into his phone one by one.

Rick grabbed the wrap from the ledge and brought it to Venus. She was exhausted from the shoot, but exhilaration still burned like coals in her eyes. In the sun's glow one side of her face was smudged with vulnerability while the shaded side was bathed in soft features, like that post-impressionist portrait. She caught his glance and stood while he wrapped the silk sheet printed in herons and lush foliage around her. 'We should move off the top.'

She reached around him for support and pressed into him, resting her head as they descended out of sight to sit a few ledges below. 'It is difficult to breathe in this heavy air, and now the temperatures are rising so quickly. Peg'sus, I am too tired to climb down.'

He rummaged in his rucksack and produced the last of the breakfast. 'Ah, pastry most delicate!' as Rami had said. He offered the dessert of soft cheese wrapped in shredded pastry and smothered in syrup. She ate greedily while he nattered on, filling in the silences. 'It's an incredible taste, part savoury, part spicy and glazed syrupy sweet. Apparently, humans have no off-button for such a taste, although the scientific programme I saw, it was discussing doughnuts and only mentioned Middle Eastern pastry in passing.'

'Poor Peg'sus. You have time to watch all these silly programmes. Now you have no dessert, either.'

'We are not finished. For energy and the most enchanting of tastes, scented most sweetly: Lokum delight.' There were two chunks, rosehip and lemon, smothered in soft icing sugar. 'Which do you prefer?'

She chose the lemon, and they finished the last of the bottle of water.

His heart pounded for fear that he might lose her to Roman and André. It was now or never: 'I am concerned that bluffing will not work. What do you say to us getting away together from this face while they descend drawing attention?'

'No bluffing? I am too tired.'

She rested her head against his shoulder, exhausted, and he, over her shoulders, watched the spread of glistening light that was flowing in waves across the plateau of Giza. The Sphinx off to the right was coming to life in glowing reds, a benign gargoyle he hoped.

Suddenly, the male duo began gesturing downwards animatedly, and talking back and forth in excitable tones. Roman turned to them. 'We are being instructed to go down. Police are climbing up. We should all go.'

'I am going separately with Peg'sus. I will take my discs,' Venus insisted.

Roman shrugged his shoulders, agreeing, and coming over, he handed over the set of discs in tiny plastic boxes. The cameraman looked concerned: there was no doubt a close bond with Venus was sundering. Rick reminded Roman about the harness and rope, and André came over to quickly show Venus how to put on the harness, after which he and Venus hugged for a long time. He let the coil of rope fall beside her.

As he pulled back to join Roman on the ledge, her eyes misted over. 'André, if I go with you, I will blow your bluff. Peg'sus and me can go down this side and we can all get away. You will be better off without me.'

Then he and Roman sat on the edge of the first ledge on the corner that Rick had ascended. Looking back, they said goodbye.

'Best of luck,' Rick wished them.

'Yes. Happy Endings.'

They lowered themselves out of sight, their packs and equipment clanking off the ancient stone. The frame was left in place and the dresser was open, as if waiting for the next Venus to ascend to the top. Roman and André would be slow on the descent. He checked his mobile: it was five-thirty. The clanking of the two was the only distinct noise, the doleful sounds of their equipment ringing off into the distance was like sheep going to their slaughter.

Time was ticking. Security was climbing up to arrest all of them. He broached his alternative to lowering ledge by ledge. 'I brought a paraglider in my rucksack to escape,' he said. 'Now that the wind has turned, we will be lifted effortlessly.'

'You go. It is not your photoshoot, and I will climb down slowly. Once I get lower, nobody will suspect me of scaling the pyramid.'

'Not without you. The parasail can well take our weight together.' He half-remembered seeing somewhere that the design had a high safety factor. Surely it would take a hundred and thirty kilos, his estimate. 'Have you ever tried paragliding?'

'Á la plage?' She shrugged, smiling.

'We can stabilise the paraglider locked together if we harness. The safety chute will be free to deploy, and I will be able to land first,' he reasoned aloud. He was not sure how all of this had come about, but he was willing to be that volunteer.

Venus agreed.

When he opened the paraglider, the wind filled each cell that combined into a multicoloured toothed circle straining on its tie-lines. The combined ridge effect and the offshore wind raised them effortlessly off the pyramid, she harnessed in front of him. It elevated them up into the vastness and pulled them back to the south over the shining desert. He could feel her hands tightening into his arms as they ascended. They circled into a thermal, spiralling upward to a height that he had never experienced, and their breathing got difficult. There they exited the ascent. When he dared to look down, the pyramids were far below like miniatures and they were gliding slowly, descending over the desert that shifted in soft undulations of shadow and sand. Where they landed was going to be potluck. The smoothness of the dunes was a false invitation, and they continued to aim for the sizeable plot of arable land near his hotel, the golf course on the opposite side of the road if they came up short. He could feel Venus fingering his arms for him to mimic. He needed to focus.

Chapter 9,

Djinn

Andy

When Andy saw the parasail rise from the apex of the pyramid, he knew that it was Rick's. He watched as the canopy with the orange-toothed fore stretched to its full width. At first it rose slowly into the cloudless sky until it was catching the colours of the rising sun and leaving them streaming behind. Such a flimsy device, a wish for flight that nevertheless swung elegantly into the graduated blues. Effortlessly, it soared in the buoyant air, spiralling ever upwards until it was a dot against the expanse. Those months of Rick taking off into rough weather along the coastline would pay off; he recalled an incident that had involved recovery after a partial collapse and two others that required deploying the reserve chute leaving Rick with only bruises and sprains. However, he could not look away until Rick had vanished from view, pulled to the southwest over the desert.

His focus then changed to the developing scenario on the face of the pyramid, to the white-clad police spread out as they clambered upwards, closing in on the laden figures descending. He feared the worst for them judging from the numbers of police involved in their capture. The man from the white land-rover, who had earlier begun climbing, was dwarfed near the summit and called back down to the police. Their advance to the summit came to a halt. Rick had escaped. He felt a certain pride that his son had outfoxed everyone. He had no doubt that Rick would now get back to the hotel, provided he did not tempt fate further – take your prizes, he had always told him.

Jubilant, he phoned Sara and told her that Rick was on his way back and remarked that Rick might even be back at the hotel before he got there. He had seen his parasail lift him off the pyramid and then turn gold as it rose against the lapis blue of the Egyptian sky.

Sara snapped sharply: 'Andy, what are you thinking. Half the police force is out trying to capture him, and all trips today are cancelled because of a terrorist threat.' In a softer tone, she asked: 'Come back as quickly as you can, and we'll plan our next move. Together, Andy.'

It annoyed him when he got the tone wrong, that instead of good news easing her concerns, he had increased them. But what a truly outrageous prank his son had pulled off, the way he himself had gotten away with stunts back in his student days. His son wasn't him – the effortless divine sublimity, though. He may have settled into programme management these days, always holding back to take a responsible overview, but who said you couldn't still marvel at such audacity?

He took a final look at events on the face of the pyramid. The two had reached the police line, had their equipment confiscated, and were each then handcuffed to a police officer. They were then jerked over the ledges, their stumbles onto bared knees ignored. He remembered his own questioning from two days earlier. Nearer the summit, the hotel security man from the hotel-carrier was lugging a pink case and a rucksack from ledge to ledge. Andy hurried to return to the hotel. Others on the lower ledges, who had no doubt come to see the red dawn spread over the Giza plateau, talked anxiously as they sneaked glances at what was transpiring further up.

The Sphinx's huge leonine limbs and human head sat both benign and poised, unpredictable, as he followed the road down that ran parallel. From the car park on, he was against the flow as traffic fused into a caravan of assorted vehicles incessantly beeping and a procession of pedestrian sellers carrying produce hung on poles or balanced on heads and shoulders. Rusting pickup trucks had everything from A-frames for quickly erecting, and awnings for gazebos, to camels that sat colourfully blanketed and swishing belled harnesses in the open backs as they bemusedly surveyed the frenzy; blinkered horses pulling decorated carriages too were in the varied cavalcade, unflappable until moved on with the flick of the whip; a line of taxis brought the early tourists poking cameras out of rolled-down windows; and then there were the inevitable converted motorbikes adding to the noise and the fumes. All argued. Cairo was back to its old self, unpredictable, garrulous, and bizarre.

He entered by the hotel's garden gate that was ajar, and strolling through the dappled shade between the babbling fountains he arrived back in reception. Sara was pacing back and forth in the din of the waterfall looking fraught with worry. He went over to hug her, but she again managed his greeting by inserting her arms onto his chest. Why was she being so aloof in public, belying the togetherness of the previous evening's lovemaking? Perhaps the worry written on her face rather than anything specific. She looked for an update.

A factual, straightforward explanation: 'Rick simply paraglided off the pyramid into sunlight and air, and then a thermal took him high and out of range. Last I saw he was performing a shallow descent. He will walk through that door any moment now wondering what all the fuss was about.'

'Where was his paraglider headed?' she returned, fraught with worry. 'Oh, I'll keep trying his mobile.'

'It was hard to judge exactly, but towards the hotel. He can't be far.'

Another question came. 'Did you see a white land-rover out searching for him? It has the hotel crest on the side?'

'That's who they were. One of the men from it climbed the pyramid but didn't reach Rick in time. Then when I looked around, the land-rover was gone.' He searched the whites of her eyes that normally carried the liveliness of her pupils outward. 'There is nothing to worry about,' he tried to reassure her attempting another hug.

Sara forced a smile. 'There's a lot to worry about, a fashion photoshoot! The good thing is that we are leaving Cairo in three days. He will have to be careful in the meantime and needs to keep a low profile. When he comes back, keep him with you – I don't care what you two do.'

'He may have his own ideas.' Andy was still annoyed with Sara, and now she had gotten inside information. 'A fashion photoshoot?'

'That's what the lights flashes looked like. Some sort of photoshoot anyway, did you see anything from below?'

'I was in close to the base, and it did look like there were surges of light. It could have been.' He let it go. 'Did you say the trip is cancelled today?'

'Yes, I asked the hotel. All trips today are cancelled. A high-level security alert in the city.'

'All day by the pool then?' he casually commented.

'Andy, please take the situation seriously. Rick is missing and there is a terrorist threat.'

He relented. 'I can grab a coffee to keep me going. He can't be far. You said hotel security was out searching?'

With that, the white land-rover with the hotel logo pulled up outside, the driver got out and opened the rear passenger door. A pair of heavily clad feet dropped tentatively to the ground and then Rick emerged into the sunlight in Raider's gear, an all-conquering hero, followed by a young woman dressed in printed silk and cut-offs, and with a silk scarf improvising a hijab. A time portal couple entering in strange attire, sullied only by Rick's eye-black staining under a bandana that sat beneath a baseball cap.

'I like his style.' Andy laughed. 'We were up half the night looking for him, and he walks out of the morning sunlight with a goddess on his arm.'

Sara beamed and rushed towards the door as the robed guard shepherded the duo through the scanner. Samir's smile was as inscrutable as ever as he nodded to the robed guard, ignoring the alarm on the personnel scanner as they went through. Rick hugged his mother and Andy in turn before turning to the young woman: 'My parents.' He then introduced her to them. 'This is Venus, everyone,' before continuing by way of explanation, 'and we have just shared sunrise over the pyramids together.'

She interjected, 'Peg'sus is making it up. My name is Mikayla.'

'Peg'sus? Can everybody use their proper name so we can get a little sanity going here? My son's name is Rick, in case you are unaware, Mikayla, is it?'

'Yes. We prefer Peg'sus and Venus,' she stated confidently.

'Between yourselves. Mikayla, are you staying at the hotel?'

'Akar is making arrangements.' She pointed to James's traditionally robed security guard at reception. 'The other man in the car told him to do so: he owns the hotel. Otherwise, I have only the clothes I am standing in,' she declared.

'I suggest you buy proper clothes soon. There's the hotel shop, you could try there. I might have a few things that might fit.' Sara's offer to share was grudging as she looked Mikayla up and down – but perhaps when an only son introduces a girlfriend.

Mikayla volunteered: 'I have a credit card somewhere.'

Rick smiled in amusement but said nothing.

'There was a pink case and a rucksack brought down the pyramid?' Andy queried.

'It is Venus's portable vanity box and my rucksack. The hotel owner has taken them away for safekeeping.'

Mikayla got called to reception. They stood with her as she produced her passport to check-in. She explained that she needed to go online to print her visa, and she was directed to the hotel computer stations in one of the arched alcoves. Andy intervened briefly to have her keep her passport with her. The receptionist then explained that check-in would be longer. Her passport needed uploading online, and there was another form that she needed to complete as a woman travelling alone. 'There was no problem. You are an honoured guest of the hotel, but you need to complete the document.'

When Mikayla had successfully logged in at a computer workstation in an alcove, they went outside to wait while she printed her visa and completed her paperwork. At a table in the coffee dock, the waterfall masked their voices. 'Will Mikayla be alright while you update us?' Sara asked Rick.

'Sure,' Rick responded.

Andy did not expect to learn much, but whatever Rick disclosed he wanted to hear. He had switched to a heightened state, like those he got into for a student protest march all those years ago, those edgy moments when every cell in his body was alive to possibility.

'Soz, gens, about the climb,' Rick proffered.

He cut him off. 'Rick, I was at the base from about four after your mother noticed lights from the summit of the pyramid and saw your rucksack was missing. Tell us what was really happening on the pyramid? This could be serious. The two guys who came down were treated roughly as they handed themselves over.'

Rick resumed. 'In brief, there was a photoshoot at the top. When I got there, long exposures of downtown lights under a night sky were underway. A supercharged *night sky* to rival Van Gogh's, *The Starry Night*. He looked towards Sara for an acknowledgement, before continuing. 'Then my Venus asked me to align her zodiac constellation about her to be photographed.' Rick gave him a perfunctory glance before looking back to Sara. 'The photographer was really pleased when I did this.'

Sara was correct about there being a photoshoot? 'Rick, the facts, please.'

'*K*. Then there were long exposures with the planet Venus arcing around her, then with her holding onto the frame posing against Turneresque flaming colours that were breaking over the city. The guy in charge said that when this one shot went viral, she would be famous. It eclipsed Marilyn Monroe's iconic red satin pose with Venus pointing upwards, he said.'

'Vertical is the new horizontal?' Sara remarked, her humour returning.

'Whatever, Mom. Dad, Venus then posed off the frame.'

Andy had already reached overload. 'Rick. I'll close my eyes now but continue to listen in while you go into more detail for your mother.' Sara was agog to hear more.

Andy tuned out and closed his eyes as Rick commenced from the beginning again. Despite a fitful snooze and the waterfall surges, he had an accumulation of half-remembered facts when he had recovered: testing by Mikayla to be allowed to watch the photoshoot, eye-black camouflage, no real names used, Rami's breakfast of eastern promise, different photoshoots and poses – and liberally sprinkled with artistic.

Rick's Venus deciding that she would prefer to parasail with him rather than descend with the two others, that was new information. It surely indicated a strong connection between them. *His Venus?* He was proud of his son looking out for her, and the way they had paraglided away together. When he had advised his son on one of Rick's paragliding expeditions, that if he met that special person, he should try to stay together regardless, he had not envisioned on the Great Pyramid with security forces chasing. 'Hang on in there, is it?' Rick had joked at the time.

It was only when Rick related that the organiser, a guy called Roman, had said that shoot would go viral that he reacted. 'Was the take on the *red-satin-pose* totally naked?' Andy asked.

'Mikayla was in silhouette.'

'Only by agreement with those two dubious organisers, and not from every angle. That might have upset the police in this Muslim country, and during Ramadan? I couldn't see this from where I was, but maybe the police could. Anything online?'

Rick uncoiled to his full height towering over Andy. 'I'll go do a search with Mikayla. '*Hfs!* Roman had André uploaded all the discs to the cloud before he went down.'

Rick was halfway across the foyer when Andy called after him: 'Delete the search after?'

Bumping into Boris, Svetlana, and their two children, Boris gave him a bear hug, and laughing heartily remarked: 'You have a new girlfriend, you mad Irishman?'

Rick, excusing himself, rushed on towards the alcove to Mikayla.

Andy went to sit beside Sara and then both he and Sara sat in silence, she continuing to stare straight ahead of her. She didn't object when he placed an arm around her shoulder and massaged her back gently. He hoped that any uploads would be innocuous.

When Rick and Mikayla emerged through the Arabic arch of the alcove, Mikayla went to reception, and Rick was upbeat when he came over, shuffling about as he spoke to them. 'There are only very dark shots posted, first with Venus standing out between the stars of Aquarius – silhouettes where I helped. Then there are images with Venus in the early dawn – also darkened. The most striking ones are against the storm of light breaking over the city. Those images are granular, more a red sandstorm. Looks *Kool*.'

'In a sandstorm? It could be worse,' Sara commented. 'Are there any of you?'

'Only my hand has made it into one of the pictures. Nothing to worry about.'

'Does Mikayla know who posted them?'

'The images are hyperlinked from the blog Venus was using. Her friend who set it up must have reopened it. The website with the images has a subscription site for an auction of original images. She sent him a "cease and desist" to have the website taken down – she is *internet savvy.*'

'The site could be selling clearer and more explicit pictures to those who subscribe. I hope the website is taken down, but nothing is ever forgotten on the internet.'

Mikayla strolled across the foyer from reception in a gait that drew all eyes. Andy added, 'Your Venus will be easily remembered.'

Sitting down beside Rick, Mikayla began explaining to him that she now had a room on their floor. They checked the room number, and it was the room beside his. Sara looked up towards reception and the receptionist smiled and waved towards her.

'Does the receptionist need you?' he asked Sara.

'Oh, I spent ages getting the rooms rearranged as I said, and I expect he is just indicating that it is in line with what I wanted. Mikayla, you can walk along the veranda to my room to see about clothes. We are not *that* dissimilar in build now that I see you – I'm more of a lithe figure, that is all. You need less conspicuous clothes.'

As they were getting up, a cannonade broke from the front of the hotel as a thunderous maelstrom exploded into the space in a crescendo of broken glass. Clouds of hot dust and debris billowed, and there were crashes of fixtures falling and furnishings being tossed about amidst shrieks and alarms going off. Andy stretched towards Sara to wrap himself around her, grabbing her covered in dust, with her arms instinctively outstretched to where Rick had been standing.

His ears were ringing as he looked about in a dim green opacity that had filled the space. The sound of sprinkler heads hissing cones of water was accompanied by wailing fire alarms and the blinds furious flapping where a window had shattered. The ceiling had fallen-in, and twisted T-bar broken into sharp angles and ceiling lights swung, and there was a pervading smell of scorched insulation, and it was difficult to breathe. People slowly emerged through a phantasmagoria of dust and rubble. Only those in the fresco of Edwardian society in the bar area remained unchanged with frozen expressions of expectation and intrigue. In a blurred light he and Sara patted each other, and when she looked up at him, her eyes had deadened in fright and worry. Rick lifted himself off the floor and began fussing over Mikayla whom he continued to shield, after which he looked over to them with a thumbs up.

Travel representatives appearing like spectres began calling their respective tours. When they recognised Rami's voice, they raised their hands and shouted to him. More swat-team in Tyvek and helmet than tour guide, he was relieved to see they were uninjured and told them to move to the garden to await updates. 'It is a small explosion on Al-Haram. Fami has gone to find out more.' He was concerned, particularly at Mikayla's state, who had been closest to the source and whose limited clothes had provided little protection. Rick grabbed a loose cover and passed it to her.

With alarms ringing in their ears, they made their way to the garden directed by Samir, burlesque and with a smile that was more of a clown's grimace. A frenzy of birds tumultuous in the canopy over silent fountains created an eerie atmosphere, and a barman operating a remote control for the TV was flicking channels. They took a table on their own and watched as others found their way outside. Kirsten came, bottles of her red wine sticking out at various angles from a bag she had quickly packed. She joined Boris and Svetlana and their children, announcing: 'There is no damage in the rooms, but I brought a change; we could be here all day.'

'And the evening.' He saw Boris eye the bottles of wine with a hearty laugh. Svetlana looked immaculate, poised on the edge of her chair, not a hair out of place as she comforted and amused the children. There was a steely resistance in her attitude that he had not noticed before.

Andy felt for Kirsten, sitting alone on what was likely to be a long day. She looked familiar, and he was sure that she was one of those he had seen on those Alpine skiing programmes. After his hurried wave elicited a similar response, he left Sara with Rick and Mikayla, and went to ask how she was.

After asking how she was, he then commented: 'Damage is confined to the foyer.'

'Yes, there was only a sweeping wind that rushed past the bedrooms, and then those evacuation bells. It is unnerving more than dangerous, I think.' The concern in her face and eyes belied her composure.

He pressed her hand on the table to reassure her.

She looked up. 'I try to leave danger behind.'

'No serious damage, but it will take time to check out the hotel. All the systems need to be shut down and then restarted safely, and then each room will need to be walked down. Checklists would allow guests to volunteer.' He smiled to himself: here he was again, proposing to go on a walk-down.

'You know about these things?'

'I know what is involved.' He didn't mention his failure to complete his engineering degree. 'I will say it to Rami, and he may be able to take up my suggestion to involve knowledgeable guests.'

'It is not unpleasant waiting in the warm shade, despite the dramatic soundtrack from our frantic feathered friends,' she remarked.

There was another thing she hadn't forgotten, eyeliner – that caught the flash in her eyes. He noticed that she was always providing a contrast in her sentences. It was none of his business, but he commented: 'Yes, and way too early to consider having wine. I'm sure they will open for refreshments here shortly.'

She looked up at him, not resentfully, somehow retaining a light in her eyes up at him. 'It was an impulsive thought. Bottles of wine to sell to Boris? I took all my jewellery, also.'

He laughed, but he felt for her, alone and holding onto something in the uncertainty of the explosion.

Sara was texting nervously on her mobile when he got back to their table. Dust from the foyer had turned her elegant clothes tawdry, he noticed for the first time, and her face was shocked pale from having removed the layer of dust; she kept rechecking her mobile.

'No problem sending internationally. Ucind is relieved we are uninjured. She says that they will round up anyone with a terrorist connection and that the rest of the holiday will be safe. No local calls or texts.'

He nodded. Why would Sara be texting locally? Maybe she had been trying to text Rick? He thought no more of it, focusing instead on the shock that was still traced on her face. He sat down beside her and tried to talk her through the explosion in the hope that this might help. Then all the TV screens about switched to an English-speaking news channel covering the explosion with the volume turned up over the bird calls. A reporter at the scene pointed to a huge crater at the base of an embankment and explained that the blast was contained between it and the side of the motorway. Consequently, the blast was diverted up and away from the local traffic, and only a white land-rover that seemed to have been the target had bodywork damage. The camera closed in on the white land-rover on the other side of the motorway, showing doors pushed in and with meshes of fractured windows. There on the door was the hotel crest. Sara startled beside him. The reporter went on, saying that there was no news on the occupants' injuries, one of whom was believed to be a developer responsible for a controversial hotel beside the Great Pyramid and major projects in New Cairo.

Sara's mobile dropped from her hand as she was checking it.

He reassured: 'The land-rover looks to have withstood the impact. Let's not jump to conclusions on injuries. The hotel owner was decent about going out to search for Rick – good things happen to nice guys.'

As she nodded, he extended an arm around her shoulder, but she leaned forward to get further details from the news report. 'I'm fine, Andy.' They sat quietly as the reporter ominously noted that if the land-rover was the target, then the perpetrators had a vantage point locally to observe the progress of the traffic, and to activate a remote device. Sara remained rapt to the screen, taking in every word.

The reported continued: a second arm of the blast had gone under the motorway to the newly built upmarket hotel and apartment neighbourhood where a warren of streets had funnelled the shock wave. The streets were mercifully empty, and many buildings had set-backs or high walled compounds that limited the impact. One group enjoying morning coffee had watched in the shadow of a tall wing as the shock wave moved past, miraculously saved from the rush of debris. The motives for the explosion were unclear, but these had been controversial developments built close to the greatest monuments in Egypt.

An interview with one of the coffee takers who had escaped followed, before returning to the possible cause of the explosion. It had been sophisticated in its planning and execution and bore the hallmark of the type of operations undertaken by organised terrorist groups. An unnamed government source has speculated that the explosion had been the work of disaffected developer, Abdul Fouad, who was known to be plotting from abroad after fleeing Egypt. There have been rumours in recent times that Fouad was intent on fostering unrest in the hope that it would instigate a spontaneous general rebellion. In a double blow he could have been targeting both the developer who had taken over his contracts in New Cairo and the developments in the shadow of Egypt's greatest wonder, the Great Pyramids of Giza. The unnamed government spokesperson had said that any attempt to copycat what had happened during the legitimate revolution of 2011 would be quashed with all the might of the Egyptian State.

The barman was about to change channel thinking the report was over until he realised the reporter was continuing. 'In another development, there are reports that a group scaled the Greatest Pyramid, Khufu, during the night. Two males of Eastern Europe origin were arrested at the scene.' The mugshots that flashed onto the screen showed swollen and bruised faces. 'They have been taken into custody where police have said they are cooperating. Authorities have been stamping down on these climbs in recent years; the last to climb received three-year sentences that had been completed by the time of their sentencing. It is expected that those arrested will receive more severe sentences, as it appears they were holding a private fashion photoshoot. Coming during Ramadan, this is considered a challenge and affront to the strictly held prohibition of such activity under Sharia law. The police are searching for an accomplice, a woman, believed to have been forced into modelling the photoshoot. A youth who scaled this ancient wonder at the same time is also being sought by the police.'

Boris, who had been standing towering over those crowded under the screen, returned to them. 'Rick, you should not draw attention to yourselves.'

'Mikayla,' Andy added, 'maybe don't connect to a phone network in case your two friends phone you. It could be a ruse to track you down.'

'Already, everyone. I am so worried about André. Did you see his picture? He is so sensitive.' She was holding back tears, clutching Rick's arm as she rested into his chest. A bigger concern, Andy thought, was how long she would be allowed to stay at the hotel. She couldn't use her passport to return home if she were being sought.

Rami called the tour group closer about him to give them an update. 'Today is cancelled,' he announced. 'This is not a cause for concern. Already it was a rest day after your journey to allow you to acclimatise to the heat and the food. It is no inconvenience. Water sprays again cool the air below the trees for your comfort, and the hotel staff will bring you whatever you desire. You can shop in the hotel shops for genuine merchandise and no haggling. Of course, haggling – we are Egyptians, and it is how we get to know you. Practise this in the shop, and you will enjoy the bazaar tomorrow and secure unbelievable bargains.

'Do you believe in Djinn? Yes? No? We in Egypt believe in Djinn. Djinn come off the desert concealed in red sandstorms that darken the sky. They are ready to rise in anger. Our Arabian tales are full of dangerous and evil Djinn who have only malice and trickery in their hearts. As Muslims, we recognise them as Allah's creations.

'This morning for us a Djinn raced along the streets from a small explosion on Al-Haram – so small it was nothing – and broke into this beautiful hotel that I have selected for your ultimate relaxation and pleasure. One of the explosion shutters did not shut properly. It was faulty, and in came the Djinn in a rush. Fortunately, no one was injured, and the damage is minor. The foyer ceiling needs repair and there is a clean-up needed. Already crews are working to restore the reception area and by tomorrow morning it will reopen. We need to applaud the hotel's response – they have already moved all catering to this restaurant and the food will be the same, no difference, I tell you.

'Djinn can also be good. You have heard of the American sitcom, *I Dream of Jeannie*: she has long golden hair tied up in a ponytail and moves her eyes to cast only good spells – like all women. You have seen the programme. She is from my hometown. I dream of Jeannie all the time – she is my wife!

'You are thinking when you can return to your rooms? I need to tell you that there are safety procedures that the hotel must perform first: each of your rooms needs to be inspected as a precaution. We have set up teams to confirm that the rooms are safe, and that will commence in the next few moments. Any other engineers or architects, please volunteer to join a team and it will speed up your return to your rooms. Everyone else, please enjoy this garden paradise where no evil can enter. There is no cause for concern. No cause for sure.'

Chapter 10,

All About the Boy

Sara

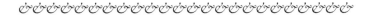

She couldn't sleep. Details of the day's explosion and Rick's safe return circulating in her mind – to say nothing of not having heard from James. She had sat through all the newsflashes until it was confirmed there were no serious injuries. Back into her life and then almost snatched away from her. Andy had handled the day much better, was in his element managing others as he rose to the challenge. He had immediately dropped off once his head hit the pillow, but only after he had explained that the cicadas did not call, they stridulated by rubbing legs together. She had liked the word and pm-ed it on to Ucind, who had texted back *so that is what it is called*. Her friend's humour was the only relief, and she laughed as she read it again. No matter the cause of the chorus, Andy's snoring joined in as it rose and fell with their drone in the humid air. He was sleeping off a lack of sleep, and not calling out to attract his new VBF – give her patience. 'Two hours in forty just didn't do it for me,' he had said, as he had put his head down 'for a short snooze' hours previously. Sweet dreams of Rapunzel in her lonely mountain chalet.

In fairness, he had not stopped going all the previous day, taking part in the room inspections where he had been allocated their floor. There must have been a dozen from the tour who raised their hands when Rami had requested volunteers to check the hotel after the explosion, and got engineers and scientists, and one architect. No surprise on the number of engineers as it was a German tour, and Andy hadn't forgotten his science degree from third-year engineering despite now working as a group manager. He did show his engineering interest now and then, as going to the BMW museum in Munich when he was returning from Asia. She had decided that it wasn't his engineering for which he was yearning though, and much better after his walk-down of the revolution, whatever that had entailed. More picking up where he left off in his student days to see what could be retrieved – an early mid-life crisis, maybe?

She hadn't met him that time in Munich when he suggested it. Her preferred German car was not a BMW but instead a Mercedes, the ease with which they sailed along, graceful and serene. James had one, one after the other, gleaming de rigour statements for the races, and always navy-blue. It had been pure luxury relaxing into the plush seats as the saloon consumed the tarmac with the passing sights reflected. Foliage so lush and shadowy, and streets colourfully inverted, pedestrians looking accusingly at her from the bonnet. She had liked lying back and looking up through the sunroof where there had always been a scatter of white puffed clouds amidst chinks of celestial blue. Everything had moved in movie reels advancing with their progress, and then James trying to take a shortcut down any boreen if it looked straight to gain time, until the hedgerows gently brushed the sides of the saloon, and they invariably came to a dead end – when his attention would turn to her. Impetuously impatient, and she had complained that at the least he could wait until she got out of her dress. The curious cattle that came over to rest their heads on a gate and breathe a discreet fog on the windows to save her blushes. Masking noises and occasionally smudging the windscreen with their wet noses – carried away with the voyeurism. Then, turning the car in a field before rushing back to catch the two-thirty off, and her scurrying off to retrieve her rigout.

Her heart had stopped for a minute when the news had shown his land-rover tossed upended across the motorway, and waiting ages for that news update, until finally it was confirmed he was safe. The land-rover must have been bullet-proofed and reinforced – always that

safety thing with him despite otherwise devil may play —
and seat belts, not just for keeping her in the passenger seat
when she might have been a mite slow undoing the buckle.
He hadn't taken a single call or responded to her avalanche
of texts. Strange, after James being the one who had
wanted her number. She was in constant fear for him —
such an obvious target as the infidel who had inveigled his
way into the inner elite. Not alone had he taken over
contracts that displaced this disaffected developer, but he
had been one of those to build a foreign luxury hotel this
close to the Great Pyramids. How couldn't he see that?

Saved him under *Cardeville,* her little play on a Cadillac
Coupe de Ville turning it into car-devil that she wouldn't
forget, like one of her other little wordplay names that she
had for her wardrobe-purchase clients. She doubted
anybody else would guess his cryptic not unless they knew
cars and hers and James's intimate history. She dialled into
the drove of demanding male cicadas and when she heard
a ringing she saw illumination from James's room. Was he
back? Her heart pounded. She tried to see through the
screen: it was dark once the backlight went off on her
mobile. She tried again and confirmed that she was dialling
his mobile in the next room. How had his mobile gotten
back there? Who was it then had answered it briefly? Could
that person have seen how many times that she had
phoned — those frantic texts?

She went back in and slumped on her bed. These were just other worries to add to those accumulated from the previous twenty-four hours, a day that started with her only son stepping into his own world and away from the safety of hers. That wasn't what hurt: it was the deceit. How had he been able to secretly plan and execute such a daring escapade? Nothing shared, despite all the times they had been out together. Andy driving all over the country for him to paraglide, and he too had been none the wiser on the climb.

To add insult to injury, her son had arrived back with a gorgeous model on his arm, fawning over her and she over him – Peg'sus and Venus, give her patience! She, his mother, left standing during the explosion while he covered his newfound. He was no longer the child she had assumed. It had never occurred to her before that he was already of voting age and the following year would be an adult. How time had passed. In a year, James could have his son without taking any part of her. Was that what the subpoena was about, him establishing his legitimate paternity of her son who could then be whisked away from her once he reached eighteen?

Was James behind having Mikayla installed in the adjoining room to her son? Were they being encouraged as an item to distance Rick from her – *adjoining for baby-making,* as the receptionist had said – or was he out to demonstrate to Rick that he as father could offer him a lifestyle of which

Rick could only dream about back home? Entice Rick into a life with him in Egypt? Akar must have relayed instructions, and why was green-eyed radiance on reception – shading brown circle around the pupils – waving with such cordial familiarity at her when he checked Mikayla in? Andy had noticed. Were Akar and the receptionist in on the same secret, and she wasn't? The way Akar had knowingly nodded to James that first evening when she sashayed past? Their vacation upgraded to bring her under his control, and now she was part of his entourage, with Akar, and the receptionist – except she wasn't? Bet the receptionist had never seen that level of colourful excitement at this staid hotel, though? On top of her being the mistress of the big baaša – not yet re-consummated – her son's girlfriend had been involved in a naked photoshoot on top of the most famous monuments in the world. Loose women in this land of arranged marriages and modest, dutiful wives.

What would James want with a woman of a certain age? For old times' sake? He said he wasn't going to go back to Ireland, but why marry – well, pursue for the moment – a woman from there? Was she his road back to legitimacy in Ireland, to rehabilitation in the eyes of the nation – but from Egypt? Could it be the fairy-tale fantastic of returning home to his first true love? She could not forget that he had discarded her before, no enquiries and no support until later, just swanning around the party circuit asserting his macho credentials. A love child to tease and tantalise the women chasing him and impress his male circle? She could be ignored again, and yet she was drawn uncontrollably to him. Ucind was right: 'File under affair, enjoy it for all its worth, but don't give up on Andy . . . for now.' If only it were that simple, and James now gone missing.

Ucind had not been able to advise on how to ensure Mikayla did not endanger Rick, but that was a situation Sara thought she knew how to manage herself. Mikayla was in serious trouble! Her partners from the shoot were in custody; photos of her from the illegal climb were circulating online with explicit photos likely to follow. She was on the run in a foreign country with no easy egress from the country, at least not until the heat had died down. That would be no trouble. All Sara had to do was make it clear to Mikayla that remaining was dependent on her goodwill. They would share everything: clothes, outings, girl time, interests, secrets, feelings – and any new developments in case James had designs on her. For certain, the latter.

Right then, all she wanted to do was check on Rick, the way she had done when he had a fever, and she went to his room to check on him. She dared not go to his room for fear of what she might stumble upon now. He was his own man who in his own inimitable style had flown into the morning light carrying off his heroine. Let them have their fun – youth was made for such things.

Andy was sleeping deeply. She got in beside him and slipped under his arm for a minute. He sensed her and wrapped it around her, and she took his hand and pressed it between her breasts – he had been a star. She and he both needed their sleep, and she wriggled out of his grasp and curled into sleep on the far side of the enormous bed. She was her own woman with an independent business – no ties unless she wanted – she reminded herself. The haunting chants of prayer came floating with the gentle breath of dawn as she drifted off, modulating into softly spoken words that rose into plainsong welcoming her to sleep.

When she awoke, there were breakfasting-noises from the garden restaurant below: she listened to the dishes and cutlery clattering, the birds, and the increasing volume of conversation. Andy called from the bathroom: 'There's been a message from Rami slid under the door that the visit to the museum will go ahead. No hurry yet. Late morning.'

Then he was beside her with a towel wrapped. She turned onto her back for a hug of wet hair and glistening body and drenched towel smelling of shampoo, as Andy bent down and gently kissed her as he ran his hand under her back. The cool water startled her into life, and then he was gone before she had properly woken. Rushing he said, 'I want to give that pair of doves instructions on keeping a low profile. It's safest if they come along, don't you think, but we should split them. Can you steal Mikayla away from Rick?'

'I would like to have a woman-to-woman chat with Mikayla. She is going to need help,' she said as the door shut behind Andy. She got up and went onto the veranda, and spotting Rick and Mikayla below, she dialled Rick. She was watching them at the same time and saw him keep her on hold as he relayed everything to Mikayla, who was dressed in harem pants and skimpy top – the hotel shop was open. She asked him to put Mikayla on. 'Mikayla, I have clothes here already laid out for you, and we need to talk. You are safest with the tour today.'

'I will ask Rick.'

'Andy will talk to Rick. Put him back on.'

She saw Andy join them and she hung up after telling Rick to discuss the day with his father. He looked up to where she was behind the screen on the veranda – a silhouette glimpsed.

When they boarded the coach, Rami immediately tried to dispel the nervousness amongst the group. 'Egypt is now safe,' he announced. 'This was not a terrorist attack. It was a surgical strike by experts to target an honoured construction developer, an attack financed by an Egyptian dissident abroad who now seeks to rally people against the government by protesting new construction close to the pyramids.' He shook his head. 'The Egyptian people are not that easily fooled. He will fail. All those in Egypt connected with him have been arrested. Do not worry that Egypt is safe already. Your tour is especially safe. Fami is always with us for your safety and security. There will be police escorts front and behind our coach.' Rami stood nodding metronomically.

The tour group was anything but reassured to realise they were in a country where revolution could easily be sparked and where street protests occurred under no obvious set of rules. Kirsten called from the back: 'Is the museum not in Tahrir Square, the focal point of protest during the Arab Spring?'

'That was another time; Egypt has changed.' Rami brushed his hands together before announcing, 'For your greater safety, we will travel north on motorways that also bring us to the museum. The police have cleared and checked this route, and we will travel safely with our escorts. When we turn and cross the Nile, you will see people in the cafes and bookshops. They are reading newspapers, meeting friends, and trying to catch the eyes of the pretty girls – it is a national pastime. If we have time, we can stroll along the corniche that overlooks the Nile.'

He interrupted himself to talk to Fami, and after conversing he said, 'Fami says not today for strolling at leisure. We will eat on a riverboat restaurant so you will not miss anything, and we will stroll another day. You will see the scarlet-orange trees for which the corniche is famous: the tree is the Flamboyant Tree from Madagascar, but Egyptians have taken it over. Our women cherish its flowers – in Egypt a man does not give a rose to show his love and instead gives the blossoms of the Flamboyant Tree that is bursting with his exuberance for her.

'Egyptian men tell many jokes and stories to amuse their girlfriends: I will tell such a joke to you that Amina, my wife, liked enough to say yes to me. At the end, there is a catchphrase for you to say: "And that is how the row started." Say it now so you will remember.'

He launched into his joke: 'A servant woman in a household went to her mistress after six months to ask for a raise.

'"Why do you deserve a raise so soon?" her mistress asked.

'"I clean the house better than you do yourself, Madaam."

'"Who said that?"

'"Your husband, Madaam."

'"Is that so," the mistress responded. "That does not warrant a raise. What else?"

'"I cook better than you, Madaam."

"'Who said that?'"

"'Your husband, Madaam.'"

"'Is that so?'" the mistress responded. "'That does not warrant a raise. What else?'"

"'I am better in bed than you, Madaam.'"

"'Did my husband say that?'"

"'No, Madaam, the gardener did.'"

'The servant got her raise, and . . .'

'That is how the row started,' the tour echoed in chorus.

Rami got on to another joke. Mikayla was sitting beside Sara, whom she had allowed to go through her whole wardrobe to thankfully select casual t-shirt and her favourite linen pants. She was able to insist that Mikayla create a hijab from one of her scarfs and to drape a wrap over her shoulders – she had informed her that Egyptian men were particularly excited by bared arms, as Ucind had said. Mikayla had examined her arms and commented smiling: 'Men have fetishes for all parts of a woman.' Despite her modesty, Mikayla had nevertheless drawn all eyes as they had walked through the foyer, so that Sara had had to check herself for a moment to be sure there was nothing amiss. It was the first time that she could remember not garnering glances, and it gave her a hollow feeling inside.

Her mobile beeped, indicating a message, and she pressed to peek, *Cardeville*. He was back at the hotel or had gotten to his mobile. She risked checking the text, squinting to see in the light. *Sara Lovely, hope you did not get too much of a shock. The hotel tells me that you are well. Sorry for not being in touch, but I will explain when I see you later in the day. Take care. James.* Brat, getting her worried like that, but his text like a child apologising – afraid to drop the 'ly' though. He must have thought of her. Road to Damascus?

She laughed to herself, tempted to muddy a trail with a cryptic reply but could not help herself sending a truthful message despite his lack of contact: *James, I was distraught with worry . . . hotel has our itinerary . . . talk then. S*

Mikayla was open, if brief, about her life once they began chatting. She had moved out of her home near Bois de Boulogne not long after her mother had remarried; it wasn't that her stepfather had done anything wrong, but that he was not her father. Then she cut short the conversation on that topic, and began asking about Sara's family and marriage, and more particularly, how she knew the hotel owner.

'Oh, James is an acquaintance from the racing circuit when I was a first-year student. That was the year before Andy and I got together. James remains a good friend.' She had said nothing about their being upgraded and played up the receptionist needing to clear Mikayla's room with her.

Then, Sara gave a long-winded and romanticised version of meeting Andy when he was a student leader, she from just outside Dublin and Andy a Dub through and through with an architect father. He was bright and steady despite his involvement in student politics, and she mentioned they had a child while still students.

Mikayla responded: 'Rick? He is wonderful, and so action oriented. I thought I was dreaming when he carried me off the pyramid. He is a true Aries, open to everything. I am Aquarius, so there is compatibility.'

'We heard from Rick about aligning you with your zodiac.'

'He was part of the shoot, positioning me. So precise and gentle. Each long finger?' She giggled into a smile. A strange conflict of emotion arose for Sara – proud of the recognition of Rick's abilities, but also jealous that it was from a rival for her son's affection. 'Andy is Rick's father?' Mikayla asked casually.

Very French, Sara thought, not to assume that Rick was necessarily Andy's. 'There was a timeline overlap,' she disclosed, 'but I do not think so. It was never an issue with Andy.'

'James?' Mikayla asked.

Perceptive! Two questions and Sara may as well have given her a full life story. 'James is long odds,' she dismissed, and then changed the subject. 'Do you follow horse racing in France?'

'Bois de Boulogne?' Mikayla suddenly became animated to have horse racing mentioned, and then with that top knot swishing her ponytail, replied: 'My house is, was, near Bois de Boulogne, and yes, I know long odds. Always at Prix de l'Arc de Triomphe.'

Clever, not letting her off the hook. Sara decided there was no sense in trying to hide anything. 'James brought me into that horse racing circle. It was the height of the Celtic Tiger boom in Ireland, bling times when everything glittered with no tomorrow. Huge bets wagered on the racing form of a four-legged animal – and with James, whose family had horses, more than that. He always placed his bets on how a horse moved by looking at it from the rear.'

Mikayla laughed until tears came to her eyes. 'Vachement!'

Sara asked if Mikayla found her room comfortable. 'It was tricky laying out the suite,' Sara explained, and then reiterated: 'the receptionist followed my instructions when you were allocated the room beside Rick's. I am keen for you to be good friends. Don't you find the view of the pyramids melts you, their indomitability and yet mutable in the light?'

'Five thousand years?'

'Rami calls them, "These beauties".'

'You are amusing, but the pyramids are reassuring and full of energy.'

'We will enjoy the tour of the museum together. You will need to cover your shoulders,' she reminded. 'A woman behaves modestly in Egypt,' – and does not upstage her hostess.

Mikayla nodded, and Sara decided to take advantage of the moment. 'Your photoshoot is headline news. You need to be careful.'

'Yes. Roman is bull-headed and would not listen, and now André is in custody because of him. Rick said they will not be released for a long time – Boris on the tour has told him. André is artistic,' she mused, looking anxious.

'You need to be concerned for yourself,' Sara reminded her. 'The police won't be long establishing your identity. Has that website been taken down?'

'Yes, I contacted a blogger that Roman has used before. It was him. He agreed to take it down. I reported the website online as a DMCA violation in case he changes his mind.'

This young woman could take care of herself, it seemed, but what about her son who would be detained along with her? The best thing would be for her and Rick to be out of the country before their identities were known – if that was an option. James would know. They crossed a bridge between rows of colourful ferries and riverboats with felucca sails gliding. Like great white-winged birds for an instant when they passed on the broad opal waters of the Nile, and she thought of being able to sit relaxing all day watching those sails move in perpetual motion like a flock of seagulls restless on the surface.

The coach entered a network of exits before coming to a military checkpoint with armoured personnel carriers and mounted machine guns, and a camouflaged tank. Signalled through, they passed a giant gun barrel poking at the windows and into a square ringed in barriers, and further military hardware that stood bronzing muscular in the central island as they circled.

'Tahrir Square,' Andy called over from where he was sitting with Rick. 'See how the streets radiate out in all directions: the city is modelled on Paris. Worth exploring the shopping. We are going over there to the building with Belle Époque Cleopatras in flowing garments.' He laughed.

TMI, give her patience, but not saying anything, as did not want Mikayla to notice tensions –enough information already.

Mikayla chirped back to him: '*Pari', my citi?*' The coach came to a halt outside the museum and Sara repeated her mantra to Mikayla: 'Modesty.' Mikayla rearranged the improvised hijab to partly cover her face and pulled the shoulders' wrap around. Was there no way this young woman could look less attractive, that body busy-ness and bursting sexual energy moving between those statement poses?

Security was thorough, everyone frisked, belts and shoes off, handbags turned out, and endless returns through the security barrier until there were no alarms. The colossal statues of Ramesses II, twelve metres or more, awaited them inside; strutting out of history with a massive physique of solid granite over which his double crowned head presided with carved royal veil and ceremonial beard, eyes focused directly ahead. Rami did not reach the knee of his forebear and was about the same circumference as the calf. 'Such masculinity!'

Mikayla dropped in French: 'Sa présence est totale. Il n'y a personne d'autre qu'une partie de lui.' (His presence is total. There is no one except as a part of him.)

Sara felt better for her son that even attractive Mikayla felt she had limitations. She loved French and ventured: 'Présences concurrentes? Il pourrait ressentir la même chose pour tu.' (A competition of presences. He could feel the same about you.)

Mikayla gave Sara a kiss on each cheek. 'Nous sommes tous les mêmes.' (We are each the same.)

They walked on, elbows linked like school friends, remarking rather than discussing, to stop at the life-size black diorite statue of Khafre, the builder of the second Great Pyramid. Seated life-size on his throne, he was a more approachable proposition, and could casually be carrying on a conversation.

'Not the same,' Mikayla commented, disappointed.

Sara differed: 'He has a boyishness, and his hand is clenched, but hard to take too seriously! I would sit on his knee, and he could whisper in my ear any time. Might unravel those silly fingers that have coiled up at whatever was annoying him. That gleaming smooth stone, Andy would know the name of the material.'

'The musculature is perfect, but I prefer Ramesses.'

Sara joked: 'Size or perfection?'

Rami interrupted them, explaining that the falcon with the open wings around the head and shoulders was the God Horus, the protector God of the Pharaoh and Egypt. Then he brought them to a tiny statue of Khufu, the builder of the largest pyramid, about which he joked that this tiny figurine built the biggest monument in the world.

The tour proceeded from attraction to attraction, Hatshepsut's rounded, happy visage for the woman who had ruled Egypt by claiming that the God Amun impregnated her mother. Sara explained about the concept of a 'miraculous conception' that she had learned at school.

'That would not be a good explanation today.' Mikayla laughed.

'No,' Sara agreed, and switched back to talk about the female pharaoh whose rounded face was laughing at the good of it all. 'Andy said that it was to give her the godly right to rule – when there was not even a female word for pharaoh. Eventually she declared herself a male pharaoh.'

'Deception and myth, she seduces a nation – perhaps very beautiful?'

Rami was explaining. 'As the pharaoh, she kept her son away fighting wars, and he, upon his ascent of the throne, removed any reference to her. Later in our tour we will visit Hatshepsut's Temple.'

Sara tried to listen in on Andy's and Rick's conversation whenever she could. They were talking about the size of the Ramesses colossi as inculcation of a superhero cult in his day that allowed him to be the longest-serving pharaoh of the ancient Egyptian world. Then they got into a discussion of the necessary qualities to inspire and rule a people. Mythologies had superheroes aplenty – did society always require these? Was the pharaoh truly a god, and did he absorb godly qualities and be capable of more because others believed he was a living god?

When they arrived at an exhibit of the Ka of a pharaoh called Kor, it was Rick who had all the facts about the Ka! When Rami suggested the Ka was like a guardian angel, he disagreed in an aside to Andy. The Ka was the life force. When a person died, a statue was placed near him for his Ka to occupy, and if his mummy were destroyed, then the Ka would retain his life force. In fact, he knew all about the ancient Egyptian soul and had opinions about how each corresponded to modern constructs of the psyche. The Ka, along with the Ba, the personality, and the Ib, the heart, were the three most important parts. 'You could not get into the afterlife unless your heart was lighter than a feather.'

But nothing, simply nothing she had ever experienced, had prepared her, or indeed any of the tour, for the Tutankhamun Exhibition, a whole floor of unimaginable wonders. Outside the main room, there were beautiful gold figurines and objects, the gods in various forms and shabti of the pharaoh's former servants that the pharaoh could at any time in the afterlife energise into their former life form to execute his wishes. Intricate gilded miniatures of four protector goddesses guarding the chests containing the organs were spellbindingly beautiful. Andy and Rick talked more about the Ka when the life-sized statues, which had stood guarding Tutankhamun's tomb, turned out to be duplicate Ka's. There were two thrones to admire, one inlaid with jewels and precious stones and the other covered in sheets of gold with a carved relief of Tutankhamun and his Queen, not sitting formal or regal but rather in a domestic interchange. She was hypnotised in awe. Of course, Andy had a conspiracy theory that the treasure had all belonged to the previous pharaoh, the heretic pharaoh Akhenaten, and that much of the haul from Tut's tomb were really objects rededicated by the priests. It was only when Andy had gotten onto this pet theory of his that she realised his alternative agenda. 'Andy, we may never get to see these again.'

'You're right.' Andy went quiet. She saw Rick smile, and Mikayla and she exchanged glances. Mikayla had separated from her, and she and Rick touched hands briefly.

When they were allowed in, Tutankhamun's mask with eyes bursting with vivacious life cast a spell over the room. Its solid gold face in royal veil drew all gazes, and his youthful eyes and flawless adolescent face went straight to her heart. She noticed every detail before she was aware that it was one mask of three similar. Beside it, lying supine, was a full-size sarcophagus of solid gold intricately carved and with a similar mask but eyes in lifeless white ovals. It looked funereal and sad in comparison with the young pharaoh holding court in the room, but the sarcophagus itself was etched in exquisite detail and hieroglyphics and with the wings of Goddess Aset wrapped around it in an embrace. On the other side was a similar full-size sarcophagus covered in gold detailing, and of course that golden mask – but looking only towards the eternal.

Sara returned to the first mask where Mikayla was standing looking like she belonged as the Pharaoh's Queen. Yes, that was it: above the coloured gems of the necklaces and the surrounding blue stripes of the royal veil, the face was clearly of a teenage boy full of the enthusiasm for life. He may indeed be wearing the regal crown and veil of the Kingdoms of Upper and Lower Egypt, golden jewelled cobra and vulture on his forehead, to single him out as the ruler of the combined Kingdoms, but this was that same tentative human face as her son's moments earlier when he had argued his case. Buried in the gaze was enthusiasm and fear in equal measure for embracing a life that needed to hold achievements worthy of eternal life. It compared with that boy in the boater in Manet's *After the Luncheon* leaning against the table with an arrogance as well as a fragility. He too was at that same moment as her son, a time in life that would determine a lifetime's endeavour.

She found herself blurting, 'I might not have had Rick.' Her eyes were moistening, and she stopped herself from bursting into sobs. Mikayla hugged her and she could feel a reciprocal tear on her cheek as they embraced. Mikayla too had suffered – losing her mother and her home to her stepfather.

Andy noticed, and having stopped his circling of the different displays, asked Sara if she was alright. Mikayla replied for her: 'It is a girl thing.'

'I am just here,' he said, placing a quick tentative hand on her shoulder.

No doubt he would have spotted all the differences between the masks for later, but it was comforting that he was there. Rick waited beside Mikayla, and she saw him take Mikayla's hand one finger at a time and steal her away from her and the eternal presence of the pharaoh. What was to be done? Rick had cast the initial stone of his own destiny and found a first love. She worried for Mikayla, who could yet be left to the mercies of her situation when the tour flew to Luxor to join the riverboat for the ascent of the Nile. She could only observe, now that she had achieved that status, *mother with adult child.*

With that, her phone vibrated in her pocket with a message. It was *Cardeville.* She needed to find a spot to check the text. After leaving Tutankhamun's youthful presence, she found a quiet corner to do so. *Sara Lovely, I have come into Cairo to a sister hotel on Gezira Island to see you. Akar is waiting at the Narmer Palette on the ground floor to take you to me. Not to be alarmist but it is better we meet in Gezira, because of the risk of another targeted explosion. Relying on you to find a way to leave the tour. Akar will wait and be available to take you back to Pyramid Dream at any time. James.* He knew her too well. Joining her in the centre was the least after going missing for a day and a half and causing her all that worry – but *big shot with sister hotel* would have to wait while Mikayla and she shopped. The tour would go to lunch on the riverboat, and, after all, Andy had pointed out the shopping area from the coach.

Sara collected Mikayla – and Rick who tagged along – to go find the Narmer Palette where Akar would meet her.

They found the grey metal palette in its display cabinet, and Sara filled in time admiring the artwork on its faces that were a template for Egyptian Art for over three thousand years. Perhaps admiring was too strong a word:

it was blood-curdling and terrifying. One side had rows of foes laid out dead, decapitated and castrated, and with the dismembered parts placed together between their legs – the first king of a united Egypt marching forth in triumph with mythical serpopards straining as they intertwined. He had united the Kingdoms of Upper and Lower Egypt to create a superpower, and she read the serpopards as representations of the two fiery civilisations uniting. On the reverse side, the King was shown smiting an impotent enemy and there were more mutilated dead enemies.

Her new *VBF* asked her son, pointing to the lines of dead: 'Does that scene send a chill?'

'Going to fight has fallen to men always, from being the hunter defending a family to the rise and fall of countries and great empires,' Rick replied, not rising to her tease. 'The great nations of the world were not easily united, and their maintenance of a central power needed to instil fear.'

Mikayla would not let him off that easily and countered, 'Now you have only a woman to fear.'

Rick smiled at her comment, seemingly at a loss to reply.

'5,000 years ago,' she interjected, to take Rick out of a spot. Mikayla was clearly on a different tack – the power she was exerting over him – and he replying factually in all innocence. *Still her son.*

Besides, Sara did not agree that a man had only a woman to fear nowadays as Mikayla had suggested. Surely, when it came down to it, nothing stood in the way of a passionately driven male no matter if a woman placed a noose around her man's neck like the serpopards on the plate – they still faced off, prepared to devour each other. Could you ever truly tame that nature? Wasn't that the charge, though, the challenge to subtly direct without his realising? The way they stood about in the cut suits at a race meeting competing to say the most knowledgeable thing, and then walking on air as if they had ridden the horse to victory. Hubris.

Akar arrived, and Mikayla adopting a statement pose, addressed him as a servant doing her bidding: 'You are bringing us to shop?'

'Your security guard, Fami, will accompany you. I could not protect you.' He smiled thinly before he added, 'He is armed.'

'Excuse me please, Ms Mikayla. I must talk to Madaam . . .' He failed to add her name.

'Madaam Sara,' she prompted him. Remembering him from their first night when he, it was, had nodded towards James. She was suddenly annoyed that he had been sent rather than James himself coming.

"If we could talk privately.' He moved to stand under one of the colossal pharaohs striding.

'James is alive,' she reminded herself, girding herself for whatever news.

'James Bey apologises for not being here himself and he said to assure you that he was not injured when the blast occurred. The carrier had much strength and withstood the explosion. It travels through the air and landing on its side does not shatter.'

A huge wave of relief went through her to have this confirmed.

'He did not come himself that he might not draw media attention.' He raised his eyebrows to convey an understanding transmitted. 'His first enquiry is that you are well, and I need to report to him once I have seen you. He would not believe the updates that the hotel has been sending him. You are as beautiful as ever, Madaam. There is no hint of what has happened on your face – the evil of the world blessedly passes over you. Inshallagh! Be assured that your master is well, and your son, he is here beside you. He is James Bey's second concern.'

Her relief that he was unharmed was replaced by an underlying annoyance that it had taken this long – *school of diplomacy, this guy*. 'Convey to James Bey that Rick is my first concern,' and softening it added, 'as a good mother.'

'Also, his friend Mikayla is well,' Akar added, ignoring her response.

He had conveyed it ambiguously – *had James designs on Mikayla* again jumped into her head. 'Rick's partner and my new best friend,' she corrected for Akar just in case.

'Yes. Madaam Sara Al—' His expression indicated that he understood, but his almost-nearly title amused her – if she and James were an item, would she be Sara Al Bahr Al Ahmar? Sara of the Red Sea sounded both exotic and interesting, stepping ashore like the *Birth of Venus*, but more Andy Warhol's portrayal, still divine but a fun seaside Venus. Auburn hair and green-eyed like herself and that still-girlish fresh face amidst the hair. Mikayla had that too, she had to admit.

Akar had collected himself. 'As you can imagine, James Bey has many new protections required for all his hotels and properties. But his concern for you has caused him to cancel all work to go to the Gezira Palace Hotel for four-of-clocks. I will drive you when you have finished shopping. He has written you a letter to explain.' At this point, Akar presented a letter with the edges embossed with an intricate design of interconnected horseshoes and snakes – at least he took the time. She was going to put it away until she found a moment, but feeling the letter, there was a card, or an electronic key placed between the pages inside. She had better look to see what it was. It was a credit card and an explanatory note in James's handwriting: *Sar, by way of apology for my enforced absence that I will explain later at the hotel. Pin is a memorable room number.* Brat, James reverting to his pet-name for her – and all those memories flooding back despite herself.

Didn't he get it? She was an independent woman now, not the penniless student who could be humoured. She had her own credit cards if she needed anything. She knew the room number he meant, and at least he hadn't forgotten. She would be quite annoyed with him if that old room number didn't work. In fact, she was annoyed with him anyway, almost a two-day gap after rediscovering her, not to mention the tsunami of an explosion through his gilded hotel where he had upgraded them. But then, he had rescued Rick and returned him to the hotel, which was something. Why was she always a churn of emotions whenever he was around? Girlish, like the Birth of Venus, all right.

She texted: '*Gone shopping with Mikayla and Rick.*' She would accompany them, and then slip away with Akar. She handed the credit card to Mikayla and gave her the pin, telling her to purchase whatever she needed.

Chapter 11,

Magic Carpet

Rick

Between their return to the hotel and the shock wave from the explosion, they gleefully joked about the consternation they were causing, even as they searched for images that Roman might have had posted. Nothing could dislodge them from the elation of their escape. Rick was no longer thinking about his becoming a legend in his school, and the only thing that mattered right now was Mikayla. They had been lucky too, he told himself, that the hotel owner impressed with their audaciousness was providing Mikayla with a hotel room – beside his! Their adjoining rooms would smooth the physical confirmation of their fledgling relationship, that, for Rick, was now an obsession.

No matter how he tried, he could not hold her gaze without it invoking a distracted sequence. He shifted uneasily under her delighted focus. At times he was sure she was toying with him in tantalising teases with that bemused way of hers. He studied her smile. She must know the effect she was having with each little adjustment of the clothing loaned by his mother, out of which she was randomly showing. To regain perspective, he surmised that their breakthrough was when he had passed her three tests to allow him to arrange her between the stars. It was then they had connected sufficiently for him to be her Peg'sus and she his Venus, and that was consolidated when the canopy of the paraglider had opened to effortlessly lift them stratospheric. She had hijacked his mind, and even that other image that had previously transported him, the lace on Cloe's top across the milky winter skin of her bust, could not compete.

To help cool himself down, he remembered the consequences of 'that juvenile tryst', as the school principal had euphemistically called it, as she set about going through the motion of expelling him. The principal had explained that she couldn't very well go to the trustees to justify his sneaking back into the school for a rendezvous with a senior girl in the school, even if his father had offered to cover the cost of the fire brigade, security, and the other emergency services. It would be tantamount to condoning their behaviour and would make her a fellow accomplice – if only the girl involved had been from another school. Then, apparently concerned for his welfare, she had asked what he was going to do when he stopped being such a joker. Ironically, this was the same question that had gotten him into this scrape in the first place. Cloe had asked him exactly this while they were hanging out that evening. Then, he had excused away his lack of ambition by suggesting that guys were not born as perfect as girls and had to make something of themselves – and he had not found the right thing. She had laughed, replying: 'Girls aren't perfect!' and the eyeshadow had narrowed her eyes to match her devilish grin. Cloe was sound out. To the headmaster, he had simply shrugged his shoulders and replied: 'It will be difficult to find such a good school. I will focus on maintaining my top grades.' That had been enough to get him a very acceptable reference for entrance to a new school, but Cloe had faded with those words he had spoken to the headmaster failing to defend her.

He was determined that he would not be disloyal to his new girlfriend, even when the aftershock swept debris through the hotel and the spell enveloping them lost its implicit power. It caused Mikayla to become swamped in worries for Roman and André, doubting their chances of ever getting home. She also foresaw the worst outcomes for Rick and herself, arrest, and imprisonment – fearing interrogation. Rick did what he could to reassure her, concerned that their tenuous unity established on the pyramid would shatter into smithereens like the glass debris on the hotel foyer floor. He tried to distract her with discussions about her life in France, but she was slow to divulge information about Paris or her family. 'It is already in my personality.' She did disclose that her parents lived on the outskirts not too far from Bois de Boulogne, and when she visited that is where she went because of the natural beauty of the surroundings. *Each flower, even the smallest, has so much intricacy and delicacy that to really experience it, she blocked out everything. It was an intense experience.* Then, standing in a statement pose, she had asserted: 'I too am as you see me; others have hidden talents that you must discover. This is me!' He then had told her about Georgia O'Keeffe's flowers and that *imho* the artist was trying to capture exactly what she had described. She seemed satisfied with his confirmation of her, 'This is me!' What the hell, he would go along.

It was the first time he had gone shopping with a woman, and that was *K*, but the way she came out to see what his mother thought was a bit of a put-down. But when she had left suddenly with Akar, he was the sole recipient, and judge – it was like a repeat of the pyramids. When Fami dropped them and Mikayla's wardrobe of clothes back at the hotel, their adjoining rooms allowed them to share the veranda while she retried selected clothes, that was K. He sat and admired, allowing him to elaborate on things he especially liked about 'This is me!' In between rig-outs he studied the perfectly symmetrical steps of Khufu rising to peak in the powdery blue sky, a picture of order, as things should be, except for that robbers' access breaking its pattern. The hotel was quiet. He had tried to work out how much older Mikayla was as she came and went – one year he hoped but easily four. The way she carried on moving between those statement poses though, that was like someone pretending to be older, and then breaking into that giggling despite herself that was girlish. Did it matter? How could he keep such a beautiful girlfriend when sooner or later it came out that he had not made it into his final cycle in secondary school? But hey, he was travelling first class, money no object, and he could ride any thermals with his genie teasing the cords. He had snatched her out of danger, and they had ascended to soar into the sun, floating on air together. She continued to call him Peg'sus, and her presence somehow took away the danger of arrest at any moment.

It was nearly two days since they met. They had shared every moment since, and concern about their outcome would deepen their relationship, another shared resonance between them. Would they go on combining until neither could say where one finished and the other started – wasn't that what happened? This wasn't the trilling and spilling the night away smoking dope under his school desk with mischievous Cloe. It was different: they were already a union, except physically. He had never done this, take on someone completely, but he guessed her troubles came with the territory? He was more than willing? The tapestry of her presence would become textured, richer, despite her protesting its superficiality. He would gather the myriad nuances of her, from each of their moments together, and from the present difficulties, and wrap them more tightly into her than the printed silk on the pyramid – like an early Cubist painting, he thought.

He needed to paint himself into the picture, not to mention that it was the only way that he could be sure that she wasn't toying with him. A plan hatched itself in his mind: he would try getting her into the mood by reviewing the photobank of her poses from the pyramid, gently shifting the focus away from André to their great adventure together. Prompted by the images of her on memory cards they would relive that magical connection between them. They could review each photo, each fine-tuning that he had made, him telling her what he was trying to achieve. She could then decide if that was really that same quality about her. Would she not be overjoyed to be the centre of her world? *This is me, or not me, who knew!* The effect on him would be no less electric: wasn't there that thing that happens to a man where he can go and go, up to twenty times – no predicting it but he did not see them stopping once they started? He came up with a strategy to deal with her concern about André: he would mention whenever André's name arose that he was right there beside her to help her through it.

The birdsong trilled again off the stone amongst the verdant greenery and floral effusion of the garden. The reactivated fountains were bubbling and babbling and the urgent drone of hotel noises mixed with the clunking of the shining silver coffee maker that brought the gritty smells of concentrated Egyptian coffee. Everyone had disappeared. Even his father, surprisingly recovered and recharged, had gone on a city walkabout with Kirsten, of all people, the same woman he had taken to task for bringing bottles of wine from her room during the room evacuation.

Mikayla did seem to be coming around when she returned to the balcony in an oversized Barsa jersey from her earlier shopping in the hotel. She got Rick to tie a knot on the shoulder, and after checking her reflection in a mirror and fluffing out the knot, she remarked: 'Yes, a rose.'

'You are subverting a famous number: Messi would not be pleased with you changing his number ten into a one and a squiggle.' When she gave him another one of those dubious looks, he added, 'But I suppose Messi is the God of Football, and you have repurposed his jersey.'

'Thank you.' She leaned towards him to give him a peck, then stood and admired the raised hem, front, and rear in the mirror. Then she told him that she would ask him another set of questions.

He agreed. She was back to her tests, and that had to be girlish.

'We need to see that you are *only-man*. There are three tests, and I will not give you the results until the end.'

'Solo man?' he asked, nudging her a little into his mindset.

'Tout-homme, *only-man*!' she repeated. Then taking the horseshoe-crested matchbox, she snapped a matchstick from the pack for him to strike on the strip. 'First, you need to strike a *lucifer* for me. *Only-man*,' she reminded, handing him the matchstick.

This was ridiculously easy, he thought. But when he tried, he found that the matchstick stubbornly would not ignite. 'What if it won't light?'

'An *only-man* would make it flame.' The oversized sports shirt from the hotel shop dropped its neckline and fell off one shoulder as she reached forward, exposing the long neckline sloping under her collarbone and onto the rise of her breasts.

Was this supposed to help spontaneously combust the *lucifer*? How would he get her damn *lucifer* to light? He thought of the desperadoes in cowboy movies striking a match off the roughness of their faces. He checked the packet of matches: the lighting strip was damp. Ftw, but that strip was never going to ignite anything. He took another matchstick and pulled the red head along the glass protector on the tabletop, and it burst into a yellow flame that sat in her eyes.

'I cannot tell until the end, as I said. For the second test, you need to look at your fingernails like an *only-man*?' She was smiling, but which smile was it?

What was next? He clenched his hand to see his nails. She leaned forward and held his hand, in a heady mixture of touch, perfume, and aromas and the rededicated Barsa shirt that had slipped some more.

'I still cannot say until the end, as I said.' She then continued to prolong his agony, smiling all the while. He caught her studying the effect this was having on him as she straightened the top. 'I need you to adjust the knot for me – it falls too much.'

'A woman dresses herself; an *only-man* undresses her.' He dismissed the request.

'Peg'sus, that is not the test. Can you help me?'

He redid the shoulder knot. Of course, the Barsa jersey now rode higher on her thighs.

As he appreciated his adjustment, she stood admiring herself in the mirror. 'It is better, yes. Now you need to stand for the next test and,' she said and waited until he did. 'Look at the sole of your foot, either foot?'

Confused again, he simply lifted his leg in front and looked underneath his foot while holding it awkwardly.

'Now we come to the decision of the judges, only one judge, me?' Laughing and tantalising, she directed her glowing eyes into his. After a moment, she said, 'In reverse: on the last test you are *only-man*, a woman looks behind her and lifts her foot so.' She looked over her shoulder, lifted a leg to look at her sole, tapping her hips at the same time. 'It does not always make sense, but it is true. She checks the line of her dress, her stockings, her shoes, who knows. So, you are one-third?'

'Which third?' What the hell?

'Later.'

Was she qualifying him for their union? 'Alive and smiling,' he replied.

'For the second of my thirds, a woman holds out her fingers, flat, in front to check her nails. You curled your hand and looked at your nails like so.' She demonstrated. 'That is *only-man* also. This is the second part of me.'

She was really playing him. 'So, I am two-thirds? Can I pick?' He had never felt this aroused – to the point where he could feel an explosion building. Wicked, evil grin: he smiled going along.

'No, it is not possible for you to pick. The judge had a difficult decision on the first question. Woman strikes a *lucifer* away from herself, so the sparks do not burn her. You pulled the *lucifer* across the glass towards you. That is *only-man*, yes. But you could not get the *lucifer* to light on the strip, that is not *only-man.*'

She was really dragging this out: but oh, she had that incredible perfume enveloping him as the oversized Barsa shirt falling off one shoulder again. 'The strip was damp,' he defended reaching out to gently hold her hand.

She indulged him and then pulled away. 'Influencing the judges gets disqualification, but I will check to see if the strip will light for me.' She made a clumsy effort to get a matchstick to light, pointing outward as if frightened of it. Casting a glance at him, she pushed the matchstick across the worn strip that had no chance of lighting – in his humble opinion.

'You are right, it is *dampe*, and you did light the *lucifer* on the glass. You are *only-maaaan*.'

Then she walked onto the veranda and stood silhouetted through the lattice against the blues, the sea dark and the sky lit from the horizon in the twilight. All three thirds – was this finally it? Mikayla liked the airiness and fragrances of the veranda, comparing it to floating on their parasail as they had glided off their pyramid. He took the Arabian rug and cushions and joined her sequestered behind the lattice pergola.

'When in Arabia, do as the Arabians do,' he remarked, as he nervously folded and moved the sun loungers along the veranda, took the Arabian rug and laid it down before softening it with a plethora of cushions. He persisted, making a big play out of positioning them for her, not allowing her to recline until they were 'perfect' that amused her.

She redirected his attention to music, giving him one earplug to listen to a track that she had downloaded. When he put the earplug in his ear, it was Rhianna's, *Shut up and Drive*. Then she leaned forward until her face was close to his ear and whispered: 'Peux-tu juste te taire et me baiser.' It was a second before he translated, remembering a word that had gone around French class. Then, just like on the pyramid, she removed her top in a single move, this time grabbing it by the rose knot that he had made. She wasn't standing statuesque rising into the sky to wield her immense beauty, but instead she was softly beautiful and inviting. Her eyes shone glittering into his, bemused and playful to a fault. As the warm evening air wafted about them, the background noises fell away. What the hell!

It was the following morning when they got around to reviewing the photobank, and immediately when the first image opened, he realised that there had been tampering. He presumed at first that it might be his laptop, but his mobile when he tried it had the same grainy effect.

She smiled weakly and yawned from her position on the veranda outside. 'No, Roman and André have altered the images to make certain that only they can retrieve them.'

'It may not be difficult to undo, but we need to know what they have done.' he reassured her, not knowing if it was or not.

'No, it will not be easy. It is to evade my copyright: the value will come from their photoshopping. Now they are in custody, and we will need to wait.' She shrugged her shoulders, pulled a resigned expression, and cosied herself between the cushions.

He began his searches for her images, relaying what he was finding. The DMCA take-down notice had been effective in stopping the original site, but nothing is ever forgotten in cyberspace. He found instances of her image under different sites; everything from the prurient humour to the tamer 'the pyramids never looked this good . . .' to the amusing: 'Interesting way to learn the harp?' caption, when she was leaning out from the frame into the sky; there were even calls for a permanent monument on top of the pyramid; that was never going to happen. 'Likes' were above 90 percent, and that was what mattered. Rick was feeling proud of her in a strange way. It was, however, the factual news header, 'Why this woman has so upset the Egyptians?' that sent a deep chill through him. He read on getting around opening a premium subscription to discover that Blasphemy carried a penalty of up to five years in prison under Egyptian law.

There was an explanation of the decrees of Islam and the more restrictive rules that applied during the Ramadan fast under the hadiths. In addition to the requirement of fasting (sawm) between the 'white thread of dawn' and the 'black thread of dusk' to elevate consciousness to experience the presence of Allah, there was a more general requirement to strictly follow the teachings of Islam. Obscene and irreligious stimuli were a direct affront, while sexual acts were specifically prohibited. Even if this happened between husband and wife, it required expiation (kafaarah) of two months fasting.

There were arguments back and forth between Islamic scholars on what the correct penalty should be in this case, and Rick's blood ran cold as he followed the internet thread. There were three questions that needed to be decided:

:was the unfortunate young woman forced?

:did the photoshoot take place during the fast, post dawn?

:was the photoshoot a sexual act?

There could be no doubt that naked filming on the pyramid both as an insult to Islam and a violation of Ramadan and blasphemy was the least crime that could be considered.

He looked towards the comfortable nest of cushions and Mikayla resting after their night together, her eyes closed to the daylight glancing through the screen. He would take care of her somehow. There was no way he was leaving her to a fate decreed by over a thousand years of religious thought being argued over on-line. Nor could she be vouched for by the hotel owner who was himself a target. He hit upon an idea. She could join their tour where her German would make her indistinguishable from others: then by the end of the tour and Ramadan, the story would have died down.

When she agreed, it was to his father that he decided to turn. Andy was not in his adjacent room, in fact had not been there overnight he was certain from the lack of activity. When he did find his father, it was in the foyer nursing a strong coffee, and looking dishevelled from what must have been a late night. Despite his state, his face froze horrified against the white cascading waterfall in the foyer when he updated him on the on-line discussions. With a gravitas he had never seen before, Andy stated in a brusque, matter-of-fact way: 'I agree. Mikayla needs to join our tour – you can't just leave her here.' It was decisive and not open to discussion, and so unlike his father's endless procrastination.

To diminish Mikayla's culpability to his father, Rick grappled with explanations, trying: 'She had no idea that the others were going to try to sell her images on the internet.'

He ignored Rick's protest, replying, 'That won't matter. Let's talk to Rami about getting her onto our tour.' His father continued, 'I am hoping it won't be too difficult. I never thought I'd be thankful for baksheesh.' His father joked, something Rick could not remember for months. As they walked along, he turned. 'Let's not deny that you know Mikayla from the internet and that you were planning to meet here all along. It's an easier sell if we are honest.'

How did he know? '*Kool.* That's fair,' he responded. His excitement at the thought of Mikayla being with him for the Nile tour was intoxicating.

'Come on. The flight to Luxor won't wait.' His father's step livened, and he led the way across the marble floor.

The radiant-eyed receptionist smiled and, anticipating their inquiry, he pointed to the garden without their asking. 'Your tour guide is relaxing pleasantly under the palms: he is beside the fountains, and you will be able to discuss much privately. I will order tea for you. But beware, the fountains will dance to music in fifteen minutes, and it is wise not to sit too close.'

Rami himself seemed to know they would be coming and rose to welcome them as if he was giving them an audience. 'My friends, I must apologise for the tour up until now, but you have seen the museum, and these babies.' He extended an arm to indicate the pyramids. 'Please, please sit!'

Rick was selecting a chair to sit directly opposite Rami, but his father moved him to another saying that he needed to discuss a delicate matter with Rami: 'You may have to leave us after a while.'

'*K.*' This was turning into a scene from *The Sopranos.* No witnesses!

His father then went into what must have been a routine, inquiring where Rami lived and if he was married.

Rami responded, 'Everyone in Egypt wants to be married, and Muslims marry young. I am blessed with a wife, Amina, and two teenage children.' He then asked how many children Andy had.

'Just Rick,' his father replied, pointing to him.

'Rick is not from earlier?' Rami queried, before quickly adding: 'Your wife, she is a beautiful woman.'

Andy leaned forward. 'Rami, I need a special service from you.'

Rami opened a hand like a sheik in a majlis of petitioners. 'Please speak.'

'Have you met Mikayla?'

Rami nodded. 'Yes, she enjoys the patronage of the hotel. She is beautiful, but young and foolish.'

'Rick knew her from the internet, and they arranged to meet here and be friends for the holiday. As you can see, she is now good friends with Sara—'

'You wish her to join the trip?' Rami was ahead of his father.

'Yes, if you think you can make that happen?' His father held a stare.

Rami sat back. 'Anything is possible. Here in the hotel or if she transfers to a sister hotel, the owner can vouch for her.' He leaned forward into Andy's face, adding through his teeth, 'She is safe. The hotel owner is a very influential man.'

Their conversation was interrupted when the fountains sprang rhythmically into life accompanied by the swirls and strains of Egyptian music over speakers. Rami relaxed, shrugging, indicating that they must wait. Andy tried to restart the conversation whenever there was a pause in the music, but each time the strains of the music restarted building to a crescendo. Rami began to smile at Andy's attempts to speak, and when the music did stop, he leaned forward, still with a smirk on his face.

'Do you recognise the music?'

'Egyptian music?'

'It is the famous music of Raqs Baladi for the belly dance. The owner is very fond of the Raqs Baladi and has his fountains dance the belly dance. It is amusing, yes. Who knows what it cost? He is wealthy.' Rami reclined looking contented, as if he had conveyed some deeper meaning for Andy to consider.

'Double spiral sprays off each rotating base, and they are synchronised like a troupe of dancers,' Andy replied as he studied the fountain's jets.

Rami's dark expression returned: 'Yes, he is fond of dancers, and has the fountains copy them.' He made curves with his hands to indicate a dancer.

Why was he telling them this? His father made no comment but clearly understood what had been conveyed.

Rami continued: 'Humbly, I cannot decide if Ms Mikayla can join the tour. It is the hotel owner who must agree to her release, and he may wish her to stay. But, my friend, when she is no longer on his property, he cannot vouch for her. Also, the shipping company will have to agree to her being on board, and if they have any awareness of the delicate situation of her circumstances, then they may refuse or require a considerable sum for this special service. It is you who will need to vouch for her good character and behaviour: I cannot accept this responsibility – Amina and my children.'

Andy leaned over, thinking that Rick could not hear. 'My son is clearly in love with Mikayla, and I cannot leave her in this compromised situation. Make the request.'

'You are a romantic.' He spread his hands and shrugged. 'It is your choice.'

His father nodded.

Rick left with his father in silence, grappling with what he had just heard. He would have to wait for the owner's reply to know if their newly formed union would survive its first challenge. Hfs!

Chapter 12,

Maze of Streets

Andy

Andy felt slighted that Sara had not turned for his support,
whatever it was about Tutankhamun's mask that had
brought a tear to her eyes. He had heard her say about Rick:
hadn't he been party to everything? Another small
rejection, in that moment turning to another rather than to
him, that nuanced distancing that was not allowing them
to reconcile and move on together. Just when they got
close, a new rebuff . . .

They had successfully cooperated during Rick's
escapade – didn't that count – and he was the one who had
held her when the explosion had ripped through the foyer,
even if she had first reached towards Rick as any mother
would. She had softly crumpled limp into his arms, and
had lain shocked, covered in dust and debris, as vulnerable
and trusting as a little girl. That sex their first night had

been as scintillating as ever, roving all over her with teases and caresses until she opened into love like her rose, as if they were rediscovering again. Sex was always the last to go – hadn't he heard that? They hadn't made love after the explosion when, after a student march of all those years ago, they'd have spent the afternoon high on the danger with their own aftershocks – but that was down to him falling asleep when he finally had the opportunity.

He was examining the perfect details of Tutankhamun in its cabinet wondering how it could possibly be crafted when Kirsten came to discuss the remarks that he had made earlier. Delighted that she was indulging his conspiracy theory, he blurted: 'A heretic pharaoh, who disbanded the priests and banned all other gods except the Aten, the sun disk; he was the pharaoh who moved the capital and changed the artistic style into his own image – a single sex perhaps?'

'It is easy to think that the priests would raid his tomb for his son, who had reinstated them and reversed his father's heresies,' she agreed.

'Not the face,' he clarified, and he pointed to the joining around the facemask where it had been attached to the headdress.

She wanted to take a photo of that detail on her mobile but, just then, one of the security guards came over waving a finger to tell her no. 'No!'

She did not try to sneak a photo, but instead stood contemplating the treasure behind the glass case, like a bold child refused in a sweetshop, who continued to point at what she wanted.

There was a familiarity about her, a playful flicker that turned to a flash in her blue eyes. What were the chances? 'As it happens,' he admitted, 'I have just taken that photo.'

She studied him for a minute, before remarking: 'Well, can you please send it to me!'

'No problem! It's on my mobile – I can send it when we are outside.'

'How did you take it?' she asked in that amused way of hers.

He smiled, taking her in again as he replied. 'By looking at one security guard through the glass cabinet and watching the other reflected in the glass.' He noticed how the lights from the glass cabinet were catching the stray strands of her fair hair that freed themselves – and those flustered hand movements that replaced the loose hairs back behind her ears. There was an athletic way to how she was standing. He wondered again if she had been one of those accelerating downhill skiers who blended seamlessly into the contours of the mountain. She might have mesmerised him with her speed, the turns – and those gravity-defying jumps?

'A schoolboy trick, I think,' she summarised.

She did have a winning determination in her eyes, and he imagined her legs crouched that low, practically folded into the run – a dash of colour streaking down the snow? Such tiny figures when at the finish you saw them against the might of the mountain that they had just conquered. Then the reveal as the helmet got removed to sit on the current leaders' bench, energised, posing with hair released over shoulders, all smiles and mitten waves. Boris liked her, and indeed everyone did, and she was a good companion interested in the history and cultural significance of everything.

He must have stared for too long because she self-consciously remarked, 'Low centre of gravity,' as she smacked the sides of her thighs.

It was a continuation of his thoughts again. 'Sorry, was I staring? You look familiar that's all. How competitive were you as a skier?'

'I have a few trophies. You might have stared also at me on the leaders' bench on your Sunday afternoons.'

Mind reader. 'I might.' There was no point in his not being honest, but why was she not giving at least some of the ski-lessons? Sounds like she had a job keeping that celeb husband on a leash. He changed the subject. 'I love the ski jump, off the ramp, magically sailing into the air. Strange, I always wanted to try than, but ski down a hill at speed, never!'

'I do not do ski-jumps, except as part of a run.'

'I don't think gravity would allow me to fly off a ski jump.' He looked towards his own build – his fitness was slipping. 'The fliers hardly fill their suits.'

Sara, who had reappeared and was always able to hear his conversations across a room, remarked: 'Kirsten, you have a groupie.'

'We were just discussing the Amarna period,' Andy defended. 'Kirsten has tremendous detail. I am hoping we have time to work around the display cabinets again.'

'You have found your new *VBF* then!' Sara repeated. 'Mikayla and I will skip the bazaar to go high-street shopping expedition to the shops you mentioned. She needs clothes – positively bursting through mine, and the less said about those harem pants she wore to breakfast. Kirsten, can you mind him for me?'

'Yes, we have the same interests.' She cast him a glance.

Andy gave directions: 'The shopping street is just out the front door, past the statues of the two gods, hang a left at the fountain with the sphinxes, cross Tahir roundabout past the military hardware, and second on the left as the streets radiate out. Right close by.'

Sara was already moving towards the exit to the room.

Andy felt fingertips touch his arm. 'Let's go through the jewellery together.' Kirsten pointed towards the cabinets. 'If you would like, I want to look at the pectorals, necklaces, and bracelets in more detail with you.'

Kirsten took her time admiring the individual pieces and discussing where the colourful semi-precious stones had been sourced and how they were mounted. The milk and brown veins on the lapis lazuli fascinated her, and she delighted in how the orange carnelian still radiated the fractured light after three thousand years of shining. She really was the class swot pushing back those unruly strands to get a clearer view – no doubt wore a headband for lab work. She must have been reading his thoughts again because she dexterously twirled the loose hair into a chignon off the nape of her neck with one hand while tying it with the other. 'How we kept our hair inside the ski-helmets,' she explained. 'Topknots like Mikayla's, that is not good?'

'Nicely intertwined,' he complimented, his voice trailing off, unsure that he should have said anything. That girlish pose again before she bent to look in more detail into the cabinet. 'What would you have been if you didn't ski?'

'Study archaeological finds, restore artefacts, I expect. We make our choices.'

The hair pulled up off the nape of her neck contrasted with the flashes that came into her eyes. He relaxed and felt he could comment quite openly on the attractiveness of the build of the four graceful, gilded statuettes protecting the canopic shrine of internal organs, and did. How attractive their curvature and rounded figures were combined with the delicate upper figures with outspread arms, flowing gowns, and exquisite faces.

'The Amarna period,' she simply commented.

At the golden throne with the reliefs, she remarked: 'How beautiful the back panel is, and such a tender moment. The queen has such elegance reaching over to him to place a hand on his shoulder.' She flashed her eyes. 'Could be an image of Akhenaten and Nefertiti,' and she touched his arms again. 'Yes, I agree, Tutankhamun's tomb could have inherited the treasures intended for his heretic father.'

Raising his head momentarily as Kirsten air-traced with her hand, he noticed over the balcony on the lower floor he saw Akar leading the trio of Sara, Mikayla, and Rick, with Fami at the rear. He could not see clearly through the dusty light of the museum, and was about to reach for his mobile to call Sara to arrange meeting later – and then decided he did not want to interrupt the time he was spending with Kirsten.

Leaving the museum, they were brought to Al-Hussein Square that was a buzzing social forum in a general clamour, and where giant inverted umbrellas opened upwards in exclamation in front of the ancient mosque. As the tour ate with their hands at the restaurant where they sampled mezzes Rami gave them a brief history of adjacent Khalili Bazaar that was originally founded as the city was recovering from the Black Death. Although the restaurants were full, no one else was eating, but instead conversed animatedly over empty tables, mopping brows with the wet towels served. He could not say if the city had returned to normal following the explosion, or if the concrete barrier in front of the mosque, and another concrete barrier concealed behind the first row of tables along the row were new, but Rami casually sent them wandering down the narrow, cobbled streets into an Aladdin's treasure throve of shops, restaurants, and workshops. They crowded through colourful and bright arrays in the noisy, sheltered passageways that held everything from the authentic Arabic and antique purchases to glittering trinkets. Their interest was at the lower end, as convivial shopkeepers directed them into their stores in English, French, and German taking no chances on their nationality.

He followed Kirsten through hooped and pointed arches examining items that caught either of their attention, while glimpsing architecture through the produce shelves piled high. Her collection of purchases gradually increased until he was carrying a clutch of plastic bags upon which each subsequent shopkeeper remarked, offering to hold for them until their return. She kept checking if he wanted to continue shopping. How long since he had felt this relaxed? He enjoyed being with her shopping as she ferreted items in each section of the market. Handmade sandals with jewelled straps and a handbag with a Cleopatra motif in the best leather, a bottle of essence as much for intricacy of the blown-glass bottle as the fragrance, myrrh from the spice market, to so many trinkets that were emblematic of Egypt. Six little leather purses for her friends that had Aset wings that opened. 'All money flies away.'

His few purchases were minor in comparison but took the longest: endless comparisons to select a bust of Tutankhamun that was the closest match to the young Pharoah holding court in his stolen photo. He was attracted to a rug of the tree of life in rich reds and blues, reaching down as high as it grew, but didn't buy. Amongst the metal and porcelain, he thought of buying a plate or tray but then got distracted by tea sets, with golden inner linings on the cups. Safiya's bangles tinkling as she poured and her beguiling looks – had they connected in that moment – but then the set also reminded him of Napoleon's divorce service. He decided instead he would buy an Aladdin's lamp for Rick, even though his son had already found his genie – that amused. Of course, he bought a multi-coloured fanoos, whose panels folded and re-folded into an envelope package.

In a café their purchasing finally came to a halt under a portrait of Mahfouz, the Nobel prize-winner about whom Kirsten enthused. They sat under amidst a row of antique fanoos and massive mirrors, for coffee and well-earned pastry on dark wooden furnishings that rivalled those of Lloyd Wright. With tongue in cheek, he presented her with a bracelet of the four protector goddesses dangling in elegance on a charm bracelet. She was a little embarrassed, remarking that her internal organs would now be protected. Then she half-joked, 'You are already becoming one of those Arabic men who buy multiple Louis Vuitton bags, one for each wife.'

'It's a trinket. We shared seeing them together,' he replied honestly.

Her eyes flashed, and this time she held his with her look. 'I will put it on.' While doing so, she asked, 'Would you like to see the historic Arabic house, Zeinab Khatoon? I have never been to a hareem.'

'Me neither,' he joked.

'Not the same, I think,' she surmised, before adding: 'You can imagine the many wives luxuriating and practising seductive routines when you are there.' She touched his arm in a combined gesture with displacing a stray strand of hair.

He was surprised at himself for having bought Kirsten a keepsake from the day, so different from his usual behaviour. What could he say – impulsive, would you believe? They passed butchers, bakeries with trays of ballooning flatbreads dropping out of ovens and being arranged onto racks, and recesses where doors unfolded to create instant 3D pop-out shops with owners who sat and watched the slow ambling of passersby. There was none of the tension from the explosion on these side-streets, but rather an affable softness in the air and an ease to activity.

The inauspicious entrance Zeinab Khatoon's observed by latticed windows above that brought them through a maze of corridors to a courtyard. 'The hareem is behind the Mashrabiyas.' Kirsten pointed to the large oriel window directly opposite. 'Then whoever arrived had to climb these stairs in view of both the hareem and the master of the house.' She hurried up the stair that led along a semi-dark narrow corridor and into a large reception room, the qa'a, where a cashier sitting at a desk in the oriel charged them for their visit. He explained that the alcove off to the oriel was where the master sat with a view of the entrance, and that a visitor was not allowed to cross the stepdown unless asked to do so by the master, and then only to sit in an alcove opposite, looking up to where the master reclined in the oriel. The other step opposite was the line demarking the hareem from where the women would attend and from where food would be served.

'The man's mother chose the first wife,' the cashier turned guide explained. 'He could go his own way; except she would then not get involved to resolve any issues. Then the first wife got to bless the second wife, and both consulted on the third wife, and so on. Again, the man could make his own choice, but he might not then get a moment's peace.'

They laughed, Kirsten disturbing those loose strands.

The cashier left them to cross the raised step and go through the door ahead, where the corridor turned left again to go between the wives' rooms and another latticed window. They stepped into one of the raised alcoves in front of a window. Kirsten looked out the window and remarked with a hint of moisture in her eyes, 'All day waiting for the man of the house to return from business elsewhere.'

Before he realised that he was doing it, his hand had reached out to hers. Had she herself waited many long hours in her gilded chalet in a snowy winter wonderland until her own celebrity returned from extended lessons? Poor Kirsten. His touch was reciprocated, and they hugged until he kissed her lips, softly eager. He could feel the bracelet he had given her dangling along the back of his neck.

Activities on Al-Hussein Square were busier when they returned, the men gregariously conversing under the giant raised parasols that now resembled avatars spreading wings, while hawkers yelled out their wares over the hubbub. Women with small children sat around the green, and the family that they remembered from earlier continued to sit on a stone bench with their marriageable daughter in full-length black burka. Her dark eyes behind a fine mesh were incredibly bored, and any attempt she made to walk resulted in her being accompanied by either her mother or father. Customers continued their discussions in the restaurants along one side over bare tables, and only the few tourists ate the food being pre-prepared in a swirl of smoke and spices on open grills. The city was drawing its breath under a spell before opening into the evening.

They noted a smattering of their tour sitting at the corner restaurant inquisitively looking in their direction as they deposited shopping bags. There might be just enough time to visit Al-Hussein mosque before evening prayer. There were separate male and female entrances, and they left each other dissolving the cocoon of togetherness they had held since the museum. They both smiled like mitching children.

When Andy had taken off his shoes, he approached one of the two burly guards at the security desk at the male entrance to this holiest of Muslim sites in Egypt. Upon asking if he could enter, he was given ten minutes, provided he did not disturb others. Most of the men were facing the same direction and he sat making himself as inconspicuous as possible, careful not to make eye contact. Men sat, stood, or bowed, read from a Quran, prayed, or simply did nothing, even lying on the carpeted floor. No images adorned the walls, and Arab calligraphic script was incorporated onto wall panels – words mattered. The only ornamentation was the ornate marble around the mihrab niche looking towards Mecca and on the stair of the preacher's minbar. It was a comfortable and convivial space, conversational with the hum of whispered prayers and voices. The softer pitch of female voices came from behind panelling with a latticed upper section, where Kirsten was.

A green light shone over the entrance in the wall ahead that must be the reliquary of Al-Hussein and where a queue bowed in prayer had formed. He should phone Sara once he was outside – she had not yet returned to the pickup point. The queue moved slowly, turning to file along the large silver reliquary between protective railings and a marble outer wall. Carried along, he stepped back towards the wall watching the faces in the green lighting. There was genuine devotion here, people who had cleansed their hearts and minds from having sat and contemplated now approaching the shine. Were they looking to be blessed with a new insight, as he was? He looked for Kirsten amongst the women on the opposite side, but not seeing her re-joined the moving body of men filing out of the space. At the desk, he thanked the guards and tapped his heart, and the burly guard smiling in amusement tapped his watch. He should find Kirsten.

Outside in the dusk, the volume from restaurants had blurred into the gabbling clamour. More of his tour group had collected, but he neither saw Kirsten, nor any of Sara, Rick, or Mikayla, and thought he would sit alone to wait. He returned to the adjacent restaurant where he thought Kirsten and he could sit more relaxed. She emerged in a throw of light from the side street, and he caught her eye, and approached, smiling. They gently kissed both cheeks in a greeting before noticing the tour focused on them. 'So much for a discreet cup of tea together. I had forgotten the optics for the tour.'

'It is international good manners to kiss each cheek.'

As Kirsten was seating herself, the waiter arrived with a huge enamel teapot, numerous cups, and a sizeable mound of leaves that he began adding to the pot. He was disappointed when he saw only the two of them. 'For your many friends to invite, I have left extra cups. It is our custom.'

'Did you see the Al-Hussein's shrine?' he asked, pouring the strongest tea and having to add hot water.

'No, but I have been given the Ramadan challenge. A lady in full-black tried to convert me to Islam at a separate booth near the women's entrance. Here is a Ramadan challenge she gave me for you; it has instructions on the other side. The kick is in the third paragraph.' She handed over a small roll of laminated paper with 'Ramadan 30-Day Challenge' emblazoned on a bicep under a sky with sickle and star.

He opened the roll and there was a sweet in the shape of an olive. 'That is temptation,' Kirsten teased.

There was remonstrating going on between the two reps in front of the restaurant. Ignoring it, Andy took the instructions to read, and quickly scanned until he came to the challenge: '. . . it is not just a month to abstain from food. It is necessary also to get rid of a destructive bad habit and to take up a good habit!' A scrawny little boy with curly hair came by and begged until he saw a huge tray of breads and other foods being carried towards a tent outside the mosque and scampered off after it.

Things were heating up between the two reps for the two restaurants, now supported by the waiters standing behind, adding comments. He ignored it. He had just read the last sentence where spaces had been left for the person taking the 30-Day challenge to complete. Kirsten had filled out: 'On Ramadan in Egypt, I Kirsten vow to take the 30-Day Challenge by breaking my habit of consuming too much wine and will maintain a new habit of *enjoying the moment again*, starting from now.'

He looked over at his Kirsten, pleased that their afternoon together had prompted her resolution. 'I think you may have given me yours.' She pushed the second rolled challenge towards him, but there was no time to fill it out.

The two reps had begun pushing and shoving and pointing at their table: a large chef holding a cleaver had now joined the fray. His travel instinct for staying out of trouble sprang into action, and in an instant, he understood what had happened. There must be arrangement made with tours with baksheesh paid to Rami. He sprung to his feet, throwing the exorbitant payment in euros from his pocket onto the table. They exited the restaurant to the adjacent one as a policeman arrived to break up what was developing into a brawl. Tensions eased.

The sun was about to dip below the skyline as strings of green lights along the face of the mosque were switched on. Food was finally being served to the tables, yet the patrons sat waiting; a gloaming twilight that spread throughout the square, was cocooning them in a timeless feel.

'Time to complete your Ramadan challenge,' she prompted him.

'I am just not sure how to phrase this.' He whispered, 'For Ramadan in Egypt I, <u>Andy</u>, vow to take the 30-Day challenge by breaking my old habit of <u>fantasizing based solely upon looks</u> and maintain a new habit of <u>connecting</u> starting from now.' He handed the scroll to Kirsten.

She looked at it and then thought about it before replying. 'What is wrong with my looks?'

He could not decipher her expression. 'Can I have my challenge back a moment, please.' He wrote at the bottom: 'Except the temptation of Kirsten.' He handed it back to her. 'I'm sure exceptions are allowed.'

'Yes, that is good.' Her laughter floated lightly on the thickening air as a deafening call to prayer broke from the minarets overhead, followed by a shuffling of bodies from the restaurants onto the square and into a reserved area beside the mosque, where all knelt. The chanting intoned out over the city until echoes of the phrases returned from every quarter.

Afterwards families and friends reunited, and soon there was only the sound of eating, conversing, and children playing. Rami came by out of nowhere and counted their numbers, as they were given complimentary mezzes to share breaking the fast before leaving.

The hotel had been fully restored when they got there, the waterfall thunder again reverberating around the marbled foyer. Andy was called over by the receptionist who, bright-eyed smiling, announced that Madaam had gone to see their sister hotel on Gezira Island, and would return later. Rick and Mikayla had gone to their rooms earlier to rest.

He returned to Kirsten, who turning to him noted: 'There is a dry white Gruner Veltliner in my room that I have been keeping to myself. It floats on the tongue and will spoil if it is not drunk at one sitting. I cannot drink more than two glasses as I promised.'

'That is an invitation?'

'A solution to a difficult problem.'

'May I join you to help with your 30-Day challenge? It would be terrible to break it on the first day.'

She looked at him. 'It is within the rules, I think.'

What might occur between them would not be within the rules, but neither of them had planned it that way. What would happen, would happen. They went to the lift and as he pressed the third-floor button, admiring them both together in the full-length mirror, a foot was placed into the closing panels and the door sprang open again. A military boot was then inserted to keep it open. There in front of him was his inquisitor from Tahrir Square two days earlier, the two others standing behind. Silence for a moment and then the same fit-looking officer with the lined angular face who had questioned him spoke. 'We have routine questions that we need to ask. Step out of the lift.'

He stepped out. Kirsten did likewise and, to his surprise, would not leave despite the officer indicating that she could go. She insisted: 'I will stay.'

'Very well. As you wish.' To Andy, he repeated, 'It is routine. It concerns the pyramid climb that was on the news program. It is not only the climb; we are aware that blasphemous obscenity was performed as part of the climb, and that there are large sums of money involved.' The rough-looking officer was clearly uncomfortable, although the more senior officer again showed no emotion, standing motionless, at ease with legs spread and arms collected behind his back.

The soldier instructed: 'Go to that alcove. It is empty.'

Andy looked to where he pointed to see that it was open to the foyer, relieved they would not be interviewed in a closed room.

There was a sense of them being part of a theatre production as they took their places in the alcove, where the three soldiers blocked the exit to the foyer, and where other guests threw curious glances. He saw Akar observe them from the reception where he was in discussion with the bright-eyed receptionist. 'There was a naked photoshoot on top of the pyramid. Egypt is a Muslim country, and it is Ramadan, and these things are especially prohibited. It is a great insult to Islam and its prophets, and there are already protests. We will find the others involved, and the person who organised this outrage.'

He stood silent for a moment, before inquiring: 'Where were you yesterday at dawn when this blasphemy was thrown at Islam?'

Andy could not admit that he was at the base of the pyramid both for his own sake, and more importantly because it would lead to implicating Rick and Mikayla. Could he refuse to answer the question: from the attitude displayed on Tahrir Square, he doubted that was an option. He would simply lie instead, and hope that Sara corroborated his story. He saw Akar approach, gesturing to the police and decided to wait.

Kirsten did not hesitate for any such development. 'It is a delicate matter. He was with me in my room.'

The officer who had no problems previously saying *I do not believe you* looked at Kirsten with a similar anger in his eyes to what Andy remembered. Akar went to the red-bereted senior officer. He pointed at Andy and then to the portrait behind reception. Both men laughed, and then the senior officer brushed his hands as he had on the Square. He spoke to his officer, barely suppressing a smile, who turned and laughed into Andy's face, remarking, 'She is not your wife!'

'That is a private matter!'

The soldiers turned and filed across reception, leaving them.

Kirsten had saved him. 'Thank you!' He hugged her.

'Es ist nichts. I am a heavy sleeper, and perhaps you were in my room to watch Alpine skiing?' She stood, that schoolgirl who had rhymed off an answer by rote.

The next time the lift door closed, Andy turned and kissed Kirsten deeply with all his resolve, and found it was returned by her soft, moist mouth.

Chapter 13,

Scrunch!

Sara

ﷻﷻﷻﷻﷻﷻﷻﷻﷻﷻﷻﷻﷻﷻﷻﷻﷻﷻﷻﷻﷻﷻﷻﷻ

It was early afternoon when Sara managed to slip away and leave Mikayla and Rick to shop with Fami's unsmiling and shaded visage in attendance. Akar's drove her much like Selim had, but with the added twist that he was intent on showing off the carrier. He tapped the dashboard and called it a Sports Carrier, and then put it through its manoeuvres. Raising the vehicle on its retractable axles he waved down at the car roofs below, and then he lowered the car on its wheels, mimicking going under a low clearance, and even flicked through the suspension options before putting it back into the off-road mode that took bumps out of the concrete motorway. When they hit traffic, he put the carrier in auto mode and stopped steering, scared her by turning completely around to face her, leaving the carrier to drive itself between the other honking cars shuttling forward. His forced humour was unsettling, more vaudeville than funny – pointed face contorted in a grimace and a deadness in his brown eyes. She asked him to drive normally. Certain people should not try to be humorous, and it was unnerving when they did.

She had not bought herself a single item on the gift credit card, but instead, had bought Mikayla a full wardrobe. Fami had to relay purchases to his carrier, as she had bought up all around her. That would teach James to install another woman only three rooms down from her. She thought about the redeeming room number that had worked with the credit card first time: 1212, a dozen-dozen that they had joked about.

It was just before he had pulled off his first big development deal when he had been helping his father train racehorses. One of these had won, a horse called *Present Option,* and there would be a massive celebration at a local hotel that was frequented by the racing crowd. The bar would be full of half-whispered tips about up-and-coming horses by men in soft felt caps leaning over pints at the bar, endless verbal reruns of the races, the bets, the odds and the winnings, cheers for winners with the possibility of drinks all round. And the whole place smelling of sweat, damp wet gear, and the faint whiff of horse dung. Models would tower above the jockeys, whom they would mercilessly tease as they tried to catch the eyes of the wealthy owners and their trainers. He had gotten a message to her that she should get a lift down by some means: it was going to be a hell of a party into the early hours. She could stay over. He had somehow gotten a room from a very obliging hotel manager, who had said she always kept a few rooms to squeeze in the winners – he was in the bridal suite, a football pitch of a room, Room 1212.

It was a wild night of anything goes in guffaws and laughter and good humour. *Present Options* had beaten a horse called *Jack the Lad*, and there were jokes about that, *Six of One, Half Dozen of the Other*. After, they had spent the remainder of the early hours in a four-poster where she had torn the delicate voile draped around the bed, and he had joked about her always scrunching her eyes when she orgasmed – he missed nothing. He was stony broke then unlike six months later, but he had brazenly paraded her at breakfast, rather than discreetly getting breakfast in the bedroom, to a murmur of comments amongst the other tables and the odd nudge and aside at the buffet bar: 'More power to ye, boy,' 'Well done on the win.'

When they got to the check-out, the manager was none too pleased. It was nothing to do with the expensive voile, but that he had only paid for single occupancy. 'Double occupancy. There is no use denying it,' she had said, clearly having had designs on being that bridal suite partner. 'I was sleeping in the next room, and you were going at it hammer and tongs all night. Full price for the room.' She named an astronomical figure for the time. He took a roll of notes that he had from a massive bet he had made on *Present Options* and pulled out fifties. Counting them out with the curious-looking avuncular man face up on the old notes, and then keeping his hand over them. He recounted, looking at the manager, and on the last note holding her eye, he remarked: 'She was worth it.' The manageress put the notes away in the cash register without taking her eyes off his and closed the drawer with a swing of her hips, forceful enough to have left bruises.

'Couldn't be up to them,' he had remarked to her walking to the 10-year-old Mazda RX-7 that still had the headlights that popped out of the front wings, those circular readouts sitting on top of the dash with rotating red dial fingers, and that red upholstery. They took off out of the car park in a blaze of stereo and roar of engine, thumping when he took his foot off the pedal before he screeched onto the roadway. That Mazda RX-7 he had kept even when he got the first gleaming Merc a few months later when the deal closed, and when the merry-go-round started.

As they crossed back over the Nile's swift waters, she floated with it and her destiny, her heart racing now with the thumping of the engine of the sports carrier. At this earlier time, when the weight of the sky still levitated in opaque paleness, the sister hotel radiated in unique terracotta colours glanced between swaying palm fronds and flowering flamboyant. It was understated until the floating golden portico at the entrance appeared, dissolving into the sun's intensity. That was anachronistic, having four Grecian marble goddesses under the arches, maybe in deference to the Greek influence – she would mention it to him anyhow.

Akar opened the door and escorted her under the ornate canopy to reception. She cleared the security gate and had her possessions returned to her by a Tyvek-clad female security officer, who continued to smile as she stepped away. The spacious foyer was huge, a mix of international styles with chandeliers, tiling, heavy brown drapes on high arched windows, a mantlepiece with mirrors, and the most wonderful marble main staircase with a heavy carpet – and walking into one's reflection in an ornate gold mirror on the landing. Too masculine, maybe move the Greek goddesses inside and add marble cornucopias and cherubs above the mantle. Brighten up those windows! Heavy drapes, where would you be going?

Through the reception, she heard 'Madaam James' from reception to the side. News had to have spread through the staff that she was Madaam James? A smiling receptionist asked, 'Is everything alright, Madaam? You are early?'

'Yes, I am fine. Overwhelmed from the museum. We saw Tutankhamun's mask, or masks. There are three with slightly different expressions, as you probably know.'

'Beautiful, Madaam. Everybody falls in love with the golden boy.'

She cut him off, not wanting to risk a repeat of her breaking down in the museum. 'Is there a message? You called me over?'

'Yes, Madaam. James Bey requests that you enjoy the hotel's facilities while you wait.'

Akar must have reported. 'The hotel entrance could be from a fairy tale?'

'Yes, the entrance looks special at this time of day because of the sun's position. It does not reflect as earlier, but instead inner glows. It is like city buildings at this time that you can see from the mezzanine lounge.'

Her visit was planned. 'Lustrous,' she quoted back first Green Eyes to new Green Eyes! James was doing this deliberately.

'Yes, I have ordered afternoon tea for you. In the meantime, please accept a coffee or tea on the mezzanine to enjoy a special city view over the river before it changes – many feluccas and the distant sounds. Like the entrance, the veranda has a golden canopy you will enjoy and a fountain that has many songs in its musical flows. Perhaps, a drink brought from the bar if you prefer?'

'Thank you! Coffee or tea will be fine.' Such thoughtfulness. A drink was not what she needed – or she really was going to become emotional – and to distract, she asked for a petit four or a macaroon biscuit.

'A selection is already included, Madaam,' he beamed and radiated. 'Will that be tea or coffee?'

'An Egyptian coffee will be fine.' She thanked him and, excusing herself, she hurried across the foyer – she had thirty minutes to compose herself – he was always punctual, ready for the *off*. Following directions, she found her way past a bar area in dark mahoganies – woeful! But then she came to an Arabic foyer leading onto the mezzanine that overwhelmed her. Another grand marble staircase but with golden banisters and a green and gold carpet was only the start. Would you believe the Celtic motives bordering the carpet despite the Arabic horseshoe arches on the wall and the contrast of colours and repeating geometric patterns, and that massive hammered-bronze chandelier? This was her James – he had arranged this for her.

She sat under the ornate canopy on the mezzanine with the fountains playing beside her. 'New Green Eyes' was right; the city buildings dissolved in different pink hues the other side of the river, shimmering into deeper colours on the river's surface, mini rainbows floating over its surface. Cleopatra entering Rome eat your heart out – here she was in her processional sedan gliding with the great river and its currents. She didn't need the lines of servants pulling her processional float – although that would have been a nice touch. She was complete in how she had gotten to this juncture in her life, and now leading merry-go-round back to the beginning, back to seventeen – well eighteen but who was counting – years previous.

The coffee was served on a gilded service on the mezzanine, and she sat in privacy behind the lattice that deflected the light without interrupting her view. She was getting used to having her private space, and she simply slumped onto a rattan divan, arranging the cushions to allow her a comfortably reach to the different offerings. She took her notepad out and began creating evening dresses in swirls with the strains of middle eastern music that she could not remember ever having heard. She began designing the bodices in pearl ivories and creams from the thickening sky to billowing, colourful skirts wafting from the zephyrs way above to combine with the shimmering surface patterns.

She felt recovered, and she put Tutankhamun's mask out of her mind. She needed to shower and compose herself on this rollercoaster of a day that would never end, and she went to Room 1212 as it had to be. The shower was a walk-in rainforest of droplets from a massive showerhead between lush waxy vegetation and that had bird calls that started with the flow. The green card described it as pure crystalline water that originated in the airy high gorges of Ethiopia and carried the secrets of the elixir of youth. It would be reused for other purposes many times before a return to the Nile to flow onward to embrace the sea – shades of Cleopatra allowing her maids to bathe after her. Dabbed in perfumes, she decided on a short number that would show the two bows on the back of her thighs – Pressie time! – and those red-soled stilettos that she had brought. A notification buzzed on her phone asking if she would accept a Bluetooth message – yes.

Just to let you know I am in the room next door – take your time.

Screen is open. Be there in a minute. To put him on his measure, she added: *Mine to invite!* She could imagine him smiling when he received it – closer now. There was much to catch up on – after all this time. She waited until she could hear him on the veranda before going to join him. She imagined the night after the race win: he was still that person, and she was worthy of their bridal suite.

Tiptoeing to the Moorish arch, she took a deep breath and then slid back the glass and appeared on the veranda in a single movement. He was standing looking at the city through the screen, casually eating cheese on broken-off flatbread from a selection on the table, wearing the casual chinos and what she now knew was a talismanic shirt.

'Wow! Sara, how can you be perfect after the two days you have had? Oh, but you are the classiest woman ever; more beautiful even than walking out of a dream!'

Brat. 'I thought your thing was to choose a winner from the rear. Are those your working clothes?'

'I'll have you know the original of this talismanic shirt was worn by an Ottoman Sultan under his armour and purported to have special powers of protection. It seems I need it these days.'

'James, are you afraid of me? Did you think we were going to do battle?' She deliberately distorted.

'It was a stormy first meeting two nights ago – if you remember. Rick is good?'

'Too good! He is preoccupied with Mikayla. She is stunning, savvy, and smart!' She added: 'My new VBF!' in case he had any ideas.

'He needs to fall in love. I didn't have time to explain, but no hotel in Egypt will allow an unmarried couple to share the same room. I hope it was okay to give her the room beside Rick's.' He smiled his new perfect new smile, and she tried to imagine the old.

'You may also have given her a full wardrobe. I put her spree on your credit card.' Caught out on that one.

'It wouldn't be anything to do with her being another woman, by any chance?'

'A teensy bit – you are indulging her,' she accused, pinching her thumb and forefinger together and tightening her smile.

He laughed that great horse laugh that brought the old him with the startled blank face.

She had to laugh, too. 'No sense denying it.'

His face turned suddenly serious: 'I was not allowed even a phone call for fear of it being traced. Was it bad at the Pyramid Dream?'

This was supposed to be for after. 'Like a news report with everyone caked in dust and alarms everywhere. It's over. One off the bucket list.' She wasn't going to tell him now about reaching out and finding nobody until Andy swept her into his arms. 'Getting back to your battle shirt. Wellington after the Battle of Waterloo, when he rushed back to Paris, twice took his lover in his boots – the expression was back then!'

'And old lovers?'

'First loves,' she corrected him, and as he moved closer, she could detect his old scent mixed with the freshness of the laundered battle shirt.

'We can't be seen,' he reassured her after their long first kiss. 'My Egyptian architect was inspired by the former shuttered boxes from the opera houses in Milan and Venice.'

She collapsed him onto the divan, sending New Green Eyes' second offerings flying. 'Nor heard, I hope?'

There was no delay, no Gerhardt pretending to protect her, no rearranging the cushions even. He reached for the bows on her thighs, and she imagined them being undone; the dress lifted and disappeared as she moved a cushion – still hadn't lost the knack. *Brat!* She could feel the hot, torpid air on her skin being swept aside by his touch; she snatched at his battle shirt, tugging at it until she pulled it over her head. His body was all over her, muscles, sinews, and bone, the country boy rippling from training his winner. Going through their paces together, building, heightening until she wasn't aware of where it started or finished, those mini rainbows over the surface of the river that came and went at their will. Losing it. She stretched into the opacity of sky above and felt it fall around her, smothering her and not allowing an escape. Yes, taken by her infidel, stripped of the pretensions of armour, the sensations shutting out the world, and closing her eyes, she felt her eyelids scrunching.

It must have been much later, when she returned slowly to the scents and fragrances of her surrounds through the chirruping birdsong from the garden way below, and becoming aware of the distant din of the city. They were lying together on the divan. She gave him a nudge and said that it didn't say anything about using a divan in the Wellington story. They still had hours before the tour would return to the hotel – and she had left that holding message at reception to give them more time together. With her fingers, she plotted the contours of his chest and abdomen – still that wiry muscularity of a country boy underneath, more angular. He must work out. She continued her survey until she knew every nuance of his body again, testing how he responded to different finger pressures and teasing scratches and trying out ways their bodies could touch. With her voice she soothed his reactions, telling him 'not to' when he appeared to be losing control – not going to complete the Wellington until they had had their tête-à-tête. She stopped when she had a full picture of him naked in her imagination and knew all his exquisite sensitivities again.

'Are you sure we can't be heard?'

'I told you they were inspired by a box at the opera when the shutters need to be closed.'

'Permanently closed…?'

'Dissipated the explosion at the Pyramid Dream, and practically no damage except on the ground floor where that pressure wave burst in.'

She hadn't intended saying anything but found herself telling him: 'I reached out to hold Rick, a mother's natural reaction I suppose, but he wasn't there. There was such a void in the pit of my stomach that he was gone, blown away. Of course, he wasn't. He had dived to cover Mikayla. Later, when I realised that my only son had instinctively reacted by reaching out to protect his one-day-old girlfriend, I felt lost, James. All day I stared numb at my mobile, waiting for a notification or message from you. But nothing.'

'I am sorry. Don't be too hard on Rick. On the high of his life. Weren't you ever in love?'

He wasn't getting away with changing the subject that easily. 'No contact? I need a better answer, James.'

'You've heard the news! My land-rover was blown across the road. Only a few bruises, luckily, but a blackout on communication as a result, until the police were certain that I was not being traced.'

'Tell me.'

'The projects I took over for the government on the New City. He had an eye on the presidency, and he was looking to foment unrest with a view to instigating another revolution. The bomb was cleverly placed to take out his non-Egyptian replacement and channel under the underpass to hit the tourist hotels built too close to the Great Pyramids. A two-forked approach. Then there was a crowd organised to create a focal point to protest an allegedly corrupt elite selling out Egypt's heritage. The bomb failed to take me out, and the damage to the area was limited. It is being portrayed as the act of a disaffected man, rather than a rallying point for a revolt. All very melodramatic.'

'I might have been right to fear the worst.'

'Ah, it was amateurish.'

Naked or not, she was not being fobbed off. 'No, my son and his girlfriend are the focus instead of you. How dangerous is their situation?'

'That's a distraction for the media. It will go no further. Rami relayed a request that Mikayla join your tour. I agree. That will take her out of Cairo until the situation has settled. I plan to cruise the river, also.'

Again, she was in his debt. 'Come on home with me, James.'

'Rick has my sense of adventure?'

Changing the subject again. 'Mine too, getting mixed up with you?' She wrapped herself tighter into him, closing her eyes to better imagine his body and hers together. She could decide on which nuanced modulation down to the way his toes curled until she scrunched her eyes and was lost in their lovemaking. It had taken all that time apart.

Acknowledgements

I was extremely fortunate to be accepted onto the program of Master of Fine Arts in Creative Writing in American College Dublin (Irish American University) and continue to celebrate each day I write at having received such a wonderful rounding of my English literary education. I would like to thank unreservedly the lecturers who shared so much of their own knowledge on the creative writing process, and the administrators of the college and all those who worked there who facilitated a conducive environment to creative writing and bonhomie. I would also like to thank my classmates whose friendship, observations, and comments added immeasurably to the course. An earlier form of this work was commenced during the Master's Program, and the assistance that I received with it had given me both the confidence and the tools to pursue its completion.

My second thank-you is to Booksgosocial.com, who unselfishly serve independent writers, and with whom I first came into contact attending the International Dublin Writers' Festival that they host annually. Can I especially thank Laurence who oversees this wonderful enterprise, and Tanja who as operations manager involved a fantastic team in the preparation of this book, even as she herself dispenses valuable advice and assistance at every turn. For proofing/editing, over and beyond and with unrelenting patience on my quasi-experimental style, Jacqui. For the brilliant cover that has been a process involving many iterations to get to the final look, thank you Masa, and to Mirna who had the challenging task of kicking off the process.

On the cover also, words cannot express my thanks to Vanessa, who despite suffering from long-covid distilled the arrangement of the cover – as well as coming up with the name of the book. Get well soon! To Aine, who got my interest going in Egypt and helped fine tune the 'blurb' into its final wording, a big thank-you.

Finally, can I sincerely thank all my family and friends for the incredible support and for sticking with me over the four long years that the three volumes have taken, despite my absences from events and commitments – and including silence when required – brought on by my all-consuming relationships with the characters in the trilogy.

Printed in Great Britain
by Amazon

25085591R00180